THE HONEY PEACH AFFAIR

DALE BRADFORD

© 2015 Dale Bradford

All rights reserved. No part of this book may be reproduced, stored in a retrieval system, or transmitted in any form or by any means, electronic, electrostatic, magnetic tape, mechanical, photocopying, recording or otherwise, without the written permission of the author.

The story within this book is a work of fiction. Names, characters, businesses, organisations, places and events are either the product of the author's imagination or are used fictitiously. Any resemblance to actual persons, living or dead, is entirely coincidental.

All trademarks used are acknowledged to be the property of their respective owners.

Cover image: Vivid Raw Super Model Doll from CalExotics photographed by the author.

Thanks to Cara, Nina, Jo, Lauren, Naomi, and Ronnie for their kind words and encouragement. And to all those who told the author a novel about the adult industry would never sell – you were right.

CHAPTER ONE: MONDAY 2ND JUNE 2003

Did anyone in the cellar bar think they were a couple? It seemed unlikely. Bruce was forty, fat and frumpy while she had a face like a Disney character's; innocently round, with oversized blue eyes, a pert little nose and plump, pouty lips. Her body would never have got past Disney's arbiters of taste though — nor proportion, as each of her enhanced breasts was almost the size of a man's head. Equally synthetic were her stiletto nails, spider lashes, caramel tan and platinum blonde hair.

Bruce looked down at his unopened bag of 'healthy eating' crisps, which were free of non-natural colourings, flavourings and preservatives and low in salt and fat. Frankly he preferred the 1970s, when the women were organic and the food was full of artificial additives.

The barmaid approached their table, which had been carefully chosen by Bruce for its discreet corner location. "Those men want to buy you drink," she said to the blonde, jerking her thumb in the direction of two inanely grinning suits stood at the bar.

"I'm with someone," said the blonde, without looking up at the barmaid or across at the men. Instead she continued texting on her mobile, which had an ostentatious gold plastic cover.

She was with someone. Bruce liked that.

"Do you get this a lot?" Bruce asked, gesturing with his eyes at her admirers.

"Fuck yeah," she said, ripping open Bruce's bag of crisps so the contents were easily accessible to them both. She made an alluring 'o' shape with her fat red lips and slowly bit into a single crisp, revealing perfect white teeth that could have just clacked their way from the set of a toothpaste commercial.

Bruce took a deep gulp of his Guinness, giving his slightly podgy face a foamy white moustache. Yes, she probably did get it a lot. He didn't. In fact he'd never had it before. But then he'd never been sat in the cellar bar of Marelli's with a beautiful busty blonde half his age before.

"Does it bother you?" Bruce asked, distracted by the gold pendant which was almost being consumed by the shadowy cavern between her breasts.

"What? Middle-aged men clocking my tits for their wank bank?" Her elegant fingers passed another crisp into her seductively sweary mouth.

"I was looking at your necklace thing," Bruce protested, hands raised in a gesture of supplication. "And don't be fooled by the grey in my hair, I'm experimenting with the distinguished look."

"I'm only teasing you, Bruce," she said. Her hand clutched the gold pendant and she leaned closer to Bruce so he could see it more clearly. "Do you like my charms?"

"They're very attractive," he replied, gazing at the two gold objects dangling at the end of the gold chain. "What are they?"

"One of them is a pot of honey and the other's a peach," she said. "They were bought especially for me by one of my fans."

Her fans. Listen to her. Anyone would think she was Madonna. The charms just looked like a ball and a stumpy little cylinder to Bruce, but he was enjoying having her face so close to his, breathing in her musky scent.

"You're not trying to take advantage of an innocent young girl, are you, Bruce?" chided a familiar voice, driving a horse and carriage through the moment. Jan, AMG magazine's editor, plonked her zebra print handbag on the table between the two of them, causing Honey Peach to back away from Bruce. Poking out of the bag's zip was the neck of a bottle of gin.

Although in her early forties, Jan looked at least a decade younger. Her auburn shoulder length hair had yet to be colonised by a single grey and her face remained fresh, which she put down to plenty of early nights. Her quirky dress sense also contributed to her youthful appearance – her distressed retro jeans had been featured in the fashion pages of Celebs & Scandals magazine the previous week – but next to Honey Peach she looked distinctly mumsy. But then so did every other woman.

"She was just showing me her charms," Bruce replied.

"I bet she was," said Jan, pulling out one of the two vacant chairs at the small round table and sitting next to Honey Peach.

Bruce sighed. No one was going to think he and Honey Peach were a couple now.

"Sorry I'm late," Jan said to Honey Peach. "I had to stop off at the off licence to pick up something for my Aunt Edith."

"Don't worry," Honey Peach said with a smile. "Bruce has been entertaining me."

"Has he indeed?" Jan said, raising her eyebrows. "I suppose he was regaling you with tales of when he was the UK Donkey Kong champion?"

Honey Peach laughed. "No, this is the first I've heard of it."

"Oh yes, in his prime he had the fastest fingers in the West Country. If anyone wanted a princess rescuing, Bruce Baker was their first port of call…"

"Can we talk about something else?" Bruce protested.

Honey Peach reached across the table and grabbed Bruce's hand. Staring imploringly into his eyes she said: "Self-love, my liege, is not so vile a sin as self-neglecting."

Jan and Honey Peach burst out laughing at Bruce's confused face.

"She's teasing you, Bruce," Jan said then, looking across the bar, added: "Oh I see Nick's finally made it through the throng. Who stands and talks on the stairs?"

Nick was threading his way down the wooden staircase through a group of chatting women in primary coloured clothing. At first they had beamed approvingly at Nick's tight T-shirt, crammed to almost bursting with muscles earned from many hours in the gym. But as he passed them their expressions changed. Although stocky enough to play scrum half – quite successfully – for his local amateur rugby club, Nick stood less than five foot four inches tall. And as he'd celebrated his twenty-ninth birthday the previous week, this was unlikely to change in the foreseeable future. The women towered above him and when they caught sight of his scrum-battered face, several of them scowled in disdain.

Marelli's was one of Bath's busiest post-work drinking destinations, catering for three different crowds. The cellar bar was originally a traditional working man's spit 'n' sawdust drinking hole but in recent years it had been colonised by the city's creative types. Above it, on street level, was a wine bar, popular with thrusting sales executives, while the first floor housed an exclusive restaurant where management could relax among their own kind, with the exorbitantly priced menu enforcing a 'no hoi polloi' policy more effectively than any doorman.

"Why are there so many corporate types down here tonight?" Nick whined as he joined them at the table, pulling out the remaining empty chair.

"That's the problem with voluntary cultural apartheids," said Bruce. "You still need borders of some kind and someone to police them."

Jan gave Bruce an amused look which appeared to say 'if you think you're going to impress the blonde with that, you're deluding yourself'.

Honey Peach hadn't been listening anyway. She had been texting on her mobile. Bruce noticed the gold case had her initials etched into it. Probably another present from a fan, unless Hewlett Packard had branched out into gaudy phone accessories.

"Where have you been until now?" Bruce asked Nick.

"Mate, I got held up," he replied. "And it took me ages to fight my way through the crowd upstairs."

"I think there's been some kind of conference in town for junior executives," Jan said. "I can confirm that they are packed like sausages upstairs, which is why we're getting the overflow down here. Don't get comfortable though Nick — as you're the last to join us, and lateness is a discourtesy to others, it's your turn to get the drinks."

Nick groaned. Despite his impressive girth, crowded bars still presented a challenge when taller heads hid you from the barmaid's line of sight.

"Yeah right, you can fuck right off," Honey Peach said to the screen on her mobile.

"Problems?" Jan asked her.

"Only Milkman, the dickhead," Honey Peach said, tapping out a reply on her mobile's keypad. "He reckons I'll have to bunk down with him tonight because his cleaner hasn't made up the spare bed. I've made one film with him and he thinks he's my manager."

"He gave me that impression too," Bruce said.

"He couldn't manage a piss-up," said Honey Peach.

"In a brewery?" Nick said.

"Anywhere," she replied.

"Well thanks again for today," Jan said to Honey Peach, changing the subject. "I thought you came across very well."

"Cheers," Honey Peach replied, stabbing the buttons of her keypad again.

Jan continued: "We've set aside four pages for the feature and..."

The rest of her sentence was drowned out by the booming voice of the slick-haired suit whose offer of a drink had been turned down earlier. He'd moved from the now crowded bar and stood, leaning against a pillar, close to their table.

"Give me advice?" Slick Hair said to his acne-faced companion. "I'm four points up so Cartwright can suck my cheesy bell-end!"

Acne Face thought this was the funniest thing he had ever heard, involuntarily spitting some of his drink out of his mouth.

"Well, there goes the neighbourhood," said Bruce. "It's usually a tosser-free zone down here."

"And he might be up four points but what's his ROI doing?" Jan added.

"What does that mean?" asked Honey Peach, raising her glass to her lips and noticing it was empty. She held the glass in front of her, emphasising its lack of contents to her companions.

"I don't know, I heard someone over there say it," said Jan.

Slick Hair had heard Bruce's comment and was now glaring at him.

"Oh I'll get the drinks then," said Honey Peach, with an irritated sigh. She pointed to the table. "Same again for you, Bruce, and White Zin okay for you, Jan?"

They both nodded.

Honey Peach rose to her feet, all five foot three of her — plus a further four inches of heel — and the busy bar collectively gasped. Her skimpy white top was struggling to contain her bulbous breasts while her short denim skirt emphasised her slender legs. Male mouths dropped like cartoon characters opening unexpected tax demands. Female eyes narrowed venomously, first at the body then at that perfect face. She grabbed Nick's arm and pulled him up. "Come on, you're carrying the drinks," she said.

As she strode towards the bar the crowd parted in awe.

"We are not worthy," said Bruce.

"She does have quite an aura about her," Jan said, taking a small compact from her bag and checking her face.

"How does she know what you drink?"

"We went out for lunch last time she came over," Jan explained.

Honey Peach was back in less than two minutes, with Nick trailing in her wake with a metal tray containing their drinks.

"That didn't take long," said Jan, as her wine was placed in front of her.

Over the next hour the cellar bar thinned out, leaving just a few renegade sales people, including Slick Hair and Acne Face, who continued standing close to Honey Peach's table despite there being vacant seats elsewhere.

Honey Peach looked at her watch, a tiny glittering thing, and announced: "Well this has been fun."

Had it? She'd barely looked up from her phone all evening, thought Bruce. And how could she tell the time on that watch? He couldn't even see the hands let alone where they were pointing.

"I suppose I'd better think about catching my train."

"You can't go yet," Nick said. "We've got to have another round, at least."

"Have you got a big day tomorrow?" asked Jan.

Honey Peach nodded.

Bruce imagined that every day was a big day when you looked like Honey Peach.

"I'm staying at Milkman's tonight because I'm cutting the ribbon on a new shop for Spaghetti in the morning," Honey Peach said. "But let's have one more for the road, shall we?"

"Shouldn't that be one more for the track?" said Nick. "Because you're catching a train…"

Honey Peach gave him a withering look in response.

"He used to work in IT before he became our graphic designer," Bruce said. "That joke would have got a round of applause in the server room."

Honey Peach stroked Nick's cheek. "Bless him," she cooed. "I quite like ugly men."

Nick blushed.

Bruce whispered to Honey Peach: "Please be careful or he might go off – he doesn't meet many women. He spends his spare time getting muddy with blokes in shorts and then they all shower together."

Honey Peach giggled and squeezed Nick's stocky thigh, causing him to blush even more.

Jan stepped in on Nick's behalf. "When you say you are cutting the ribbon on a new shop for Spaghetti, you don't mean the shop specialises in pasta, do you?"

Honey Peach laughed. "No, I'm opening the shop for him. He's got the local paper coming and he's invited a load of his customers. Milkman is driving me there, which is why I'm staying with him tonight."

"Spaghetti is a person?" Jan looked confused.

Bruce stepped in. "His real name is Gerardo Sachetti. If you haven't heard of him you have heard of his shops – there's a Love Shack in the town centre, not far from the station."

"Is he Italian?"

"With a name like that I think it's probably safe to assume he is, at the very least, of Italian descent," Bruce said.

"And everyone calls him Spaghetti?" Jan said. "Doesn't he mind? I thought we'd moved on from casual racism towards our European neighbours. That would be like me calling Nick 'Frogs Legs' because he's French."

"I'm not French," Nick said.

"He's called Spaghetti because he's like Spaghetti Junction," Honey Peach said.

Bruce, Jan and Nick looked blankly at each other and raised their eyebrows in expectation.

"Because you don't ever want to cross him," Honey Peach explained. "They say he can't make an omelette without breaking legs."

Fuelled with four pints worth of confidence and spotting the break in the conversation, Slick Hair finally made his move. "I think you mean eggs, love," he leered at Honey Peach as he wiped sweat off his forehead with a handkerchief. "You can't make an omelette without breaking eggs."

Bruce and Jan exchanged amused glances as Honey Peach stared up at Slick Hair. "Excuse me?" Honey Peach said to him.

He wiped the sweat from his forehead again. "You're excused, we all make mistakes," he said in his booming voice. "Let me get you a drink, I know just the thing for you."

"Would it be a rude-sounding cocktail, by any chance?" Honey Peach said. "A Slippery Nipple or a Screaming Orgasm?"

Slick Hair grinned. "What about a Quick Fuck?" he said.

"Yeah what about a Quick Fuck?" echoed Bruce, in a perfect impression of Slick Hair's voice.

"Mimicry is one of his few talents," Jan said to the surprised Honey Peach. "Some say his only one."

"It sounds absolutely mad but it's completely genuine, I promise you," Slick Hair persisted, guffawing at Honey Peach while simultaneously scowling at Bruce. "It's made from one part coffee liqueur, one part Midori and one part Bailey's…"

"Have you ever had a Throbbing Bollocks?" Honey Peach asked Slick Hair.

"Can't say I have," he boomed, a huge grin spreading across his face as he moved closer to her.

"Here you go then," Honey Peach responded, jabbing her elbow hard into Slick Hair's crotch, which was just a few inches away from her.

Slick Hair doubled over in pain but before he could react, Nick leapt out of his chair. Chest expanded, arms spread and muscles tensed, he said: "Come on mate, we've all had a drink, let's not spoil the night."

As she watched Acne Face help Slick Hair up the stairs of Marelli's, encouraged by Nick, Honey Peach said: "Funnily enough, I do fancy a cocktail now. How chilly is that!"

"Chilly?"

"Yeah, something that's cooler than cool. It's my new saying and I'm going to try and make it catch on."

Nick returned from ushering duties and Honey Peach stood up and hugged him. "My hero!" she squealed.

Blushing again, Nick said: "Are we having another round then, or what?"

Jan nodded. "Cocktails this time, please," she said. "You can choose."

Nick walked off towards the now much emptier bar and Honey Peach followed him, holding onto his arm, before taking a left turn into the ladies'.

Jan looked across the table at Bruce. "Well this has been…"

"Chilly?" Bruce said.

"That's the word I was looking for," Jan said. "She's definitely got something there."

"Oh she's certainly got something," Bruce said. "Imagine what it must be like, always being the centre of attention."

"I can't imagine," Jan said.

"If it's any consolation, I think Acne Face had his eye on you with a view to a foursome."

"I'm not terribly good at reading signals like that," Jan sighed. "Perhaps that's why I'm still single."

"Don't worry," Bruce said. "You might collect china frogs and have a cat called Buffy, and you might be in your mid-forties, but I'm sure you'll be a great catch for someone…"

Jan narrowed her eyes at him. "I am not in my mid-forties…"

"Perhaps we could have a reader competition?" Bruce suggested. "Win a date with Adult Movie Guide's editor!"

"Dating one of our more gauche readers has always been my dream," Jan said, in the style of an overwhelmed talent show winner.

After a pause, she said in a rather wistful voice: "Actually the only dream I ever had was to buy a camper van and just bugger off around Europe and see what happens."

"Why didn't you?"

"I suppose I never found the right person to go with," Jan said. "Don't suppose I'll ever get around to it now."

Bruce was wondering if he should attempt to lighten the mood when Nick returned to the table with four glass tumblers, each filled with a murky red liquid. He gave one to Bruce, one to Jan, took one himself and placed the final one on the table for Honey Peach.

"What have you got for us?" asked Jan.

"It's a Red Hot Dutch," said Nick.

"I've never heard of that," said Jan.

"I saw vodka, tomato juice, grated Edam cheese and chilli powder go in," said Nick, chugging his Red Hot Dutch down.

Bruce and Jan exchanged resigned glances and did the same, leaving a residue of lumpy yellow-red goo at the bottom of their glasses.

"Who puts cheese in a cocktail?" said Jan, inspecting the dregs.

"For me, the cheese aspect is very much a secondary concern," said Bruce, his face gurning with disgust.

"It might have chilli in it but it certainly isn't chilly," Jan said.

Bruce mimed applause, which Jan accepted with a bow.

When Honey Peach returned from the ladies' she picked up the final Red Hot Dutch. "Is this a cocktail?" she asked dubiously.

"Oh yes my lover," said Bruce in an exaggerated West Country accent. "Tis the chilliest in this here fair city of Bath."

"You're funny," said Honey Peach. "It doesn't smell too good."

Nick said to Honey Peach: "We didn't notice, we all drank ours down in one."

"Stick around," said Bruce. "We're going to be putting our hands in the fire next and we'll be counting on you to do the same."

Honey Peach threw Bruce a curious look.

"She has no cultural reference point," Jan said quietly to Bruce. "I think mothers stopped saying that to their children in the 1960s."

Honey Peach took a deep gulp but then quickly slammed down her glass, her perfect face distorted with revulsion. "That's vile, I am not drinking that," she said, ferreting in her leather handbag for a gloss stick to wipe the taste off her lips.

"Waste not, want not," said Bruce, picking up the half-drunk cocktail and offering it to Jan.

"Nobody says that anymore either," Jan said to him, taking two large gulps of the Red Hot Dutch. "Dear Lord, it actually gets worse."

Bruce took the glass from her. "Stand back feeble old woman, this is man's work," he said, finishing the drink. Jan was right, it tasted even more offensive the second time around.

"Well, on that rather depressing note, I think we should call it a night," said Jan, getting to her feet. "We've all got to be up for work in the morning. Bruce, you and Nick had better escort Honey Peach to the station – she's not really dressed for walking the streets alone at this time of night."

Bruce shook his head. "I'm going to have another drink first – to get rid of the taste of that abomination."

"She's got a train to catch," Nick said, gesturing at Honey Peach. "And like Jan says…"

"Anyone else want another one?" Bruce said, ignoring him.

"Oh go on then," Honey Peach said. "Make it a brandy. A good one."

"In that case I'll join you," said Jan, sitting back down at the table.

"What about her train?" Nick protested.

Honey Peach looked at her watch. "I've got a few minutes yet."

"Well I'm not having anymore," Nick said.

"Oh come on," Bruce said. "It's not like you've got anything to go home for."

After she had finished her brandy, Honey Peach looked at her watch again. "I really must go now," she said. "I've got to change at Newport to get to Chepstow."

"Are you alright to drive?" Bruce asked Jan, feeling beads of perspiration prickling his forehead as the group marched up the stairs.

"Absolutely not," Jan replied. "I've got to get my gym bag out of the car but I'll catch a cab."

By the time the four of them made it up the stairs, through the still bustling wine bar and out into the night air, Bruce started to feel a little woozy.

"You're not driving either, are you Bruce?" Jan asked with genuine concern. "Because you're starting to sway."

"No, I'll walk home and leave the car in Vicky Park," Bruce said. "Hopefully someone will steal it."

Jan exchanged embraces and air kisses with Honey Peach and walked off towards Royal Victoria Park, where her car was also parked. It was one of the very few places in central Bath where it was possible to park all day free of charge, if you arrived early enough in the morning.

Bath Spa railway station was just a few hundred yards further along Manvers Street from Marelli's, and Bruce and Nick positioned themselves either side of Honey Peach as they headed towards it.

"Honestly guys, there's no need," she said, waving them away as she removed her phone from her handbag.

"I'll just walk you part of the way there then," said Nick.

"I'd really rather have some privacy," she said. "I want to make some calls."

Bruce could see the lights of the train station twinkling in the distance. Out of the corner of his eye he could also see two familiar suits, leaning against the wall of Marelli's. They were both devouring burgers and staring at him.

"Are you sure you don't want us to walk you to the station?" Bruce said, though the words came out a little slurred. He tried to focus on her but his vision was blurred. Slurred and Blurred, that would be a good name for a cop show featuring two alcoholic detectives...

"I'm really sure," Honey Peach said, from somewhere distant. "It's only like a couple of yards down the road..."

Suddenly Bruce felt a huge blow to the side of his head. He crashed to the pavement and then everything went black.

CHAPTER TWO: TUESDAY 3RD JUNE 2003

Bruce woke with a start. Every part of his body ached, especially his head. He was lying in a shop doorway just down from Marelli's and a bearded man in a bobble hat and stained overcoat was squatting by the side of him, holding a steaming cup of coffee under his nose.

"Hey pal, I got this for me," the man said. "But you look like you need it more."

Bruce took the plastic cup gratefully, his hands trembling. Dawn was breaking over Bath and with it came the sound of clattering diesel engines as delivery trucks made their way around the city. Bruce greedily gulped the coffee down.

"Well this is a new low for me," Bruce said, holding his throbbing head and taking in his surroundings of cigarette butts and ketchup-smeared burger wrappers.

"This is one of the nicest doorways in Bath," the man corrected him. "A couple of streets over and you could have been robbed, beaten up, butt-fucked..."

"Thank you," Bruce said, holding his hand up in an attempt to stop the man speaking.

"And that's just if the police had found you," he cackled.

Bruce's head felt like someone was kicking him in the temple. He slowly got to his feet, leaning on a wall for support. He dug three pound coins out of his pocket.

"Can I pay you for the coffee?" Bruce said.

"That's very princely of you," the man replied, taking the cash. "Is this all you got?"

Bruce brought out some smaller denomination coins and offered them to the man. "Now if you'll excuse me," he said, attempting to walk. "I need my bed."

"Oh that's right, rub it in, you flash bastard," the man yelled at Bruce as he hobbled away.

The walk back to his flat took Bruce past the forecourt of Reeves & Jeeves, purveyors of fine quality motor carriages to the residents of Bath for several generations, and he stopped to admire their 'Car of the Week', a maroon Jaguar XK8 convertible. He peered through the side window at the black leather upholstery and wooden trim and then at the long, elegant bonnet, beneath which was a V8 engine with the power of three hundred horses. He stared in wonder at the £29,999 price sticker on the windscreen.

"Imagine driving a car that costs more than your salary," Bruce said to a man in a hi-visibility vest who was picking up litter. "You'd be frightened to park it anywhere."

Bruce noticed the man had earphones in, so he hadn't heard him. Then he vomited a horrific looking torrent of red, yellow and black liquid over the Jaguar's gleaming bonnet.

***

Six hours later Bruce was back in Bath city centre, pushing open the heavy wooden door of the four-storey Georgian building which housed Adult Movie Guide's office. The property had once been owned by a firm of solicitors but it had been converted into separate office suites in the 1980s, with only the grand staircase and the imposing oak reception desk on the ground floor remaining from the original features. All of its tenants paid towards the cost of the receptionists, who answered their phones, signed for their mail, greeted their guests and gossiped about them behind their back.

"What time do you call this?" said Dee, the perky blonde, interrupting the text message she was composing on her mobile. "Some of us are getting ready to go on lunch."

"As the weather was so glorious I took a few liberties," Bruce said with an air of confidence he didn't feel. He was alarmed to discover that he slurred the word 'liberties'.

"I've put through several messages for you…" Dee yelled after Bruce, as he slowly climbed the stairs.

AMG magazine lived in One East, the smallest suite in Legal House. The other tenants included architects, accountants and a public relations firm, each of which rented the part of the building which best suited their bank balance and sense of self importance. One East, along with two other suites, was located on the third floor and every step of the stairs was an effort for Bruce this morning. There was no lift.

"Bruce!" Plum barked at him when he eventually crossed the threshold of One East. "My office!"

Bruce staggered through the open plan area to Plum's glass-doored lair, where utilitarian functionality gave way to the luxurious indulgence of thick carpet and cherry wood furniture.

"Close the door," Plum said, an edge of irritation in his smooth as chocolate public school voice. He flicked his foppish greying fringe out of his eyes, in a manner which may have been considered endearing thirty-five years ago, and pursed his thin lips.

Bruce sighed as he gently pushed the glass door closed.

"We need to have a chat," Plum said.

"Do we have to do it now?" Bruce whined, staring at the excess weight that always collected around Plum's neck when he sat back in his chair. It's like a cravat, Bruce thought, a cravat of fat.

"Time is of the essence," Plum said. "I need to appoint an acting editor."

"Why would you do that?" Bruce said, pulling a confused expression.

"Well call me old fashioned but with the incumbent currently enjoying an unscheduled city break at the Royal United Hospital, with the very real possibility of following this up with a stay at Her Majesty's Pleasure, I rather thought I'd like my business to continue functioning. "

"Plum, what are you talking about?"

"I'm talking about Jan of course," Plum said, thumping his desk with his fist. "The stupid cow got sloshed last night and wrote off her car."

The words stung Bruce like a slap in the face. His stomach lurched and his throat tightened. "Is she alright?" he finally said, almost collapsing into the chair reserved for visitors which was positioned opposite Plum's desk.

"That depends on your definition of 'alright' — if it stretches to being taken to hospital unconscious with a myriad of broken bones then yes, she is absolutely chipper."

"That's unbelievable," Bruce said.

"Isn't it? Nick has rung in sick too and here you are, waltzing in half-way through the day. A good night, was it Bruce?"

"No – well, yes it was but it wasn't a session. We only had a couple of drinks and we were all fine when we left."

"Much as I would like to believe that, your tardiness and shambolic appearance today hardly inspire confidence in you as a credible witness," Plum said. Pointing to the large lump on the side of Bruce's head, he added: "And what's that? Have you been in a fight?"

"Jan wouldn't drink and drive." Bruce said, shaking his head.

"Tell that to the police who attended the scene," Plum said. "Or the doctors who pumped her stomach. In the meantime we have got next week's magazine to put out and we need an acting editor."

Bruce put both palms to his head in an effort to ease the pain. "Obviously I'll be happy to take on extra responsibilities," he said.

"I'm glad to hear that because I'm putting Alex on the masthead until we know what's happening with Jan. She's going to need a lot of hand-holding, as I'm sure you'll appreciate."

"You're making Alex the acting editor?" Bruce spluttered. "But she sells the ads."

"And?" Plum said, looking down at the fingernails of his left hand.

"And she can't write. And she's been here less than six months. And I've been here since the magazine started," Bruce protested.

"She's very bright…"

"She brightens the office up, I'll give you that," Bruce said, his voice getting louder. "But so would a couple of poinsettias."

"Alex is popular with the advertisers," Plum said. "Now keep your damn voice down."

Too late. The disturbance had attracted her.

"I take it you've told him the good news then?" Alex said in her Coronation Street accent as she barged open Plum's door. Her eyes were immediately drawn to the lump on Bruce's face. "Ooh, what's happened here, Bruce? Did you upset the wrong person this time? That looks really sore. I hope it is."

"Would you mind pissing off, Alex?" Bruce said to her. "I'm having a discussion with Plum and words are likely to be said that you might find upsetting."

"Plum!" Alex bellowed, her face losing its smugness. "Are you going to let him speak to me like that?"

"This doesn't concern you," Bruce said, holding the glass door open for her and attempting to usher her through it.

Alex glared at Bruce. "If it's anything to do with the magazine, it does concern me," she said. "Because you've alienated so many of my clients."

"I'm afraid she's right, Bruce," Plum said. "It's like I always say – selling pages pays the wages. We can't survive on just newsstand sales. We need advertisers, and handing over the reins to you, even on a temporary basis, wouldn't have gone down terribly well."

"How can I sell space to someone when you've said that their new film is shittier than the bogs at a chilli festival?" Alex said, pointing her finger in Bruce's face.

"Alright that's enough," Plum said, before Bruce could reply. "The decision has been made. Needs must when the devil drives, so in celebration of Alex's ascendancy to the big chair…"

"Jan's in hospital and you think we have something to celebrate?" Bruce said.

"It's onwards and upwards, Bruce," Plum said, pointing to a framed motivational poster of those very words on the wall behind his desk. "As I was saying, in celebration of Alex's ascendancy to the big chair I'm delighted to inform you both that lunch will be on me today. I've got my regular table booked at Marelli's restaurant and you are welcome to join me."

"No thanks Plum," Bruce said. "I don't really have the appetite for celebrating."

"We'll also be going over the soft proofs of the issue," Plum said. "Though your glazed eyes and toxic breath suggest you wouldn't be able to tell a restrictive pronoun from a relative clause."

"That's right," Bruce said. "Best leave that to Alex, eh?"

After Plum and Alex had left for Marelli's, Bruce flopped into the chair at his desk. The red light on his phone was flashing, indicating that several messages had been left for him, confirming what Dee had said. Ignoring them, Bruce called the hospital to enquire about Jan. After being passed between departments he eventually learned that her condition was stable and he should be able to visit her between seven and nine this evening.

Relieved, he turned his attention to his messages. The first was from Milkman, asking Bruce to ring him back as soon as possible. The next message was from Zara, film director and chair of BATA – the British Adult Trade Association – who claimed to have 'exciting' news. He returned Milkman's call first.

"I've been trying to get hold of you all morning," Milkman said, in his distinctive Welsh accent.

Bruce powered up his computer. "Why?"

"What time did Honey Peach leave?"

"About nine, I think."

"What happened?"

"Nothing happened," Bruce said. "She was only here a couple of hours. After Jan interviewed her we went out for a couple of drinks and then she caught her train."

"Well she never arrived with me," Milkman said. "Did she say anything last night?"

"What about?"

"About me."

"Oh yes, she said how much she was looking forward to spending the night in your bed."

"Is that supposed to be funny?" Milkman said. "Spaghetti's been on the blower and I've had to tell him I didn't know where his guest of honour was. How do you think that makes me feel?"

"Like dancing?" Bruce suggested.

"She won't be doing no dancing if Spaghetti gets hold of her," Milkman said. "No wonder she's not answering her phone today."

"Maybe she caught the wrong train," Bruce said. "Or maybe she just changed her mind and went home instead."

"It wouldn't surprise me, women are so bloody flaky," Milkman said. "But even so, you'd think she would have had the decency to let me know what's happening."

After Bruce established to Milkman's satisfaction that he could provide no more information about the whereabouts of Honey Peach, he returned Zara's call. Her 'exciting' news was that BATA had written to the Department of Culture Media and Sport enquiring about funding for an overseas trade mission to the world's biggest adult industry expo in Las Vegas.

"Imagine how brill that would be!" Zara trilled. She added that she had met with representatives from the department last week and had received a sympathetic response, once she had explained about the unfair restrictions the UK adult industry faced.

Bruce smiled. Zara must have been wearing her tight white blouse, pencil skirt and fishnet stockings ensemble. He jotted down the details, closed his eyes and sat back in his chair with his feet on his desk.

Unfortunately his recuperation was continually disturbed. Dee was aware that every other member of staff was out so she directed all calls for AMG to Bruce's extension. In every case it was one of Alex's friends trying to get in touch with her. She had left her mobile charging on her desk, along with the latest issue of Celebs & Scandals magazine, and Bruce concluded that she had sent out a blanket text to everyone in her contacts list informing them of her promotion before she left the office. And it seemed everyone she knew wanted to congratulate her. He swiftly put her mobile in silent mode but when that went unanswered they called the AMG number. And Dee put them through to Bruce.

With each successive call, Bruce's 'she's not here' script became more abrupt. He could have just let them go to his voicemail but then he would only have to endure listening to their screechy little voices at a later date. Removing the handset from its cradle resulted in an irritating warning tone being triggered so he decided to unplug his extension from the wall. As he was following the cable's route to the socket it rang again.

"Hello, AMG magazine," he parroted.

"I'm trying to find my sister," said a female voice that could have belonged to a Radio 4 continuity announcer.

"I suggest you ring Marelli's in Manvers Street," Bruce said. "Just ask them to take the phone to the woman with a face so smug you'd think she's learned to cunniling herself."

Bruce didn't hear the response to his improvised verb because on the stroke of 'herself' he pulled the telephone cable from the wall socket.

Rather annoyingly, even though the office was now peaceful apart from the sounds of the street below wafting in through the front window, Bruce's aching head prevented him catching up with his sleep. He resolved to get the lump looked at during his visit to Jan. But why did Slick Hair and Acne Face assault him? For doing one lousy impression?

The small hand on the office clock went from two to three and now it was approaching four. He walked across to the rear window, which looked down onto the private courtyard. He pushed the sash window up as far as it would go and sat on the ledge, with his head and body outside but with his legs still safely inside, and lit a cigarette. Legal House had a strict 'no smoking' policy but Bruce would often get around it in this manner if he was in the office alone. Strictly speaking, he wasn't contravening the policy – as the cigarette and all the smoke it emitted was outside the building – though he suspected that he might be breaching Health and Safety regulations by sitting outside, forty feet up.

After he stubbed the cigarette out on the stone window ledge and clambered back inside he paced around the office. With neither Jan nor Nick in, Alex's monitor was the only one besides his displaying signs of life. It revealed that she had taken over All About Me, the inside back cover page that closed each issue. All About Me asked an industry personality a standard set of questions which allowed them to show off their self-deprecating sense of humour and plug their latest product. In Alex's case she was the product as she introduced herself as AMG's new editor, though there was scant evidence of a sense of humour. Her childhood ambition was to have a pony; the three words her friends would use to describe her would be fun, flirty and fabulous; she liked to relax away from work by taking her dog for long wanks on the beach...

Hang on, how did she like to relax away from work? His eyes scanned back up the screen and checked — yes, she really had typed what he thought he'd seen. Normally he would have instantly corrected the typo but he didn't feel particularly normal today. Besides, maybe that was how she liked to relax?

Feeling a little happier, Bruce decided to finish early so he could sneak in a snooze before visiting Jan. It was after four o'clock and it didn't look like Plum and Alex would be getting much done today, assuming they even returned, so he closed the windows, turned off the lights and locked the One East door with the spare key that was kept on a hook in the event of the designated keyholders, Plum and Jan, not being around to lock up. Company policy, in this situation, was for the last person out of the office to lock up and leave the spare key with the receptionists.

Clomping down the grand staircase he heard raised voices coming from reception. Dee was trying to placate a woman wearing a pink beret. As soon as Dee saw Bruce, her face lit up. "Bruce, there's something wrong with your pigging phones and you've got a visitor," she yelled in her broad West Country accent, causing Pink Beret to visibly recoil.

The woman turned to look at Bruce. She had an unremarkable but quite agreeable face. "Are you Bruce?" she asked in a confident and cultured voice.

Bruce nodded and wondered why any woman who wasn't a student would wear a pink beret with a billowing lime green skirt.

Pink Beret's response was to slap Bruce so violently in the face that Dee dropped her mobile in astonishment. She had been composing an epic three-screen text, and she watched in horror as her Motorola bounced off the reception desk and landed on the hardwood floor, separating itself from its back cover and battery.

Pink Beret raised her hand to her mouth, seemingly shocked by her own actions. "I am so sorry," she said. "That was inexcusable, regardless of the provocation."

Bruce gently rubbed the side of his face. Why did it have to be on the same side as yesterday's blow? "What provocation?" he asked.

"You were so horrid and dismissive of me and then you hung up," she said. "I tried ringing back but your receptionist wouldn't put me through…"

"Hang on there, sweetheart, I explained to you that no one was picking up," said Dee.

"Nobody has ever spoken to me like that before," Pink Beret continued. "So I decided I had to let you know exactly how I felt."

"Well I think it's safe to say you can now tick that particular box," said Bruce, lightly massaging the side of his face. "Now if you'll excuse me..."

"I will most certainly not excuse you — what about my sister?"

"I told you — Alex went to Marelli's."

"Alex?"

"Isn't she your sister?" As soon as he said it, Bruce knew that she couldn't possibly be, not with Pink Beret's Sloaney accent.

Pink Beret shook her head.

"Is Jan your sister?" Bruce asked, suddenly concerned.

Again Pink Beret shook her head.

"Well I'm sorry but that's the only two possible candidates we have at AMG," Bruce said.

"I never said she worked at AMG," Pink Beret said, retrieving a rolled up copy of the magazine from a denim bag. "But if you'd given me the opportunity I would have said that she was recently featured in it."

She flicked through the magazine to the inside back cover's All About Me section and held it up to Bruce.

"Your sister is Honey Peach?" he gasped.

"I know what you're thinking," Pink Beret said, gesturing with her eyes at her slender frame and flat chest. "I should have demanded a recount when it came to the family tits allocation."

Bruce chose not to comment. He didn't want another slap for being overly familiar.

"I need to get in touch with her," she continued. "It's a family emergency."

Bruce rubbed the side of his face again. That girl knew how to slap.

"Bruce I'm so sorry, I've completely forgotten my manners," she said, offering him her hand. "I'm Rachel, and I'd really appreciate it if we could grab a coffee and have a chat. I know you were on your way out but could you just spare me a few minutes?"

***

As Bruce led Rachel through Bath's bustling streets crammed with tourists, she threaded her arm through his. It had been a long time since anyone had done that. Her fine fair hair flowed out from below her beret as she walked alongside him. When she turned her face to smile at him, Bruce noticed very slight laughter lines around her mouth and he guessed she was in her early thirties. He smiled back, enjoying the unfamiliar feeling of having an attractive woman on his arm. When tourists occasionally slowed to take in the splendour of Bath's Georgian architecture, Bruce indulgently slowed too, instead of tutting loudly and impatiently marching around them in the manner of many Bath residents.

Bruce spotted the bearded man who had brought him coffee early in the morning. He was sat on the edge of the pavement selling magazines. Bruce stopped, causing people walking behind him to tut, and took a ten pound note out of his wallet. Bending down, he offered it to the man.

"I can't split a tenner pal, I'm sorry," the man said, staring at the note.

"I'm not asking you to," Bruce replied, taking a magazine. "Thanks again for your act of kindness this morning."

There were no free tables in the coffee shop Bruce usually frequented, so he took Rachel to Marelli's. Outside the building, he looked up to the first floor restaurant and saw that Plum was sat at his favourite window table, alongside Alex. Even from street level, Bruce could see Plum's florid complexion, indicating that several bottles of Merlot had been consumed.

The cellar was much quieter today, with just a couple of shabby old men sat morosely at the bar — the creative types tended to spill in after five so Bruce and Rachel practically had the place to themselves for the next half hour. They had plenty of seating options but Bruce chose the same corner table as the day before.

"What will you have?" Rachel asked. "I know I asked you out for a coffee but it seems a bit of a shame to enter licensed premises and not sample the vino."

Bruce smiled. Rachel was his type of girl. He imagined it would be bad form to watch her drink alone, so when Rachel ordered a glass of house red, Bruce had one too.

"Well, this is rather rustic," she said, gesturing at her surroundings as she brought the drinks to the table.

"Cheers," he said, taking a deep glug. It was surprisingly drinkable, he thought, for a house red.

"Gosh, this is evil," said Rachel, wrinkling her nose in distaste.

"So you're Honey Peach's sister," Bruce said. "You're so different."

"It's a long and winding road of a story — same mother, different fathers, neither of which could stand the pace."

"You don't look anything alike."

"She has always been the attractive one in the family," Rachel said.

"You're just as attractive as her," Bruce replied.

Rachel moved her head backwards and threw him a quizzical stare.

"Perhaps in a less obvious way."

"A 'less obvious' way? Isn't that what you journalists would call being damned with faint praise?"

"That's not what I..."

"Look, if you don't mind, can we talk about my sister rather than mousey old me?"

Bruce shrugged. She wasn't mousey. Or old.

"I really need to speak to her but I don't have her number. You must have it?"

Bruce explained that he didn't. "If only you'd asked me yesterday," he said.

"Why? Would you have known it then?"

"I could have asked her for it. I was sat at this very table with her last night."

"She was here?" Rachel looked around the gloomy bar.

"She's been here a few times actually. Last month she popped in and signed a load of posters for us to give away as competition prizes."

Rachel frowned. "What was she doing here yesterday?"

"She was being interviewed for our Performer Profile section, which is an in-depth piece, charting her career highlights."

"Career highlights?" Rachel almost snorted. "What have they been?"

"Well, as I'm sure you know, she's only done one film — Legend of the Amazon Women — but that made a quite a splash when it was released earlier this year."

"Did it have a compelling storyline?" Rachel sneered.

"Yes it did," Bruce said. "It was about a bunch of women who buy a lot of books from a mail order company."

Rachel stared at Bruce and slowly started to smile. "You're quite the card, aren't you?"

"Well, I'm sure you know all about her chosen line of work, being her sister."

"Unfortunately we lost touch a while ago," Rachel said. "And now I really need to speak to her because Mummy is seriously ill."

"Sorry to hear that," Bruce said, taking another glug of wine. It still tasted perfectly drinkable to him.

Rachel looked at him imploringly. "So will you get her number for me?"

Bruce said he would.

The quiet cellar bar suddenly erupted with braying laughter as four men in grey suits stumbled down the stairs and ordered a magnum of Marelli's most expensive champagne. They cheered as the barmaid poured its contents into crystal flutes. The men looked around and made straight for Bruce's table. They all appeared to be in their fifties and already drunk.

"I say, you brighten this old dive up," one of them said, pointing at Rachel. "Got dressed in the dark this morning, did you?"

His companions laughed like road drills hammering concrete.

"I'd still give her a dig in the ribs though," the man said.

"Guys, do you mind?" Bruce said, standing up. Was something like this going to happen every time he brought a woman to Marelli's?

"Do excuse us old fruit, we had some luck on the gee-gees this afternoon," the man said. "Will you two share some bubbles with us?"

Rachel suddenly stood up and snapped: "We're in the middle of something here so just fuck off, will you?"

Chastened, and slightly shocked, the men retreated to the bar. Bruce was also a little taken aback. The harshness of Rachel's words contrasted sharply with her cultured voice — but then he remembered that he too had been on the receiving end of her displeasure a little earlier.

"Do you always get such lascivious types in here?" she asked.

Bruce's shrug suggested he didn't know how to answer that.

"Time for me to go then," she said, pushing her unwanted glass of wine into the centre of the table. She retrieved a tiny slip of paper and a pen from her bag, wrote a number down on it, and passed it across the table to Bruce.

Bruce was delighted to see she used a fountain pen. He carefully folded the piece of paper and put it in the breast pocket of his shirt, alongside his phone.

"Promise me you'll call me when you get her number?" Rachel said.

Bruce promised. She hugged him. He didn't want her to go. She kissed him lightly on the cheek. Now he really didn't want her to go.

As she walked across the bar towards the staircase Bruce decided that she was actually more attractive than her sister. She'd certainly struck a chord with the four toffs, one of whom directed a lewd comment at her as she passed them.

She smiled coquettishly, then grabbed one of the champagne flutes from the bar and threw its contents into the face of the offender. And without saying a word, she stomped up the stairs.

Bruce sunk as low as it was possible to go into his chair and hoped the toffs wouldn't notice he was still here. They did. They marched across the bar towards him and, hooting with laughter, poured what was left of their champagne over his head.

CHAPTER THREE: WEDNESDAY 4TH JUNE 2003

The stench of stale booze assaulted Bruce when he was forced awake by his stretched-to-capacity bladder. He realised why when he opened his eyes — he was lying on his sofa, still wearing the previous day's clothes. Last night had been another late one. He had ended up getting completely blotto with the toffs, who turned out to be enormous fun – particularly when advising him of the best way to keep that 'filly' of his under control.

He removed his mobile and the piece of folded paper containing Rachel's number from his shirt pocket. The phone's tiny keys were sticky from the champagne. The LCD screen was blank, hopefully only because the battery was exhausted. Rather unsteadily, he got to his feet and stumbled across the lounge to his television. As the screen burst into life he noticed the digital clock in the corner was approaching nine o'clock. That wasn't what he wanted to see. He couldn't be late two days in a row. Well, he could, but he shouldn't...

A shower, shave and taxi ride later and he was in One East, only to find it deserted. At first he wondered if the celebration of 'Alex's ascendancy to the big chair' had turned into a session, and he was the first one in, but if that had been the case the office would still be locked up. Then he heard voices coming from the boardroom. As he approached, he could see through the glass door that Plum, Alex and Nick were deep in discussion around the mahogany table that dominated the small room.

"What's going on?" Bruce asked as he opened the door.

"Sit down, Bruce," Plum commanded. "You're late. Again."

"Late for what? We had the Next Issue Planning Meeting on Monday."

"AMG has a new editor now and, following ideas we kicked around yesterday at lunch, she's outlining some changes she's planning to make," Plum said.

"Changes?" Bruce started to protest.

"Look, the best thing you can do is sit down and be quiet. I'm not at all pleased with you, Bruce — you got Jan sloshed, you left the office early without permission yesterday, and now you've been late two days in a row."

Alex said nothing but Bruce noticed she was wearing a particularly smug smile. It transpired that one of the changes she intended making was to add the news pages to Bruce's workload. Another was to introduce a diary page in which she would namecheck everyone she had been socialising with that week.

"Any comments, Bruce?" Plum asked.

"If I'm going to be doing the news now, as well as contribute to features, then I'm not going to have time to do all the film reviews," he said.

"Why not?" Alex said. "All you do is read the back of the box isn't it?"

"Yes, that's exactly how I review films," Bruce said. "You'll find The Guardian's movie critic does the same."

"We could get a freelancer to do them if it's going to be an issue," Alex suggested. "Or we could just cut down the number of review pages."

"Is this a hidden camera stunt?" Bruce said, looking around the room in a theatrical manner. "Alex, are you aware that the name of the magazine you have been made acting editor of is Adult Movie Guide? We exist to review adult movies, that is our purpose, which is why over half of our pages are devoted to them."

"That doesn't mean..." she started to protest.

"And as for your diary idea, why would any of our readers want to know which parties you have been to? Aren't their lives depressing enough as it is? They buy a weekly guide to masturbation material, for goodness sake. Don't you think they already know that your life is so much better than theirs, without you ramming it down their throats?"

Plum stood up. "Right, I think we'll adjourn this meeting for now. I'd like a word in private with you, Bruce."

Alex and Nick filed out and Plum closed the door behind them.

"Bruce, I simply can't have you speaking to Alex like that," he said, waggling his finger. "I said she would need your support, and you agreed to take on extra responsibilities."

"Are you trying to get rid of me?" Bruce said, a slight tremor creeping into his voice. "Because it feels like you're making my position untenable."

"Oh Bruce, you take yourself far too seriously," Plum said in a conciliatory tone. "AMG's position in the market is simply to point people in certain directions. Buy this book if you like reading about spanking, buy that film if you like seeing naked housewives, visit that website if you want to know more about goats..."

"The expression is goatse," Bruce quietly corrected him.

"I know you like to think you're 'the voice of the reader' but more of our income comes from advertising than cover sales, so our priority is to keep our advertisers happy, and that's why Alex will be an ideal editor."

"Ideal in what way — she's cheap?"

"In all candour, I'll concede that economics did play a contributing part in her appointment," Plum said. "Granted she doesn't have your urbane way with words but she wears short skirts and low tops and the advertisers love getting sloshed with her. This is actually a great opportunity for the magazine. Jan had the air of a maiden aunt about her. And there's nothing wrong with that when you're the editor of a needlework title – which of course she was, and a damn fine one too – but I've often wondered if bringing her to AMG was a mistake."

"It sounds like you've wondered that about me too."

Plum spread his arms and shrugged.

"Well thank you for that resounding vote of confidence."

"This is a much smaller business than video games and it really is all about relationships," Plum said. "The trouble with you is you've made a name for yourself as a hatchet man. You're the guy who tells it like it is. And that talent doesn't transfer particularly well to other areas of the business. The advertisers already know and like Alex. They like being with her, they like…"

"Excuse me, I'm going to be sick," Bruce said, walking out of Plum's office.

***

After a calming cigarette in the bright morning sun of the courtyard, Bruce made his way back up the stairs to the office. Plum was back in his den, Alex was on the phone and Nick was quietly dragging page elements around the screen on his computer.

"The world's gone mad," Bruce said, rolling his wheeled chair along to Nick's desk. Nick's extra-large monitor displayed pages two and three of the next issue. Page two contained an advert while page three housed the editor's Welcome column, a list of the magazine's contents and the flannel panel, which provided details of the AMG staff. Nick was reducing the size of the flannel panel.

"It certainly has, mate," Nick agreed, still looking at his monitor. "I was flabbergasted Plum made Alex editor instead of you."

"You were flabbergasted?" Bruce replied. "How do you think it made me feel?"

"Like dancing?"

"Not quite," Bruce said. "And that's my line."

Nick shrugged.

"What happened to you yesterday?" Bruce said.

"Yesterday? I wasn't in work yesterday."

"Yes, I was aware of that, which is why I asked – why weren't you in work?"

"Nothing serious mate, just a dose of the squits," Nick said quietly. "Must have been the kebab I had Monday night."

"Listen, about Monday night..."

Nick's face was screwed up in concentration as he resized the flannel panel box by a tiny percentage. "Mmm?"

"Don't ignore me," Bruce said, poking Nick in his arm and causing his mouse pointer to dash wildly across the screen.

"Oi, don't touch the guns," Nick warned him, forming a fist. "They might go off in your face."

"What happened, after we left Marelli's?"

"I told you, I had a kebab."

"Did you see what happened to Jan?"

"How could I? She went in the opposite direction and I was watching Honey Peach to the station..."

"You make it sound like an act of chivalry," Bruce said. "You were heading that way anyway because it's on the way to your flat."

"What's your point?"

"You didn't see anything happen to me, did you?" Bruce asked, pointing to the lump on the side of his head.

Nick stared at it. "You picked that up Monday night, did you?" he said. "It looks quite tender, mate. Have you had it checked out by A&E?"

Bruce shook his head.

"You should," Nick said, staring at the lump and prodding it. "You can get brain damage from a blow to the head. That's why we wear scrum caps in games these days."

"Don't finger it," Bruce said, in response to Nick's prodding.

"Who gave it to you?"

"I'm not sure."

"You're not sure? How smashed were you?"

"I wasn't smashed, I only had a few pints..."

"Did you report it?"

"How could I when I didn't see who it was?"

"They'll only have a couple of thousand suspects. I suppose it goes with the territory when you make a living from pissing people off."

"I didn't piss anyone off," Bruce protested.

"What about those two blokes?"

"You were the one who escorted them out of the bar. If they were going to attack anyone it should have been you."

Nick grinned and tensed his bulging biceps. "Mate, nobody is going to mess with these bad boys. Now let me take another look at that lump on your head…"

"Will you stop poking it?" Bruce yelped. "We've already established that it's sore."

"There's something awfully sad about middle-aged people who get smashed in public places, don't you think?" Nick said. "I tried to talk you out of that last round but you wouldn't listen."

"I told you, I wasn't smashed," Bruce said. "And one brandy wouldn't have made a difference anyway."

"I didn't say you particularly," Nick said. "I might have been talking about Jan…"

"Jan wasn't drunk either. You were there – you saw how much we had."

"You might have done shots or something before I got there…"

"We did not do shots – we're not teenagers."

"Well maybe she stopped off somewhere before she went back to her car?"

"She wouldn't do that."

"Maybe you don't know her as well as you think you do. She told us she was going to catch a taxi, didn't she?"

Bruce nodded.

"Well she obviously didn't. And did you see she had a bottle of gin in her bag? Perhaps she drinks alone every night…"

Before Bruce could reply, Alex interrupted her phone call to shout across the office: "Bruce, instead of gossiping like an old woman, get chasing up news stories for the next issue — you do know our deadline is Friday?"

"Funnily enough I was just thinking about that," Bruce replied. "I was thinking that every news story should be about you this month – how great you are, how great your friends are, how great your life is, that sort of thing. What do you think?"

She pouted and glared at him, before making another call.

"How can Plum make her acting editor?" Bruce said to Nick. "It's not that I even wanted it, I just hate to see her with it. I wouldn't trust her to write a shopping list."

They both stared across the office at Alex, who was perched on her desk, her short skirt showcasing her legs to great effect.

"I think you're just saying that because you fancy her," Nick said to Bruce.

Bruce mimed putting his fingers down his throat. "No thanks, she's repulsive."

Nick gave Bruce a quizzical look. "Mate, how can you say that? She's young, slim, she's got a pretty face..."

"She's repulsive on the inside," Bruce stopped him.

Bruce couldn't look at her any longer. Turning his attention to Nick's monitor, he said: "How much longer are you going to be dicking around with this? You are familiar with the phrase, overegging the pudding? And why are you cutting everyone's pictures from the flannel panel?"

"Alex says there's no need for them," Nick replied. "And with the extra space we can have a large picture of her above the Welcome column."

Bruce sighed. "Of course we can. Even though Jan's profile pic was always the same size as everyone else's. Let's hope we've only got to put up with her for a few issues."

After a pause of a few seconds, Nick said: "Have you been to see Jan yet?"

"No, I haven't had chance," Bruce said.

"Same here," Nick said. "But when you do go, in all seriousness I think you should get them to check your head while you're there. It looks like you took quite a hit."

"Bruce!" Alex yelled in his direction. "Can you please get on with the news?"

Bruce stared across the office at Alex and contrasted her with Rachel, the woman he had met yesterday. Even though Rachel had demonstrated that she had a feisty side, she was also elegant, chic and she used words like 'lascivious'. And she was attractive, even if it wasn't in an obvious way...

Back at his own desk, he flicked through his collection of business cards and considered who to chase for information that could be churned into news stories. He picked four candidates from the pack and shuffled them, deciding who to call first, but now her name had cropped up he kept thinking about Rachel. He would much rather talk to her again, but before he could do that he needed to have Honey Peach's number. And to get that he would have to see Jan – unless he could get it from Milkman…

"Has she turned up yet?" Bruce asked when Milkman answered his phone.

"No she hasn't," Milkman said. "I'm starting to worry about her now. She didn't say anything to you, did she, about going somewhere else?"

"No, but you couldn't blame her if she did," Bruce said. "Sending her a text saying she was going to have to share your bed…"

"That was only a bit of banter," Milkman said.

"And you've tried ringing her?"

"Dozens of times."

"Would you mind giving me her number?"

"Do you think she will answer the phone to you and not me?"

"It's not for me," Bruce said. "I only want to pass it on to her sister."

"Her sister?"

"She came to the office yesterday trying to find her. Some kind of a family emergency. I said I'd get her number so she can let her know…"

"I didn't know she had a sister," Milkman said, suddenly interested. "How big are her tits?"

"In your eyes they would be disappointingly diminutive," Bruce said. "And I don't think she's your type anyway. She looks about thirty-five."

"Thirty-five!" Milkman snorted dismissively. "Fuck that shit! I'm not into grannies."

Bruce was about to point out that Milkman was at least twenty years older than Rachel when the old roué read out Honey Peach's mobile number to him.

"If you do speak to her, tell her to ring me," Milkman said. "We've got other things we're supposed to be doing for Spaghetti and I need to know where I stand."

Now Bruce could speak to Rachel again. To his surprise, the thought of doing this gave him butterflies in the stomach. That was a feeling he hadn't had for a considerable time. To savour it for as long as possible he decided to chase up his news contacts before calling her. The first three calls he made yielded a few little snippets he could write up, leaving him with just Julian Gregan, CEO of pressure group CRSP – the Campaign to Restrict the Sale of Pornography.

CRSP was formed as a direct result of the year 2000 legislation which allowed hardcore pornography – given an R18 rating by the British Board of Film Classification – to be legally sold in the UK through licensed sex shops. The aim of CRSP was to get this legislation overturned and Julian Gregan was occasionally quoted in the mainstream media if they ran an anti-porn piece. Some of his more alarmist public statements were occasionally reproduced and ridiculed in AMG.

Bruce scribbled four questions down on his pad, based on his notes from yesterday's conversation with Zara, and dialled Gregan's number. He answered immediately, like he always did.

Bruce adopted a Home Counties accent and introduced himself as a journalist. He did not say which publication he worked for but he went on to explain that he was looking for a reaction from CRSP regarding the government awarding grants to makers of pornography.

"They're doing what?" Gregan spluttered.

"I must stress there has been no official announcement yet," Bruce cautioned, mangling his vowels in the same way he imagined a Royal Correspondent for Tatler would do. "But, assuming there will be in the foreseeable future, does CRSP think it appropriate for the government – which, by definition, really means the taxpayer – to subsidise pornographers' overseas jaunts when there are pensioners living in poverty and life-saving drugs are subject to postcode rationing on the NHS?"

Gregan did not think this was appropriate. After asking for more details, Gregan composed himself and gave Bruce an official 'on the record' quote: "I find it inconceivable that a serving government would stoop so low as to court popularity with pornographers by using decent, hardworking families' taxes to help them peddle their sordid wares in other countries."

Thank you Mr Gregan, that'll do nicely. Now to put a different spin on it for AMG's readership. Something about the enemies of freedom attempting to stifle an already overregulated industry, putting British jobs at risk, preventing UK firms from reaching their potential, frustrating the industry's attempts to help the country's balance of payments...

After typing up the story Bruce dragged it across onto the network drive and sat back, feeling a little guilty. Gregan actually had a perfectly reasonable point – why should pornographers be subsidised by taxpayers? But then he remembered that it wasn't actually a real story...

Now he could call Rachel. He ferreted in his shirt pocket for the precious piece of paper with her number on. Pulling it out, his heart sank. It resembled a twenty pound note he'd once found in his jeans pocket after it had been through the washing machine. The champagne which the toffs had poured over him had soaked through his shirt and into the paper. It tore as he unfolded it, revealing that the ink had run into an indecipherable confusion of squiggles.

CHAPTER FOUR: THURSDAY 5TH JUNE 2003

Bruce opened the door of the ancient fridge in AMG's tiny kitchen area. He removed the plastic container that housed his lunch and took it to his desk, where he popped the top.

"Been out, have you mate?" Nick asked, from across the office.

"Indeed," Bruce replied. "I do occasionally leave these premises during the lunch break – though I can understand the appeal of staying in the office alone so you can wank like a safari park chimpanzee over the latest batch of film releases."

"You do realise you're describing yourself there, don't you?" Nick said. "Where did you go?"

"I went to see Jan."

"Oh, how is she?"

"She's in a pretty bad way actually," Bruce said. "And she won't be returning to work anytime soon."

Nick sighed.

"Her face is bruised and swollen, she's got a catalogue of broken bones and the nurse said she's in constant pain."

"The nurse said?"

"I don't think Jan knew I was there. She's so full of drugs that she can't even speak."

"So it's not all bad news then?" Nick laughed.

"That's not funny," Bruce snapped.

"I meant about the drugs, not that she can't speak," Nick protested.

Before Bruce could reply he was interrupted by his phone. It was a woman called Roz. She had sent AMG an email inviting the magazine to visit a new fetish fair she had launched but she hadn't received a reply.

Roz emphasised that her event was taking place the following day, in Brighton. Despite Bruce explaining that Friday was AMG's deadline day, Roz insisted the magazine had a duty to send a reporter to cover it. That's your job, she told Bruce. He asked her to re-send the mail direct to him and he would see what he could do.

The email from Roz pinged through seconds after their conversation concluded and Bruce immediately deleted it. Pushy bitch. He was tucking into his bacon and brie sandwich when his phone rang again. He ignored it. It was probably Roz, wanting confirmation he had received her email. He had no intention of ever speaking to her again.

"Mate, answer your phone," Nick grumbled.

Bruce ignored it even more intently, slouching lower in his chair, which prompted Nick to stride across the office and answer it for him. "Bruce's phone," Nick said with mock enthusiasm. "Yes he is here, I'll put him on now."

Bruce glared at Nick as he accepted the receiver. "This is Bruce," he said sulkily.

"Gosh you sound like a barrel of fun today," said Rachel. "What did you have for lunch, a Valium?"

Hearing her voice, Bruce instantly sat upright in his chair. "Hello!" he squealed with delight. "I was really hoping you would call."

"Well it seems one of us has to make an effort," she chided. "I was a bit disappointed you didn't ring me yesterday, given the situation."

"I tried to ring you," Bruce said. "Well, I was going to but the ink ran on the piece of paper…"

"Did it really?" she said, her voice heavy with sarcasm.

"Honestly, it did," he said. "After you made your dramatic exit, those old blokes doused me in champagne. And if you remember, you'd written your number down with a fountain pen which meant…"

Nick looked across at Bruce with concern. "Are you alright, mate?" he asked. "Your voice has taken on a strange new tone. If you weren't such a cantankerous old bastard I would say it sounds like you're flirting."

Turning his head so he couldn't see Nick, Bruce explained that he had obtained her sister's number but Milkman had told him that she wasn't answering her phone.

"Who is Milkman?" she said.

"You haven't heard of Milkman?"

"Should I have?"

"A lot of people have – he used to be a well known porn star and he directed her film," Bruce said.

"And why is he called Milkman? Is it because – let me guess – you can rely on him to deliver the white stuff?"

Bruce laughed. "Nothing that creative, I'm afraid – it's because he was actually a milkman in his younger days."

Rachel said she would try calling Honey Peach now, using another line, but she asked Bruce to hold while she did so. After a few moments Bruce could just about make out a tinny version of Honey Peach's familiar voice in the background saying she was too busy to come to the phone but to leave a message. Rachel did not leave a message.

Instead, she ended the call and said to Bruce: "She's not picking up so can you get her address for me?"

"Her address?"

"Yes, you know, the place where she lives."

Bruce exhaled loudly, like a mechanic giving an estimate for an engine rebuild.

"In her All About Me piece you asked her what she enjoyed reading the most and she said letters from her fans and AMG," Rachel said. "Apparently she looks forward to it popping through her letterbox every week."

"I don't know if she actually used those exact words," Bruce cautioned. There was every chance that Jan had embellished, if not fabricated, that answer, as it had a touch of the double entendre about it whilst also promoting the magazine.

"But you could look on your subscriber database for me, couldn't you?" Rachel said.

"I could, if I had access to it."

"I'm sure you can get it, Bruce. I wouldn't ask if it wasn't an emergency..."

After a little more cajoling Bruce said he would try to get it but he couldn't promise.

"Thank you so much, I'll be in your debt forever," she said. "Call me back as soon as you can – anytime after five today is good for me. Here, take my number down – and promise me you won't throw it away so bloody casually this time."

After she hung up Bruce realised he hadn't asked Rachel what name he should search for, as he doubted very much that Honey Peach was her sister's real name. To find her he might need to look through every record in the file but that would not be the most difficult part – getting access to the AMG mailing list would. It existed solely on Plum's computer and he was fiercely protective of it.

Although AMG only had a couple of thousand direct subscribers – most of its sales came through newsagents – advertisers had often asked if they could use the subscriber list for their own mailings. Plum would always say the Data Protection Act prevented this, which was true, but another reason was if a list containing the names and addresses of consumers with an interest in pornography fell into the wrong hands, and they knew how to exploit it, life could be made very uncomfortable for AMG's subscribers. And that was why no one else in the office – not even Jan – had ever seen the mailing list.

"Who was that?" asked Nick.

"Honey Peach's sister," Bruce replied, still smiling.

Nick did not return his smile. "She has a sister?"

"She is trying to get hold of her because her mother is ill."

"When did you meet her, and what was that about being doused in champagne?"

"It's a long and winding road of a story," Bruce said.

"Is she fit?"

Bruce ignored him and called Rachel back but it went straight through to her voicemail. He didn't leave a message. Instead he called Milkman – he would know Honey Peach's real name – but he too was unavailable. Finally he interrogated his favourite search engine. The results for Honey Peach were less than helpful, with most matches being crude fan sites featuring images grabbed from the Amazon Women movie. The online homes of the lads' mags mentioned her many times but generally only to emphasise how much they would like to bang her.

The bright afternoon sunlight which had been flooding into the office was suddenly eclipsed by the corpulent figure of Plum, who was standing between Bruce's desk and the window. "How are the news pages coming on Bruce?" asked Plum.

"Okay," Bruce replied. "I've still got a bit to do."

"Have you got a lead?"

Although it would be easier to put an attractive image on the cover, like every other adult-themed magazine, AMG was formatted as an A3-sized newspaper. It resembled the 1970s' incarnation of music magazine Melody Maker, which Plum had greatly admired during his early teens, and it featured a news story on its front page. Jan had been responsible for collating AMG's news pages, and sourcing a suitable lead story each week had always taken up a considerable amount of her time.

"I thought we'd go with just the one word – Rejoice! – alongside a big picture of Alex."

"Let me see what you've got," Plum said, ignoring the sarcasm.

Bruce opened the text document on his computer. The headline read: 'Killjoys call for the stifling of British enterprise'.

Plum quickly skimmed through the piece. "Actually I'm pleasantly surprised," he said putting a hand on Bruce's shoulder. "The headline needs work but the piece itself is not bad at all. Is this an exclusive?"

Bruce informed him that it was all his own work.

"Excellent!" Plum said. "In that case we'll organise a sale or return promotion for the newsagents. It might get the buggers to order a few more copies. Right, on that extremely positive note, I'll off to my Rotary lunch and I don't expect to be disturbed for anything less than the end of the world. Understood, Bruce?"

***

Over the next couple of hours Bruce churned out another dozen news stories, most of which were based on company announcements so they just needed tidying up and reformatting in the AMG house style. He collated them all in one folder and sent them across the network to Nick's computer, where the magazine was laid out.

Job done, despite the intrusive CD that Alex had inflicted on the office stereo in Plum's absence. The current number featured the singer screeching: "I'm doing what I'm good at, doing what I'm good at, doing what I'm good at, and that's fuck all…"

Over and over and over again.

"Not too challenging for you, Bruce?" Alex asked at one point.

"Not at all," Bruce replied. "It makes a pleasant change to hear a whole CD without a single tune on it."

"Being as you're now Plum's blue-eyed boy I'll let you put some Glenn Miller on tomorrow," Alex said. "Now I'm using my editor's privilege and popping out for a while to do some shopping – don't tell Plum."

Bruce looked around the office, which was now empty apart from Nick, who was engrossed in paginating the magazine. The film and book reviews were finished and the features had been collated earlier in the week so now he could address the big issue – how to access Plum's computer.

He sauntered over to the water cooler. Seeing the courtyard was dotted with staff from other offices, having their afternoon smoke break, Bruce took his cup outside the front of Legal House. The pavement was packed with summer pedestrians so Bruce sat down on the curb while he pondered the problem.

After a few minutes the street vendor he had given a tenner to earlier in the week sidled up alongside him, dumping a pile of magazines on the pavement. "Hey, is this your pitch?" he asked.

"No, I'm just…"

"Only joking, pal," the guy said, offering him a handshake.

He introduced himself as Nosh and explained that Bruce's tenner had been the biggest tip he had received all summer, adding: "If there are more like you around here then maybe I should set up camp here?"

Bruce offered Nosh a cigarette and took one himself. While the two of them smoked, Bruce said: "If it was me, I would go for the upmarket coffee shop near the end of the road."

"I'm not pan handling for spare change," Nosh protested.

"I know," said Bruce. "You're selling reading material and although the coffee shop is a popular meeting place, it doesn't have a newspaper rack. I know I'd feel more comfortable waiting for someone if I had something to read…"

Nosh understood. He grinned, thanked Bruce and shook his hand. "Nice one, pal. You'd have to go for a long walk in this city to find someone as decent as you," Nosh said.

Bruce watched Nosh gather up his pile of magazines and make his way further down the street. That may just have been the nicest thing anyone had ever said to Bruce.

Suddenly inspired, he stubbed out his cigarette, leapt to his feet and raced up the staircase back into the office, oblivious to the commotion his cup of chilled water caused after a Japanese tourist in a hurry had accidently kicked it over a traffic warden.

"Has the All About Me section gone to press yet?" Bruce asked Nick, gasping for breath.

"It went to production this morning," Nick replied, without looking up. "But it won't be on the presses yet. What's the problem?"

Bruce sat at his desk and called Plum.

"This had better be good," Plum said.

"What's the procedure if we want to recall a section from the printer?" Bruce said.

"Why would we do that?" Plum snapped. "That costs time or money. Or both."

"There's a tiny issue with Alex's All About Me page," Bruce said.

"How big is tiny?"

"It's only one letter but…"

"In that case it's fine," Plum said. "We're not the Sunday Times."

"Well alright, if you're sure," Bruce said. "I just thought Alex might prefer us not to tell the world that she likes to relax by taking her dog for long wanks. But if you're happy for it to go to print, and you're prepared to confirm to her that I did bring it to your attention…"

Plum swore repeatedly and he asked Bruce to put Alex on the phone.

"I'm afraid she's not here," Bruce replied. "She's gone shopping."

Plum cursed some more. "I'm not swearing at you Bruce," he assured him. "But that section goes on the press in less than an hour and if we miss our slot we'll be shunted to the back of the queue."

"Can you come back to the office and amend it?" Bruce asked, aware that the only computer connected to the printer's FTP site was Plum's.

"No I bloody can't," Plum replied. "The mayor is making a presentation soon and it would be the height of bad manners if I left now."

"Oh dear," Bruce sympathised. "I can see that wouldn't go down well. I suppose we'll just have to delay our publication day for next week's issue."

"No we won't," Plum said. "You'll have to go into my office and make the changes on my computer."

"Well, I could..." Bruce replied reluctantly.

Plum explained where the pages for the current issue were located on his hard drive. "The only other thing you need to know is the password," Plum said. "When the prompt comes up, type in 'young boys'."

"Every time you turn on your computer you enter young boys?" Bruce queried.

Plum confirmed that was indeed what was required to obtain access to his computer. "If you must know I have an affinity with the Swiss football club, Young Boys of Bern," he said. "My parents had a lodge in the mountains not far from there when I was growing up."

"I don't doubt that for a minute," Bruce replied.

Bruce performed his mission with military-like efficiency. After inputting the password the hard drive was a doddle to navigate. The subscriber list turned out to be a spreadsheet rather than a database but each entry was very detailed. The 'trade' section numbered just a few hundred and the records were helpfully broken down into sub-sections of manufacturer, distributor, retailer, publisher, performer and other. Bruce metaphorically doffed his cap at Plum's efficiency, sorted the list under the performer tag and scanned through it.

He was prepared make a copy of the entire list, so when Rachel told him her sister's real name he could look her up, but Honey Peach was actually listed as Honey Peach. She had been a subscriber for four months and she lived in Brighton. Bruce scribbled the address down and closed the program, ensuring he declined the offer to save the workbook in the new configuration he had ordered it into.

Then, begrudgingly, he opened the desktop publishing program to make the amendment to Alex's All About Me section. He converted the new page into a PDF and uploaded it to the printer's FTP site, replacing the previous version. He kept a copy of the original page too, so if Plum queried it he could see Bruce had been telling the truth.

Bruce felt a warm glow of satisfaction. Most obviously because he could now give Rachel what she wanted but also, he suspected, because he had done the right thing. Even though it meant relinquishing the best opportunity to publicly humiliate Alex he was ever likely to get. She would have been on the receiving end of comments like 'You must have the happiest dog in the country' for years to come. And he'd let her off the hook.

***

At the stroke of five Bruce rang Rachel and, feeling almost smug, he informed her that he had her sister's address.

"That's great Bruce, thank you so much. Could you text it to me please?"

"When are you thinking of going to see her?"

"In the morning."

"Would you like me to go with you?" Bruce said.

"Go with me?" she said, surprised. "It's a bit out of your way, isn't it?"

"It would be but by a remarkable coincidence I am actually going to Brighton tomorrow for a fetish fair," he said. Well, I am now.

"That is a coincidence," she agreed. "It sounds awfully kinky. What will you be wearing?"

"Sorry to disappoint you," he said gravely. "But I'm only reporting on it. However I could pick you up and we could go there together."

"Pick me up?"

"You're in Bristol, aren't you? It wouldn't be much of a detour."

"No, I'm in London," she said.

Bruce tried not to sound disappointed, though a part of him was thinking that it would be far more difficult to develop a relationship with her over that distance. "Oh, I thought…"

"I was in Bristol on Tuesday but…"

"Well we could still meet up down there for a coffee or something," he persisted. "We could even visit her together as I'd like to, er, ask her a couple of supplementary questions following her interview on Monday."

"Well okay," Rachel said. "How about you meet me outside the Grand at noon?"

"The Grand at noon," Bruce confirmed. "I'll be there."

"But don't forget to text me the address as well, just in case."

Bruce composed an internal memo to Plum, Alex and Nick, informing them that he would be out of the office the following day to report on a fetish fair for the next issue. He sent the memo and heard it ping into everyone's computer.

Nick read the mail and looked across at him. "You're going out on deadline day?"

"Yes I am."

"Shouldn't you confirm this with Plum first?"

"Oh you know what? I'd really love to," Bruce said. "But he's not here, is he? Neither is Alex. Besides, I've completed all my sections."

"What about the news?"

"I sent you the news hours ago," Bruce said.

"No you didn't. You only sent me the front page lead."

Bruce sighed, swore and sent the folder across again.

"What's wrong with you?" Nick said, just seconds later. "This folder only contains the piece about Julian Gregan."

"No, it contains that story and a dozen others I put together this afternoon," Bruce said, opening the folder which he had saved the stories in on his computer. His stomach flipped when he saw that it did indeed contain just the one story. Trying not to panic, Bruce searched his computer's hard drive for the missing documents, swearing as he did so.

"Calm down mate," urged Nick. "You're going to give yourself an aneurysm."

The stories were not there.

CHAPTER FIVE: FRIDAY 6TH JUNE 2003

The drive down to Brighton was long but uneventful. Bruce's little Mazda convertible wasn't at its best on motorways but the Friday morning M4 traffic kept him well within the speed limit. Folding down the MX-5's canvas roof had exposed him to far more sun than his pale skin was accustomed to so he stopped at the first services on the M25 to yank it back up. His face was glowing crimson, which is rarely a good look for overweight blokes of his age.

The last few miles along London Road into Brighton city centre were bumper-to-bumper, and Bruce was regularly overtaken by pedestrians. He'd woken up at six but had been unable to get back to sleep, possibly because he was looking forward to seeing Rachel, so he decided to hit the road early. Which was just as well as this final leg of the journey was taking an age. Luckily he still had an hour and twenty minutes until his appointment with Rachel, which should allow him sufficient time to make a flying visit to the fetish fair.

It was taking place on the promenade, a few hundred yards further down from the ruins of the West Pier, and eventually Bruce emerged on the sea front and found a pay-and-display parking space relatively quickly. The price appeared exorbitant for a few hours, which explained why there were so many vacant spaces, but Bruce didn't mind. He could put it on expenses.

The fetish fair consisted of around twenty stalls selling leather clothing, corsets, whips, floggers, restraints, lotions and potions and erotic imagery of dubious artistic merit. A few dozen customers milled around, though there did not appear to be much buying going on.

Bruce liked to travel light when on reporting duties, packing just a digital camera and a tiny mini disc recorder into the pockets of his shirt. He usually used the camera to capture images of things he thought were of interest, negating the need to make notes, and he collected quotes on the mini disc. Today he had taken around a dozen images when he felt a hand on his shoulder.

"What do you think you are doing?" said an aggressive female voice. It belonged to a short stocky woman in a black and white polka dot dress. Her dyed black hair had the texture of wheat that had been shredded and she sported thickly drawn eyebrows and bright red lipstick.

"You don't take pictures without permission," she said. "Now give me the film out of that camera."

"It's digital."

"I don't give a monkey's what make it is…"

"Are you Roz by any chance?" Bruce asked.

"Who wants to know?" The woman asked defiantly.

"I'm Bruce from AMG magazine. You invited me here."

Her attitude immediately softened. "You should have made yourself known, love, and you should never take pictures of people at a fetish event without asking them first. I've got to look after my stallholders and protect their customers' right to privacy."

"Would you mind giving me a quote for the report?" he asked, taking the mini disc out of his shirt pocket.

"I can only give you a few minutes," she said, looking around.

"Oh don't worry, that should be fine," Bruce reassured her, plugging a small microphone into the mini disc, which he then held up between him and Roz. He pressed the record button and said: "I'm with Roz, the organiser of Leathers, Tethers and Feathers. Is this the first time you have staged this event?"

She confirmed it was. Bruce went on to ask about support from exhibitors, visitor numbers and why she chose an open air location, when a closed-in space would have seemed more appropriate, given the nature of the products on display. Her responses were short and defensive.

Bruce decided to wrap it up, saying: "Leathers, Tethers and Feathers is quite a good name for a fetish fair but…"

"It sums up what we are…" Roz said.

"But this is not what I would call a fetish fair," Bruce said. "It's a BDSM-themed jumble sale, and not a particularly good one at that."

Roz glared at him. "Is that a serious question?"

"No," Bruce replied, winding the microphone cable up and turning off the mini disc player. "It's a serious statement. I can't believe you got approval to stage it here and I can't believe I've wasted my time coming down to see it. If you hold another one, please do hesitate to let me know."

The three hour car journey had been worth it just to see the disagreeable woman's mouth drop open in amazement. She was still stood rooted to the spot staring at him as he walked off in the direction of the Grand Hotel, further along the sea front.

As his fetish fair visit had been concluded much quicker than expected, he was twenty minutes early for his appointment with Rachel. He leaned back against the promenade railings, lit a cigarette and looked up in admiration at the imposing Victorian building while enjoying the breeze created by the stream of fit young things on bicycles that tore down the promenade's cycle lane. He was getting restless as noon came and went and his thoughts returned to the missing news stories of the day before. He was still furious that he had to write them again, though he wasn't sure who to be furious with. After another smoke and a further twenty minutes wait he decided to call Rachel.

Her phone went straight to voicemail. He left a message asking her to ring him. Then he sent her a text asking the same thing.

A further fifteen minutes passed. Should be call her again? He did, and again it went to voicemail, though this time he didn't leave a message. Instead, he asked an old lady who looked like a local for directions to Honey Peach's address.

"Take the first left after the Grand then follow the road to the station," she said. "As the road curves to the left, keep going and it's one of the side streets. You'll know if you miss the turning and go too far. Everyone will smell of lavender and you'll be in Hove."

Bruce thanked her and set off. Although it was a gentle gradient, the road leading to the station was still a hill – and almost half a mile long. As he slowly trudged up it, the imposing five-storey buildings close to the sea front gave way to more modest dwellings until the street was lined with the type of houses small children drew, with four windows and a door in the middle.

Eventually he arrived outside the address he had sacrificed the opportunity to humiliate Alex to obtain. It was a pleasant red brick residence with bay windows up and down and a small gravelled forecourt providing distance from the pavement. Above the front door was a tiny balcony with wooden railings. Very nice, certainly compared to his tiny flat, which currently had an ant infestation in its kitchen.

He paused and rehearsed what he was going to say if she answered the door. 'Hi, I've broken the law and risked my job by misappropriating your address from our computer and driven over 130 miles to see you because your sister who I've never met before this week but who I think I fancy has been trying to get in touch with you but she appears to have stood me up and so I've come to see you on my own...'

He played about with it a bit but every permutation sounded like the actions of someone who needed sectioning under the Mental Health Act.

He felt like a foolish adolescent. He had actually said, in his head, that he thought he fancied Rachel. He barely knew her. Besides, men of his age didn't use terms like that. He should drive back to Bath before he made an even bigger fool of himself. He had what he purportedly came for, the raw material for a feature on the fetish fair, and he could fulfil the secondary purpose of his visit – letting Honey Peach know her sister was trying to get in touch with her – by simply popping a note through her door. No one would know that his real purpose in coming to Brighton was just because he wanted to see Rachel again.

Using the waist-high forecourt wall to lean on, he wrote 'Honey Peach, please contact your sister re: your mother' on the back of one of his AMG business cards. That would do. That would allow him to draw a line under this juvenile episode whilst fulfilling any moral obligation he might have towards Honey Peach or her sister. The metal gate screeched as if in pain as he barged it aside and approached the rather shabby front door, which had a frosted glass panel above the brass letterbox. He was about to post the card when the door was wrenched open from inside.

"You finally made it then?" said Rachel. She was wearing tight white jeans and a yellow T-shirt which had the words 'Mildly Amusing Slogan' printed on the front in a large black font – which Bruce's inner geek recognised as Impact. Her hair was scraped back into a ponytail and purple-painted toenails peeped out of her green flip-flops.

"Well don't just stand there like a stalker," she said impatiently.

Bruce followed her through the almost empty hall into the compact kitchen. A set of patio doors led out to a small garden, which was separated from its neighbours' on each side by a brick wall of around the same height as the one at the front. A glass-topped round table and two chairs took up most of the kitchen's available floor space.

"Well?" said Rachel expectantly, pulling out one of the chairs and sitting at the table.

Well what? This was confusing. Bruce looked suitably confused.

"Why didn't you let me know you were going to be late? I was stood around waiting for you for over an hour," she said.

"Rachel, I was the one stood around for over an hour," Bruce replied. "I didn't move from outside the hotel and I rang you several times."

"The battery in my phone is dead," she said. "What hotel?"

"The Grand. On the sea front. Where we arranged to meet at noon."

"I meant the Grand Pavilion," she said. "That's where I was."

"I didn't know there was a Grand Pavilion in Brighton."

"Oh," she said. "You gave me the impression you knew the place quite well."

"I have been here a few times over the years. Isn't it called the Royal Pavilion?"

Rachel shrugged and her tone softened. "Whatever it's called, it's where I was. Now are you going to continue to bitch about this or do you want a coffee?"

"I'd prefer a glass of cold water," Bruce said.

"Yes, you do look like Mr Sweaty," Rachel said, running the tap and looking around for a glass. "Mug alright?"

"Fine," he said, accepting it gratefully and gulping it down. "I assume you've caught up with your sister and everything is sorted?"

"Why would you assume that?"

Bruce made an expansive gesture with his arms. "Because you're in her house."

She shook her head and pouted.

"How did you get in then?"

Rachel didn't answer.

"Was the door open?"

"Not exactly…"

"What's going on?"

"I don't think she's been here for a few days. The milk in her fridge has the 3rd on it and she's got four ready meals in there which have also passed their 'best before' date."

"That doesn't prove anything. I've always got out of date food in my fridge."

"Maybe, but I bet that isn't all you've got in there, is it?" Rachel theatrically flung the fridge door open. "Look, there is literally nothing else in there apart from some low calorie drinks and a bottle of plonk."

Rachel then popped the lid on the chrome pedal bin and pointed down at the interior. "And look, no rubbish at all. Does this woman exist solely on ready meals?"

Bruce stared at her. She sounded like a prosecuting barrister. This woman. I put it to you, m'lud, that this woman exists solely on ready meals.

Rachel moved to the cooker and opened the oven door. "This has never even been used. This woman has not cooked a meal in her life so if she's been here for the past few days, what has she been living on?"

"Takeaways?" Bruce suggested. That's what he frequently did.

"No wrappers of any kind in the bin," Rachel countered. "Besides, people who eat takeaways on a regular basis don't tend to look like Honey Peach."

"Is Honey Peach her real name?" Bruce said as he finished his mug of water.

Rachel opened the freezer door. "And all that's in here is ice," she said.

"I mean, I just assumed it was her made-up porn name but she's actually down on our mailing list under that name…"

"Bruce, please stop wittering, I'm afraid something might have happened to her," said Rachel. "I think she's in some kind of trouble…"

The sound of a car reversing into the space outside the front of the house suddenly cut Rachel off. She dashed into the hall and peered out through the letterbox. The empty hall allowed the sounds of outside to seep in, echoing off the black and white chequerboard tiles. Bruce heard the engine shutting down, a car door opening and then closing, followed by the creak of the metal gate and then footsteps on the stone path.

"Oh bugger," Rachel hissed. "Someone is coming."

"Is it her?" Bruce said.

"I'm afraid not," Rachel said, scampering back into the kitchen and fumbling with the key in the patio door lock.

"What are you doing?"

"Getting out," she snapped. "And I suggest you do too unless you want a breaking and entering charge on your CV."

She opened the doors leading into the garden. Bruce stared at the front door. Even from the kitchen he could see through the frosted glass panel that the approaching shape was most definitely masculine. Hang on – did she just say breaking and entering?

"How did you get in?" Bruce asked.

"The old credit card down the edge of the door trick, I'm afraid," Rachel replied. "Look, can we talk about this later?"

She darted to the wall on the left hand side of the garden and then to the right. She kicked off her flip-flops and cleared the wall like an army assault course champion, to Bruce's astonishment. She continued into the next garden, cursing as her foot landed on something painful, but it didn't stop her.

"Are you coming or what?" she shouted back to Bruce.

With his heart beating faster than he could ever remember, he decided that, on balance, he was. He was neither as agile as Rachel nor as elegant in his execution, clambering awkwardly over the wall. The garden next door contained an old lady sunbathing topless on a tartan blanket and she stared up at him disapprovingly. Before she could say anything he was over the wall into the next garden. By the time he'd done it four times he had built up a sort of rhythm, though he was falling further and further behind the nimble Rachel. Thankfully most people who lived in this row of houses were spending their Fridays somewhere other than their garden.

Bruce knew he had reached the last garden in the row because the final dividing wall was over six feet tall, too high even for Rachel to vault. It did have an access point though – a three-quarter height doorway had been knocked out of the wall and plugged by a wooden gate. Rachel was desperately struggling to loosen the rusty bolt that kept the gate closed when Bruce caught up with her.

"Can I help you with that ma'am?" he said, wheezing.

She stepped aside gratefully and Bruce grappled with the bolt. When it snapped open, it forced his hand into the sharp metal surround, drawing blood.

In complete contrast to the last few minutes, life on the other side of the gate was utterly calm and conventional. Cars and people were going about their normal everyday business in a sedate and civilised manner. Rachel was perfectly composed as she strolled away from the scene of the crime. Bruce wasn't.

"Hang on a minute," he wheezed a few dozen yards down the road. He leaned back against the front wall of another house. His chest was burning, his lungs were gasping desperately for air and rivers of hot salty sweat were gushing down his face. His whole body was trembling and his stomach was telling his brain that it wanted to be violently sick. And his hand was bleeding.

Rachel, displaying no obvious adverse effects from their escapade, ambled back towards Bruce and looked at the bottom of her bare right foot. "Landed on something sharp back there," she said, retrieving a screwed up tissue from her jeans pocket and absorbing the blood with it. "Smarts a little, if I'm honest."

Bruce said nothing but held up his hand, causing the blood from his open wound to trickle down his forearm.

"Picked up a battle scar as well, did you?" she said with a laugh. "Well we can't hang around here. Let's find somewhere to fix ourselves up."

***

The interior of Da Vinci's restaurant was air conditioned and dark, both of which suited Bruce in his present condition. They had cleaned up their injuries in the toilets and their waiter had kindly liberated a plaster for Rachel's foot and a bandage for Bruce's hand from the first aid kit.

Rachel wound the bandage around Bruce's cut and secured it by ripping the trailing end down the middle and tying it into a knot. "He'll be expecting a big bloody tip for this," she said, nodding in the direction of the waiter.

He was all smiles as he brought their drinks, a glass of the most expensive red wine on the menu for Rachel and a pint of lager for Bruce. Were they ready to order yet? They weren't.

"I resent eating in Italian restaurants," said Bruce. "They don't really do anything I can't cook at home."

"Dab hand in the kitchen, are you?" Rachel said, without looking up from her menu.

"When it comes to warming up pizzas or microwaving pasta I am," said Bruce, taking a large gulp of cold lager. "But before we engage in a normal conversation can we talk about what happened today?"

"Livened up a dull Friday afternoon, didn't it?"

"Where did you learn to break into houses? Are you a criminal?"

"It's a long and winding road of a story but yes, you've rumbled me, I am Rachel Raffles, the Camden cat burglar. Nothing's safe when I'm around, guvnor."

Bruce stared at her across the table.

"Bruce, I'm teasing you," she said, playfully punching his arm. "I'm a boring old sales rep who sells women's things to pharmacies. I was locked out of my flat once, and some guy showed me how to get in with a credit card. Though he did turn out to be a burglar, now I come to think of it…"

"What if we'd been caught?"

"Oh you would have gone down for it," she said, taking a glug of wine. "I would have blamed it all on you."

He looked hurt.

"Oh Bruce," she said, smiling. "You really are not used to being teased, are you?"

"Who was the guy?"

"Who taught me the credit card trick?"

"No, the one at the house. The one we just ran away from."
"I don't know, but I'm going to find out."
"Did he see us?"
"I don't think so. He didn't chase us over the gardens, did he?"
"I've never done anything like that before. It nearly killed me."
"Yes, I noticed you were puffing a bit. It was fun though, wasn't it?"

Actually it was far more than that. It was exciting, it was thrilling, it was like being a teenager again. And even though he'd said it nearly killed him he couldn't remember when he'd last felt this alive. Or used such a hackneyed cliché in an internal monologue.

The obliging waiter returned to their table, pen poised above pad. "Are you ready to order now?" he said.

Rachel shook her head and dismissed him with a wave. She closed her menu and looked around the empty restaurant. "Actually I'm not hungry. Shall we just go?"

"We can't do that," Bruce protested, pointing at his bandage. "Not after he helped us."

"You really are a soft touch," she said, pinching his cheek affectionately.

Eventually they did order. They had a Bruschetta starter followed by a pizza to share, though Rachel only had a single slice. "This is no better than something you'd get from a supermarket," she complained. "I see what you mean about Italian restaurants."

Standing just over six feet away, the waiter heard Rachel's comment and frowned at her.

"What will you do now?" Bruce asked.

"I might have another drink, if you're buying," she replied, looking around. They had been joined by a group of four on another table and other diners were standing outside, perusing the menu that was stuck to the window. "Just to wash away the taste."

"I meant about your sister."

"I'm going back to the house to find out who that guy is," she said. "Although, having said that, I am dressed rather distinctively, if anyone saw me there the first time. Did you notice the old bird next door, sunbathing with her tits out?"

Bruce nodded.

"She obviously saw me so maybe I should buy a change of clothes first."

She removed the elastic band that held her pony tail and shook her hair loose. "I'm going to need something for my feet too, as I left my flip flops behind. Tell you what – how about if I borrow your trainers and get myself some clothes while you're finishing your food? There's a charity shop around the corner and most things fit me – I can get a whole new outfit for a tenner."

Bruce obediently slipped off his trainers. "Shall I see you back here?"

"Sure," she said, tying the laces tight so they wouldn't flop too much. "Are you alright to get the bill?"

He nodded and watched her leave. One day their grandchildren would ask them about their first date and they would look at each other and smile at the memory...

He was dragged back into the present by the ringing of his mobile. He groaned inwardly when he noticed the Bath area code of 01225 in the display. He didn't want to speak to anyone from Bath right now. He considered ignoring it but he was supposed to be here on magazine business so he reluctantly answered.

"Have you finished at that fetish fair?" Plum asked.

Bruce confirmed he had.

"Well can you come back and get it typed up as quickly as you can? We're a feature short."

Bruce's heart sunk. "This is supposed to be for next week's issue," he said. "Can't Alex toss something off if we need filler that badly? I'm sure she could give you two pages on something like how to get promoted beyond your ability."

"Don't be so disrespectful, Bruce," Plum said. "Jan's Performer Profile on Honey Peach was scheduled to go in the issue but she obviously hasn't done it."

"In all fairness, there are mitigating circumstances," Bruce said.

"That's a matter of opinion but we have to replace it with something else – as I would have told you if you'd been in the office this morning. What was the fair like?"

"Disappointing."

"Of course it was. I don't know why I asked. Get back here and get the piece written up."

Bruce finished the pizza, downed the last of his lager and paid the bill. He then carefully made his way to the charity shop, the pavement burning his bare feet with every step. When he asked about Rachel, the old lady behind the counter said she had not seen any young women this afternoon. She looked about a hundred though. He bought a pair of old-man sandals and ran, as fast as they would allow him to, back to Honey Peach's house and rattled the letterbox.

There was no answer. After waiting a few minutes he went back to Da Vinci's but Rachel had not returned during his absence. Where was she? He waited for fifteen minutes but the place was filling up and the waiter was giving him 'you've outstayed your welcome' glances.

Bruce hated the thought of abandoning Rachel but after another ten minutes he scribbled a note on the back of one his business cards, explaining why he had to leave, and asked the now rather huffy waiter to give it to Rachel when she eventually returned.

He went back to both the charity shop and Honey Peach's house again but there was no sign of Rachel. With a heavy sigh he trudged walk back towards the sea front where his car was parked. He had a long drive back to Bath ahead of him.

CHAPTER SIX: MONDAY 9TH JUNE 2003

When Bruce arrived in the AMG office he was disappointed to see that Nick was still laying out his Brighton fetish fair feature, with Plum stood over him.

"I gave up my Friday night to write that up," Bruce complained. "I needn't have bothered. I could have done it today."

"No you couldn't, Bruce," Plum said testily. "Mondays are for Previous Issue Post Mortems and Next Issue Planning Meetings."

Turning to Plum, Nick asked: "Is there nothing else we have on file that we can drop in instead of this? I really don't think it brings much to the issue or does us any favours."

"Thanks Nick," said Bruce. "It's so nice to work in an environment where your efforts are appreciated. And where the guy who does the layout critiques the editorial."

"Sorry mate," Nick continued. "But you make it sound really depressing."

"Which it was," Bruce said. "Do you want me to lie?"

"In which case, why are we giving two pages to a 'cynical money grabbing exercise by an organiser who exuded all the easy charm of a Blue Krait'?" Nick asked.

"That's an Indonesian snake that hunts and kills other snakes," Bruce explained. "It's regarded as one of the world's most venomous."

"I really am getting thoroughly fed up of your sniping attitude, Bruce," Plum said. "We should be cheerleaders for these events not assassins."

Alex was attracted by the sound of Bruce being reprimanded and wandered over to join in. She stared at Bruce. "How can you write something like that?"

"You just tap the corresponding keys on the keyboard and words come out," Bruce replied. "You might like to try it sometime. In most offices dedicated to journalism I think you'll find it's known as work."

"And why aren't there any quotes from the organiser?" said Plum.

"I did speak to her but she had nothing of worth to say," Bruce replied. "Which was just as well because the mini disc didn't record, for some reason."

"You only took one?"

Bruce nodded, sheepishly. Due to a previous incident of this nature, AMG's standard policy was for every interview to be conducted using two mini disc recorders, in case one failed.

"How many times is this going to happen?" Plum thundered, the volume of his voice rising as his face reddened with anger. "Belt and bloody braces!"

Bruce hung his head. Oh why couldn't he have just left it as she had nothing of worth to say?

Scenting blood, Alex joined in: "Wasn't that one of the reasons you and Jan spent £800 on that tiny video camera? So you would have an additional backup?"

Thanks Alex.

"Didn't you take it?" Alex persisted. "Or didn't you use it? Because I'm not being funny but whichever it was it hardly reflects well on you, does it?"

When they broke for lunch, Bruce said to Nick: "Thanks for your support and encouragement with the Brighton piece."

"Sorry mate, but it was awful," Nick said, adding, in a fair imitation of Bruce's voice: "Do you want me to lie?"

Hearing this exchange, Alex put aside her Celebs & Scandals magazine and walked over to Bruce's desk. "On the same subject, thank you for noticing the typo in my All About Me piece," she said.

Bruce shrugged in a 'just doing my job' kind of way.

"More to the point, thank you for bringing it to Plum's attention and making sure he knew I was out of the office all Friday afternoon," she said.

"Hang on, let me get this straight, are you annoyed that I noticed it?"

"Why didn't you just quietly mention it to me when you saw it? And when did you see it? How come it had gone to production before you flagged it? Why did you only do something about it on Friday?"

Bruce stood up. "Alex, rest assured that next time I see anything like that in your 'work' I will handle the situation very differently. Now, if you'll excuse me, I have to leave before I kill you."

***

Bruce had intended taking his packed lunch to Royal Victoria Park but the coach parties of foreign tourists and pensioners tramping through it, on their way to be photographed in front of the sweeping majesty of Royal Crescent, were particularly annoying today. Exiting on to Weston Road, he decided to consume his sandwiches while walking around the perimeter of the park, away from the summer crowds. As he walked he relived his adventure with Rachel in Brighton the previous week, and compared it to his dull weekend – in bed with aching legs all day Saturday, hungover all day Sunday – and the awful morning he'd just endured. Seemingly unwittingly, he followed the road until it became Weston Lane and he realised he was now just a few hundred yards from the Royal United Hospital.

Bruce was pleased to see that Jan had improved significantly since his visit the previous Thursday. Although she was still on serious quantities of medication she was conscious, sitting up and she looked genuinely pleased to see him. She was in a ward with five other women, all of whom had bedside cabinets packed with cards, flowers, fruit and confectionary. Jan's cabinet had just one card, from her Aunt Edith. And all Bruce had brought with him was his empty lunch box.

Bruce noticed that Jan looked a little older without makeup, though he thought it prudent to keep the observation to himself. After a rather awkward initial exchange in which he asked the traditional hospital visit questions regarding how she was feeling, what the food was like and whether she was being looked after, Bruce slouched into the chair by the side of her bed.

"I walked up," he explained. "My legs are going to be aching in the morning."

"Shall I see if they can find a bed for you?"

Bruce's out of condition legs were still aching from his exertions in Brighton with Rachel. Thinking of Brighton and Rachel brought an involuntary smile to his face, which Jan attributed to her comment.

"I miss having someone to talk to," she said.

Bruce smiled weakly but said nothing.

"I suppose that's one of the drawbacks of being single," Jan added. "I'm beginning to think we should run that reader competition."

All Bruce could offer in response was another smile.

"Like I said, I miss having someone to talk to."

"Sorry," Bruce said. "Work is…"

"You're right, that's quite enough about me. How's everyone in the office? No one has been to see me yet, apart from you."

Bruce groaned and explained that Plum had appointed Alex as acting editor.

"That must be nice for you," she said. "Having a bit of totty ordering you about. Has she sexually harassed you yet?"

Bruce shook his head and groaned again. He stared at Jan's lonely card. "Look, I'm sorry I didn't bring you anything but I hadn't actually planned to come."

"How nice of you to tell me that. Got lost did you?"

"Actually I came to see you last week but you were out of it and, well, life has become a little more complicated since... you know..."

"My accident?"

Bruce nodded.

Jan's eyes started to glisten. "It's had a bit of an impact on me too," she said.

"You said you were going to catch a cab."

"I know," she said, reaching for a tissue. "I fully intended to."

"So why didn't you?"

"I don't know," she said.

"You can't remember?"

She shook her head. "The doctors say that's normal, after a traumatic blow to the head..."

Thinking more about the incident he was involved in than Jan's accident, he asked: "Do they expect your memory to come back?"

"It might, in time," Jan said. "Apparently I drove out of the park onto Marlborough Lane but I didn't make it to the bottom of the hill. My car veered to the left and scraped along the wall before embedding itself in a stone pillar. The tracking was out apparently, otherwise I would have made it to the main road and I probably wouldn't be here now."

Bruce felt like he ought to say how lucky she was but he wasn't sure she would agree.

"I just don't understand it," she said, shaking her head. "I would never have driven after all those drinks we had."

"Did the police take blood samples from you?"

She nodded. "I'm really scared though. Nobody is saying anything about what happens now."

"Have you spoken to a solicitor?"

She gave him a withering look. "I haven't exactly been up and about these last few days."

Bruce looked around the ward. "Is there a clock in here?"

"Sorry, am I boring you?"

"You're not boring me," Bruce said. "It's just that it's a long walk back into town."

"And Monday afternoon is the Next Issue Planning Meeting," Jan said. "Plum won't be happy if you're late for that."

"Can you believe that Alex has pushed the news onto me as well?" Bruce complained. "So now I'm doing the reviews, the news, at least two of the features…"

"You're a saint, Bruce," Jan said. "Oh, and while I think of it, the Honey Peach interview disc is in my drawer. You can transcribe that in your spare time too."

Bruce considered telling Jan about his adventure with Honey Peach's sister but decided to save it for another time.

***

Bruce was indeed late for the Next Issue Planning Meeting and Plum was indeed not happy.

"Honestly Bruce, the sheer contempt you show for your position and all your colleagues is beyond belief," Plum said when Bruce arrived in the boardroom. "Your attitude alone could be construed as misconduct and that's without taking into account your increasingly erratic behaviour."

"What erratic behaviour?"

"Alex said you threatened to kill her and then you stormed off without so much as a bye your leave."

"Threat to kill is a criminal offence," Alex piped up. "I looked it up. And anyone who commits a criminal offence in the workplace…"

"Shut up," Bruce snapped. "I did not threaten to kill anyone…"

"You did," Alex said.

"Seriously Bruce," Plum addressed him. "When I hear things like this, how do you think it makes me feel?"

"So young? Like spring has sprung?"

Wrong audience. Plum's mouth curled a little at the corner.

"Look, I did not threaten to kill her and the only place I 'stormed off' to was the hospital to visit Jan," Bruce said. "You might remember Jan, she was editor of AMG up until last Monday. She's improving, by the way. I know that was of great concern to you."

Bruce took his seat and, after a few seconds of awkward silence, he said: "How far did you get without me then? Have you allocated me any more jobs? Am I expected to come in at seven to put the Hoover around and water the plants now as well?"

Plum held up a copy of a leading right wing newspaper, nicknamed The Daily Hate for its scaremongering editorial policy and antigovernment agenda. "Have you seen this, Bruce?" Plum said, pointing to the front page.

The headline screamed 'Now they want YOU to pay for porn peddlers' overseas jaunts!'

The lead paragraph said: "Britain's pornographers will be laughing all the way to the bank with your money if a scheme to subsidise their travel costs is approved by the government. The Department of Culture Media and Sport is believed to be pushing the Treasury to sanction the proposal which, critics say, proves the left wing liberal elite running the country are completely out of touch with the man on the street. Julian Gregan, CEO of pressure group CRSP — the Campaign to Restrict the Sale of Pornography – commented: 'I find it inconceivable that a serving government would stoop so low as to court popularity with pornographers by using decent, hardworking families' taxes to help them peddle their sordid wares in other countries,' while opposition spokesperson Barbara Burke-Reynolds added: 'This is further evidence that this morally bankrupt government is determined to drag this once proud nation into the gutter with it'."

Bruce gasped as he snatched the newspaper from Plum. "That's the quote that I cajoled out of Gregan!"

"By the time we hit the newsstands our front page splash will look ridiculous," Plum said. "You told me this was your story, Bruce."

"It was," Bruce said. "I made it up."

"And on that basis I upped our print run and paid our wholesalers to promote it and offer the newsagents sale or return," Plum frowned. "We're going to take a big hit now."

"You've ruined my first issue," Alex added. "How can I show it to any of my friends now? First time we trust you with the front page and you balls it up."

"This is not the first time I have written the front page lead," Bruce protested. "As you would know if you'd been here longer than five minutes. And I did not balls it up."

"Of course you have," Alex countered, pointing at the Daily Hate story. "You've put a bloody press release on our cover – it's even got the same quote, word for word..."

These exchanges continued for a few more minutes, with neither side backing down.

"Well there's nothing we can do about it now," Plum said eventually. "We'll return to the subject when we get the sales figures in. Now, what have we got planned for the next issue?"

Alex gave a rundown of the number of pages she had sold and then reeled off a list of anodyne features she had planned, adding: "I know this is really short notice but can we also get a freelancer to cover the Love Shack open day? I've been trying to get them to advertise with us for months and it would help if we could give them some coverage."

Alex explained that Love Shack had taken on a PR executive who had told her it was about to launch a range of new products. The firm had conducted research which revealed that many people were unaware that hardcore pornography had been legal to buy in the UK for almost three years, so it had booked an entire hotel for a day and a night and it was inviting representatives from mainstream publications and television channels to meet the company and enjoy a complimentary mini break at the same time.

"I'd go myself if it wasn't so far away," Alex said, showing Plum a printout of her emailed invitation. "But I've already made other plans."

Plum placed the invitation on the boardroom table. "They're holding it tomorrow - it might be difficult to get a freelancer prepared to travel there at this short notice," he said.

Bruce noticed that the invitation said guests would be able to meet and interview Love Shack's senior personnel and there would be porn stars on hand for photo opportunities, including Wanda Wette, Cherry Chicolo and Honey Peach.

"I'll go," said Bruce.

"No thanks," Alex said immediately. "Imagine if I had to ring Leathers, Tethers and Feathers for an advert after they see your piece in this week's issue…"

Plum stopped the discussion escalating by clapping his hands. "How about this - Bruce covers it but Alex, as befits the editor, will have copy approval."

If Plum had suggested this last week Bruce would have erupted, but he let it go. He had got what he wanted.

After the planning meeting broke up, Bruce returned to his desk and saw that a message had landed on his answerphone during his absence. It was from Zara, banging on about the Daily Hate story and asking him to ring her back. Instead Bruce called Love Shack to discuss tomorrow's event.

"And can you confirm that Honey Peach is going to be there?" he asked.

"Yes, she's one of our key attractions," Gina, the Love Shack PR executive, replied. "We're launching a range of products based on porn stars, including lifelike casts of their vaginas, and the girls will be there for photo opportunities and to autograph boxes for media that want to use samples as competition prizes."

They'll love one of those at Country Life magazine, Bruce thought.

His next call was to Rachel.

"I'm sorry I had to go on Friday," he said. "There was an emergency at the office and I was called back."

"You must be very important," Rachel said.

"Oh I am," he said. "They worship the ground I walk on. Did you get my note?"

"Your note?"

"I left a note with the waiter at the restaurant."

"No, he didn't give me anything," she said.

"What a git. You must have thought I'd deserted you. Did you go back to the house?"

"Yes, in some horrid smelly clothes from that shop but there was no one in."

"Did you use the credit card trick again?"

"No, the woman opposite was sat out on her balcony watching me. I gave up in the end and caught my train back to London."

"Well I've got some good news," Bruce said. "I'm sure your sister is fine because she's making a personal appearance tomorrow at an industry bash."

"Really?" Rachel said. "Are you going to it?"

Bruce confirmed that he was.

"How do you fancy taking me as your date?" she asked coquettishly.

Bruce fancied that very much. He passed on the details of the hotel's location and arranged to meet her in reception at noon. Bruce chose not to mention that, courtesy of Love Shack, he had a double room booked and would be staying over. It seemed far too forward. But, if they were both still there in the evening, and they were getting on famously, it would be a cool thing to reveal. No, it would be cooler than cool. It would be chilly.

***

As he would be out of the office tomorrow, the day which he usually set aside to write features, he decided to tackle Honey Peach's Performer Profile piece. Wandering over to Jan's now vacant corner he pulled out the single deep drawer that was part of every desk's construction. It contained the usual office detritus – a box of her business cards, a stapler, a hole punch, paperclips, blank CDs, ancient floppy disks – plus the mini disc archive of previously recorded interviews and a quantity of brand new discs, still in their cellophane wrappers. He located the disc with Honey Peach's interview on it and also grabbed a blank for use tomorrow. Actually, better make that two...

Returning to his desk he retrieved the mini disc player from his drawer, plugged in the earphones and inserted the Honey Peach interview disc and was just about to press the play button when his phone rang. It was Zara.

"Finally!" she blurted. "You're a difficult man to get hold of – it's like trying to get an audience with the Pope. Did you get my message?"

"Sorry, I was tied up in an editorial meeting," Bruce said.

"Ooh, were you a naughty boy? Did you get spanked?"

"Yes, that's exactly what happened."

"Well I'll let someone else bid for the film rights because you'll never guess what..."

"What?"

"I'm only going to be on Today's Talking Point tonight!"

"What's that?"

"Today's Talking Point! It's a topical discussion show on Radio 4 with that Welsh bloke."

"You're going to be on Radio 4?"

"You betcha. I'm going to be debating with that nutter who was quoted in the papers today. How fab is that? This is really going to put BATA on the map..."

"By 'that nutter', do you mean Julian Gregan?"

"Is that his name? It's the bloke who runs the anti-porn group."

"That's Gregan," Bruce confirmed.

"This could be a real turning point for the industry," Zara gushed. "The Department of Culture Media and Sport must be really behind us to have leaked the funding story to the press..."

This story – his story – was taking on a life of its own and AMG's front page really was going to be horribly out of date when it appeared on Thursday. But as he considered this he suddenly realised that, for the first time since he joined the magazine, he didn't actually care that much about it. The airbrushing out of Jan and the promotion of Alex had given his loyalty to AMG a kicking.

The small hand on the office clock moved down to the four. Bruce looked forlornly at the mini disc player. Bugger it. There was no point starting to transcribe now. Instead he announced to the office he was leaving early as he had to organise a few things in preparation for tomorrow's trip. This was true, if the definition of organising a few things could be stretched to include buying new underpants and checking if he had any condoms which had not exceeded their expiration dates – just in case.

***

Bruce stumbled into his flat's kitchen, his stomach stretched to full capacity by six pints of Guinness, and picked up his ancient radio. After checking it for ants, he took it into the lounge, tuned it to Radio 4 and slumped onto his sofa. The programme had already started.
"But these women are forced into making these films," Julian Gregan was saying. "The pornographers get them hooked on drugs and..."
"Oh please, that's complete rubbish!" Zara interrupted. "How many performers do you know? I've been making films for over two years and..."
"Zara, please," said an urbane Welsh accent. "Let Mister Gregan finish. You will be given the opportunity to respond."
"Thank you," Gregan said. "As I was about to say, the women are no different to prostitutes and the people who make the films are their pimps..."
"You're calling me a pimp?"
"If that's what you do then that's what you are. You and your kind should be prosecuted for living off immoral earnings..."
"Oh that's ridiculous..." Zara started to say, before being hushed again.
"I'd like someone to explain to me the difference between prostitution and what these women do," Gregan continued. "Because as far as I can see they are both being paid to have sex outside of a normal loving relationship. Does putting a camera in the room suddenly elevate a harlot into a movie star?"
"Would you like to respond to that point, Zara," asked the host.
"The difference?" Zara snapped. "Pornography is adult entertainment..."

"Entertainment?" Gregan said with a sneer. "That's the last word I would use to describe this filth and it's about time that this government was held to account for legalising it."

"It's the government we are here to discuss," said the host. "Because, according to one daily newspaper, the Department of Culture Media and Sport is going to be funding the making of pornography…"

"Not the making of it," Zara corrected him. "We have applied for a grant for an overseas trade mission."

"We asked for a DCMS representative to appear on tonight's programme," continued the host. "But no one was available and the department also declined to comment on the issue…"

"Deplorable," said Gregan. "We should be arresting these people, not throwing money at them…"

"Mr Gregan, please," the host shushed him. "However, our senior political correspondent has told this programme that, in his opinion, although all applications are judged on their own merits it would be 'extremely unlikely' that any such application from such a sector would be given a green light…"

"If that is the case then why would someone from the DCMS leak the story about our application to the press?" said Zara.

"Why do you think the story was leaked, Mr Gregan?" the host asked. "Do you think the department might have been briefing journalists in advance to gauge public reaction?"

Gregan paused for a few seconds before replying: "Oh I know why it was leaked."

"Do you?" the host said. "Would you care to enlighten us?"

"Because some of us can remember what happened to the country in the 1960s, after Labour's social reforms and the abolition of censorship," Gregan said smugly. "It wasn't the Department of Culture Media and Sport who informed the newspapers, it was me."

"You?" Zara was confused.

"I had a phone call telling me about this last week," Gregan said. "Naturally I was appalled. But nothing subsequently appeared in the newspapers so, to ensure there was no cover up or sweeping under the carpet, and given this government's track record I considered that a very real possibility, I decided to take the bull by the horns and contacted the media to make my objections known."

"How do you feel about that, Zara?" the host asked.

Her tone suggested she was crushed. "I'm shocked," she said. "Shocked and disappointed, obviously. But how did you know about our application?"

Gregan said: "It was a journalist who informed me about it."

"A journalist?" Zara was incredulous. "Who…?"

Gregan could be heard shuffling paper. "Here it is," he said. "He rang me on Wednesday 4th of June to get a quote from me. When I didn't hear anything more about it, I assumed someone had silenced him. He said his name was Bruce Baker."

Unfortunately Bruce did not hear the first time his name was mentioned on a national radio station. His comfortable sofa and stomach full of Guinness had sent him to sleep.

CHAPTER SEVEN: TUESDAY 10TH JUNE 2003

Bruce pulled into Strensham Services just before eleven o'clock. He was still a little groggy from last night's Guinness so he bought a black coffee. Sat outside in the family area, he wondered how Rachel would express her appreciation for him reuniting her with her sister. But before he could get too creative he was dragged back to reality by the ringing of his mobile.

Polly – or it could have been Molly, it was tricky to hear with the constant roar of the M5 so close – said she was a journalist and she had been given his number by the office. AMG was often asked to assist the mainstream media when it ran stories about pornography – which delighted Plum as it usually resulted in a credit for the magazine.

Bruce explained to Polly/Molly that he was not in the office and it therefore wasn't convenient for him to talk, adding: "My signal is week because I'm in the shadow of the Malvern Hills and there's a motorway within spitting distance."

"I'll only keep you two seconds Bruce," she said. "I just wondered what your thoughts were about Julian Gregan's statement. Do you think he has a valid argument?"

Bruce paused for a few seconds, appreciating the absurdity of being asked for a quote by another publication for a story he had fabricated. "No," he eventually said.

Polly/Molly's disposition changed from enthusiasm to irritation by his reluctance to give her free copy: "Can you expand on that?"

"No, he doesn't have a valid argument."

"Well that's what I'd expect an advocate for hardcore pornography to say."

Bruce took a long drag on his cigarette. He wasn't going to bite.

She continued: "You are an advocate for hardcore pornography, aren't you? You must be, given how you earn your living, so you obviously support the pornography peddlers?"

"Calling them pornography peddlers is not particularly helpful," Bruce said. "They are dealing in a perfectly legal product so why shouldn't they have the same opportunities as other legitimate businesses?"

"But CRSP maintains that it shouldn't be legal," Polly/Molly said.

"That's another argument – it is legal and the sector is already overregulated," Bruce said.

"But pornography degrade women," Polly/Molly said. "You can't deny that."

"Some does," Bruce conceded. "But you could equally level that accusation at any other form of popular culture…"

Polly/Molly's voice became screechy with astonishment. "Are you saying you believe that pornography is a form of popular culture?"

"You say the word 'pornography' like it's the worst thing in the world," Bruce responded, raising his voice and attracting stares from a coach load of pensioners who had pulled in for a wee break. "I can buy a DVD of someone torturing young girls or blowing men's heads off from my local supermarket. But if I want to see adults having consensual sex I have to go to a shop with blacked out windows which is hidden away in a secondary location. And that's if I have a licensed sex shop near me. If I don't, I'm stuffed, because I can't legally buy an adult film from a UK mail order company…"

He paused and realised that Polly/Molly was no longer on the end of his phone. Either the signal had dropped out or she had hung up on him.

***

Although the M5 traffic was quite heavy Bruce pulled into the hotel's car park ten minutes before he had arranged to meet Rachel. He strode purposefully through the hotel's glass and chrome revolving door and approached the counter in the lobby which had a Love Shack sign above it. A slim woman in her early twenties, with a mass of dark curls, was sat behind it.

"Hello Gina," Bruce said, reading her name badge. "I'm Bruce, from AMG magazine."

Gina explained that the Love Shack bash was taking place in one of the function rooms and that complimentary refreshments were being served on the hotel's lawns. She wrote Bruce's name and the title of his publication on a blank badge and offered to take him through.

"Is it okay if I wait for a colleague first?" he said.

"Sure. You didn't come together?"

"No, she… it's a long and winding road of a story."

"It's a her? That's awesome. I'll get her badge ready. What's her name?"

Bruce smiled. That's a good question. Her name is Rachel. But Rachel what?

Gina looked up at him expectantly, felt tip pen poised. "Her name?"

"It's probably best if she tells you," Bruce said.

"Huh?"

"I don't really know her that well…"

"You don't know her well enough to tell me her name?" Gina looked sceptical.

Bruce closed his eyes. He hadn't thought this through. He paused for a few seconds and then inspiration struck: "She's a freelancer. A freelance photographer. That we've booked through an agency."

"Oh right," Gina said. "Now it makes sense! Well, I hope she's broad minded, we've got some pretty scary looking new lines on show here today."

Out of the corner of his eye Bruce spotted Rachel emerging from a taxi that had pulled up outside the hotel. She swished through the revolving door and ran up to him.

"Bruce, darling," she said, hugging him. "How wonderful to see you again!"

Gina stared at her. "You guys do know each other!"

"Of course we do," Rachel said, returning the stare.

Gina said: "You haven't brought a camera?"

"Why would I bring a camera?"

"It's okay," Bruce said, pulling his small digital out of his jacket pocket. "She can use mine."

"Look, if you guys have got something going on, that's cool," Gina said. "You don't have to…"

"Thank you Gina," said Bruce, ushering Rachel towards the function room.

"Wait, photographer lady!" Gina called after them. "You need a badge to get in."

Bruce groaned. They returned to the desk and Rachel spelled out her name for Gina, who wrote it in the space provided and handed it over with a thin smile.

"Rachel Rogers?" Bruce said, staring at Rachel's badge as they walked towards the function room.

"Do you have a problem with alliterative names, Bruce bloody Baker? At least they are easy to remember."

He laughed. "No, but I thought you'd be a Peach."

"That sounds a bit like a chat-up line. Are you trying to seduce me, Mr Baker?"

"I meant your surname," Bruce spluttered. "I thought it would be Peach."

"Same mother, different fathers," Rachel tutted. "Don't you listen to anything I say?"

A sign on the door of the function room read 'Restricted access – invited guests aged 18+ only' and a hefty man with a shaved head and goatee beard stood guard. He glanced briefly at Bruce and Rachel's badges and, moving only his left arm, held the door open for them.

As they went through, they were greeted by another hefty man with shaved head and goatee beard. The function room was bigger than Bruce expected and decorated in the style of a Venetian ballroom, with flocked red and gold wallpaper and elaborate chandeliers dotted around the ceiling. Three booths had been constructed down one wall and opposite them was a series of desks with Love Shack representatives sat behind them. To the rear were two sets of doors, leading out to the lawns.

A few dozen people were milling around inside and talking in hushed tones. They turned to look at Bruce and Rachel as they entered but, failing to recognise either of them, quickly returned to their conversations.

"Why would they stage a shindig here, in the arse end of the country?" Rachel asked Bruce.

"This is hardly the arse end…"

"They're never going to get the London media to travel to a regional event. If something is important it takes place in London."

"You're remarkably well informed for a sales rep…"

"Oh come on Bruce, it's common sense," she said dismissively, heading for the booths.

Each featured a table at the front stacked with posters and DVDs and a sign indicating the name of the performer – Wanda Wette, Cherry Chicolo and Honey Peach. All three were unoccupied. Behind the tables were stacks of plain cardboard boxes, containing the new products.

"Where are they?" Rachel asked.

A young girl in a black Love Shack T-shirt wandered over and said brightly: "They will be back in about twenty minutes."

"What are they doing, having their implants serviced?" Rachel said.

The young girl's enthusiasm was undimmed by the catty remark. "They're outside having some photos with the press. Can I help you with anything?"

"We'll wait," Rachel sighed. She approached the Honey Peach booth and picked up a Legend of the Amazon Women DVD. Reading the back cover blurb, she wrinkled her nose.

"You go and do your work," she said to Bruce, shooing him away with a hand gesture. "I'll stay here and brush up on my porn abbreviations."

Bruce dutifully whipped out his camera and took a series of pictures.

Gina approached him with an A4 envelope. "Hey Bruce, here's a press kit for our new products, which we're calling the Signature Series. The Head Master, Spasm Chasm and Hand Job are lifelike casts of each girl's head, vagina and hand..."

"Has there been much interest?" Bruce asked, accepting the pack.

"It's still kind of early," Gina said. "We're expecting more people this afternoon."

"Maybe it would have been better to hold it in London?"

She raised her perfectly sculpted eyebrows at him.

He added: "You know, as far as the London media is concerned, if an event is important it takes place in London."

Before she could reply they were both distracted by the piercing sound of a glass being smashed and raised voices. A short stocky man in a black suit was dragging a taller man in through the doors by his hair. The shorter man had pulled the taller man's head close to him and he was swearing quietly in his ear.

"Oh Lord..." Gina said, covering her eyes with her hand and lowering her head.

The two men continued through the function room where the short one flung the tall one towards the bouncer, and made a gesture which appeared to suggest he wanted him removed from the building.

"Will you excuse me?" Gina said to Bruce. "You're going to be here for some time, right?"

Bruce nodded.

"Cool, because before you go, Mr Sachetti wants to meet you," she said.

"As long as that isn't him," Bruce said, gesturing at the short man.

The look she gave him told him that it was. "I'm afraid he can be a bit old school."

Bruce jumped as he felt someone put their hand on his shoulder and he was relieved to see it was Rachel.

"Well there's nothing like a PR disaster to liven up a dull Tuesday afternoon," she said.

"What happened?"

"The turnout is so disappointing there are heaps of unopened bottles of wine on the tables outside," she said. "That reporter from a local freesheet decided to stuff his bag with a couple."

"Really? That's a bit off..."

"That's what journalists are like," she said. "No offence but they're freeloaders, especially lower down the orders. Taking exception to it is like walking into a public toilet and complaining it smells of pee. Speaking of which, do you know what's in those boxes on the stands? Rubber casts of each girl's fanny – how gruesome is that?"

"That's shocking," Bruce agreed, trying to suppress a smile.

"How sad must some men be to buy rubber body parts to shag?"

Bruce shrugged. No good could come from him answering this question. "Shall we go outside and see if the photographers have finished?"

They hadn't, so they sat at one of the round pub-style tables. Rachel examined the label of the white wine chilling in the chrome ice bucket centrepiece. Several long oblong tables on the terrace were covered with white linen tablecloths and offered a variety of salads, sandwiches and cold meats, though they were slowly spoiling in the summer sun.

The wide expanse of lawn ran for several hundred yards down to a man-made lake where a small crowd congregated. One of the girls had been persuaded to wade in and splash in the shallow end for the photographers.

Rachel grabbed two glasses and unscrewed the cap of one of the wine bottles. "I know it's very low-rent but I actually quite like fruity Germans," she said, filling the glasses.

Bruce raised his glass to his lips and, shading the sun from his eyes with his hand, looked across at his companion. Her attractive face was accentuated by the backdrop of lush green lawns and bright blue summer sky.

"So what's a nice boy like you doing in porn, Bruce?" she said. "Before I met you I thought you'd be some lecherous old creep."

"I don't work in porn, I work in publishing..."

She guffawed. "Okay you keep telling yourself that, darling!"

"It's true. I'm doing the same job I was doing when I was writing about video games."

"You were in the video games industry?" she said.

"No, I was in publishing then too," Bruce replied, spotting the trap she had set for him.

She laughed. "So what happened?"

"One of my bosses left to start Adult Movie Guide. Hardcore pornography had just been legalised to sell in licensed sex shops and he thought porn could be the new video games, so he invited me to join him."

Rachel removed a DVD from her bag. Staring intently at the case, she asked: "Do they honestly expect people to believe that these are real nuns? Since when did nuns have tattoos and pierced nipples?"

"Are you telling me they don't?"

"Thank the Lord, it looks like they've finished the photos," Rachel said, standing up. "Is it me or does this have the air of a really bizarre wedding?"

Bruce stood up too. The group was walking noisily up the lawns from the lake. As they approached, Bruce could see that the entourage consisted of two T-shirted Love Shack girls, a few shabbily dressed photographers and two porn stars. And neither of them was Honey Peach.

"She's not there, is she?" Rachel said.

"It doesn't look like," Bruce replied.

Rachel's face flushed with anger. She sat back down and downed the contents of her wine glass. "You told me she would be here, Bruce," she said, emphasising each word. "I've taken time off work to be here today."

"I'll sort it out," he said, walking towards the group.

Rachel huffed.

"Hi, I'm Bruce from AMG magazine," Bruce said to one of the Love Shack girls. "Is Honey Peach about?"

"Have you met Cherry Chicolo and Wanda Wette?" the girl said, gesturing to the two performers, who were now snogging for the benefit of the photographers.

"I specifically came to see Honey Peach," Bruce said.

"Unfortunately she's let us down," the girl said. "We're as disappointed as you are."

Bruce doubted that.

"But we've got Wanda and Cherry!" the girl said with a flourish, gesturing again in their direction.

The group reached the terrace. Some of the photographers followed Cherry Chicolo and the Love Shack girls inside while the others sat down at a table and made a start on the wine.

Wanda Wette approached Bruce. "Did you just say you were Bruce Baker?"

Bruce nodded. "Hi, how you doing?"

Wanda calmly picked up the open bottle of wine from the table, looked at the label for a few seconds and then poured it over Bruce's head. "That's for what you said about me last month."

The photographers cheered. One asked her to do it again so he could photograph it.

"What did I say?" Bruce spluttered.

"That you've seen more attractive sacks of potatoes than me," Wanda said.

Bruce considered how to respond as the cold sticky wine ran down his chest, causing his white linen shirt to become transparent and stick to his skin. The commotion had brought people from inside the function room out onto the terrace. One of the Love Shack girls saw what had happened and quickly stepped in to steer Wanda away from Bruce.

"Bravo Bruce, you certainly sorted that out," said Rachel, applauding in a slow, mocking manner.

Bruce picked up a paper napkin and wiped the wine off his face. "Just one of my fans," he explained.

"You picked the wrong one to have a go at there," said a familiar Welsh accent. "She's got a bell in every tooth, that one."

"Oh hello Milkman, I wondered where you were," Bruce said, rubbing his eyes.

Rachel's ears pricked up at the mention of his name.

"I've been having a dump, I have," Milkman said.

He was wearing a beige jacket which hung off his tall, wiry frame, and matching slacks with brown sandals.

"Where's Honey Peach?" Bruce said. "She was supposed to be here."

"I wish I knew," Milkman said. "Spaghetti's tamping mad. This is the second time she's let him down. It looks bad for me."

Rachel stood up and joined them.

"Who's this lovely lady?" Milkman said, looking her up and down and digging a business card out of his pocket. "Are you a model?" he asked as he handed it to her.

She laughed.

"Don't laugh, you should be. You look very fetching, I must say."

Bruce was distracted by the approaching figure of Gina. She was holding a large fluffy white towel which she offered to him. "I've just been told what happened, Bruce," she said. "I am so sorry. How can we make this up to you? Is there anything you have seen here today that you would like to take home with you?"

There was actually, Bruce thought, glancing across at Rachel.

"We have a room booked for you so you are more than welcome to use it to shower and freshen up. You can also order a massage on room service, use the gym and the pool and run up a huge bar bill at our expense..."

Bruce thanked her and took the towel. "I don't suppose you've got something I can change into, have you?" he said, pointing at his shirt.

"I can give you a Love Shack T-shirt," she said. "What size are you, XL or XXL?"

"Can you get me one of each?" he said. "So we cover all bases?"

While Gina went to get the shirts and a room key for Bruce, he performed an 'I'm just going to have a shower and change my shirt' mime for Rachel, who was still being schmoozed by Milkman.

When the hotel lift brought Bruce back down into the reception area, Gina left her post to accompany him back to the event. Rachel and Milkman were still talking, though they were now stood near the empty Honey Peach booth.

Seeing Bruce and Gina, Milkman extricated himself from Rachel and joined them. "Where did you get her from?" he said, gesturing towards Rachel. "She's been giving me a right ear bashing."

Before Bruce could explain that Rachel was Honey Peach's sister, Milkman's gaze landed on Gina. His lecherous smile told Bruce that he had already forgotten all about Rachel.

"You're gorgeous, aren't you?" Milkman said. "Are you a model?"

Gina smiled coyly and shook her curls.

Milkman handed her one of his business cards. "You should be. Why don't you give me a call sometime and we can set something up?"

"You already asked me this when I signed you in," she giggled.

"Oh you're the one from the front desk, are you?" Milkman said. "Have you done something with your hair? You look different."

Rachel grabbed Bruce's arm and pulled him away from the pair. Gesturing at Milkman, she said: "He may be the sleaziest man in the entire world."

Bruce shrugged and said in a convincing Welsh accent: "Are you a model? You look very fetching you do, I must say."

Rachel laughed. "That's actually a pretty good impression," she said.

Bruce bowed.

"Did you drive up?" Rachel asked him.

Bruce confirmed that he had.

Rachel strode across the function room to the spot where Milkman was talking to Gina. When she was just a few feet away, she tripped on the carpet and fell forward into Milkman. She grabbed at his jacket in an attempt to stay upright but Milkman's slight physique was easily bundled over by her momentum and the two of them became entangled as they collapsed on the carpet.

Rachel got to her feet and stared at the carpet in search of whatever had tripped her. "Somebody should take a look at that," she said.

With the support of two onlookers Milkman shakily got up, glaring at Rachel and cursing under his breath.

Rachel offered Milkman a cursory apology and rejoined the open-mouthed Bruce. "Right, let's go," she said breezily.

"Go?"

Rachel showed Bruce the business card Milkman had given her. "Take me to Chepstow, South Wales, my good man, and don't spare the horses."

"Now?" he said. "But I've got a room..."

"Yes! Now!" she said, tugging his arm.

"At least let me go back outside and get my press pack then. I left it on the table..."

"Oh that's all just corporate bollocks," she said, pulling him in the direction of the entrance. "Now are you coming with me or am I going to steal your car?"

***

Rachel insisted Bruce keep the Mazda's roof down during the journey – she loved the feel of the wind in her hair, she said – which ruled out conversation. Bruce didn't mind. The Beach Boys' Greatest Hits was blasting out from the CD player and he was roaring through England's green and pleasant land in a convertible with a pretty girl in his passenger seat.

Chepstow was only around thirty miles from Bath, and Milkman had thoughtfully printed directions to his office and a basic map on the back of his business card. It was located near the end of a row of shops and had been a retail outlet in a former life. It still had a full sized shop window but off-white Venetian blinds now kept the interior of the premises private from the street and the original shop entrance had been replaced with a solid wooden door.

They parked down a side street and Bruce twisted his body and pulled the Mazda's lightweight canvas roof up with one outstretched arm. Rachel didn't notice this feat of dexterity and strength unfortunately, as she was rearranging her windblown hair in the driver's rear view mirror.

"And we're here because…" Bruce said.

"We're paying Milkman a visit," Rachel said, touching up her lip gloss.

"But he won't be here."

"Oh, won't he?"

Bruce stared at Rachel.

"While you were off changing your shirt I was asking him about Honey Peach and it was obvious he was hiding something," she said. "Now, turn that Love Shack shirt inside out so the logo isn't on display."

Rachel opened the car door and strode purposefully towards the former shop, while Bruce did as he was told, sparing her the sight of his naked torso. When he was decent, Bruce locked the car and hurried after her, hoping she wasn't going to do her breaking and entering trick on a busy road in broad daylight.

Rachel pressed a buzzer on the small aluminium intercom plate that was built into the frame of the front door. "Randy Milkman Enterprises?" she read aloud. "What is this, the 1970s?"

"Can I help you?" A distorted female voice asked through the intercom.

Rachel looked at her watch. "We've got a four o'clock appointment with Mr…" She looked at Bruce and raised her eyebrows expectantly.

"Jones," Bruce whispered.

Rachel sniggered but managed to keep it out of her voice. "With Mr Jones. We're from Her Majesty's Customs and Excise."

The intercom buzzed, releasing the lock on the door and allowing them to enter.

"Never fails," Rachel said.

The door opened into a narrow lobby area. Running parallel to the shop window was a plasterboard partition, with a doorway leading inwards. A white-haired woman sat behind the only item of furniture in the lobby; a scruffy desk which contained an elderly BT phone, a large format desk diary and a vase of strong-smelling white lilies.

"Mr Jones never said anything to me about anyone visiting today," the woman said, staring at Bruce's inside-out shirt. "There's nothing in the diary and he's away on business."

"Well this is unacceptable," Rachel said. "We gave him ample notice that we would be inspecting his books today. But I suppose we can do it without him being here."

The woman looked concerned. "I'm not sure about this," she said. "Can I see some form of identification?"

"Of course," Rachel replied, ferreting in her bag. From her purse she produced an official looking laminated plastic card which had her photograph embossed on it.

Bruce's eyebrows arched in surprise.

"Do you mind if I ring Mr Jones?" the woman said, staring at the ID card. "It's not that I don't believe you but you can't be too careful these days. You hear such terrible things…"

"Please do," Rachel said.

Bruce stared at both women in turn, his eyes growing wider by the second.

While the woman was pressing each number on her phone, Rachel said: "So, what's your name?"

"Megan," the woman replied.

"Are you employed full time here, Megan?"

"No, I only come in for a few hours a day. I just answer his phone, sign for his mail, do a bit of cleaning… It gets me out of the house."

"Well, as long as he's not paying you cash-in-hand," Rachel said with a smile.

Megan suddenly looked concerned, suggesting that was exactly what Milkman was doing. She had finished dialling Milkman's number and all three of them could hear the sound of it ringing.

Rachel's phone began to ring a few seconds later. She removed it from her bag, looked at the caller display and said: "Will you excuse us? We have to take this call."

Bruce followed Rachel through the front door out onto the street. "What are we going to do now?" he hissed. "She's actually ringing him."

"What you're going to do is get into character," Rachel said. "Come on – do the accent. Are you a model? Very fetching you do look I must say…"

"What for?"

"Because you're going to have to be Milkman," she said, offering him the ringing phone.

Bruce backed off, shaking his head, but Rachel pressed the answer button and handed it to him anyway.

"Hello?" Bruce said.

"Mr Jones?"

"Yes Megan," Bruce said, partly covering the phone's microphone with his hand.

"There are two people here who say they have an appointment with you."

"Oh damn," Bruce said, trying to channel the spirit of Milkman. "I forgot about them."

"There's nothing in the diary," Megan said indignantly.

"Alright, calm down, you've got a bell in every tooth you have."

Rachel's face beamed with delight at Bruce's characterisation.

"They've been asking if you pay me cash-in-hand," Megan said quietly. "Should I let them go through into the office?"

"Yes, just let them get on with it. Listen, I've got to go now, the signal's getting weaker," he said, moving the phone further away from his mouth.

Rachel kissed him, causing Bruce to blush for the first time in several years. She took the phone from him, opened the Randy Milkman Enterprises door and pretended to still be holding a conversation of her own. "Yes, I understand that but I'm sure it won't be necessary to involve the police," Rachel said into her phone. "People of her age don't last long in prison. I'll ring you back when we're finished."

Megan looked worried.

"Sorry about that," Rachel said, putting the phone into her bag. "That was the office, wanting to know how we're getting on. Have you spoken to Mr Jones yet?"

"Yes," Megan said. "Everything's fine."

"Good," Rachel said. "Now can you show us his records?"

Megan opened the door in the internal partition and beckoned them to go through. They emerged into a square space containing a rather tatty Chesterfield sofa, several filing cabinets and a large wooden desk crammed with computer equipment. To the rear was a tiny kitchen and a flight of stairs leading up to a first floor. The air was thick with the odour of damp - which perhaps explained the lilies.

"Would you like me to make some tea?" Megan asked.

Rachel declined the offer and guided her gently back into the lobby.

Bruce raised his finger in the air. "I have a question," he said to Rachel. "Why do you carry fake ID?"

"Who said it was fake?" Rachel replied. "Lots of companies issue staff with passes to get into buildings. Do you really think Megan would know the difference between my company pass and one from HMCE?"

"Okay, it was a bluff, I can understand that," Bruce said. "But I have another question – how have you got Milkman's phone?"

Rachel nonchalantly walked behind Milkman's desk and booted up his computer, adjusting her hair in her reflection on the monitor. "I thought it might come in handy."

"Would I be right in assuming that collision between you and Milkman was no accident?"

Rachel said nothing.

"And what if Milkman rings Megan now?" Bruce whispered.

"Oh don't worry about him, there are enough nubile young girls at the hotel to keep him busy for the rest of the day, especially if he goes through his routine more than once with them."

"But what if he does ring?"

"He hasn't got a phone. Now stop fretting like a little girl. Go through his filing cabinets and I'll see what I can find on his computer."

"What are we looking for?" Bruce asked, a slight tremor in his voice.

"Anything to do with Honey Peach," she said.

Bruce rubbed the still sore lump on the side of his head.

"What's the matter, Bruce?" Rachel said in a high pitched voice. "You're not scared of Megan, are you?"

Moments later her tone had soured. "Bugger, it needs a password," she said, thumping the computer's keyboard in frustration.

She turned her attention to the filing cabinets, yanking out each drawer and speed-reading the sections' headings much quicker than Bruce. After a few minutes she removed a document: "Bingo," she said.

CHAPTER EIGHT: WEDNESDAY 11TH JUNE 2003

Bruce was woken by his phone thirty minutes before his alarm was scheduled to assault him. It was several feet away on his dressing table so he ignored it. But he was awake now and aware that his bladder needed emptying. When it rang again he glanced at the caller display on his way to the bathroom, just in case it was anyone he wanted to speak to. To his surprise, it was.

"I can tell everyone that I know a celebrity now," Rachel said, sounding very bubbly.

"Can you? Who's that?"

"You are funny, Bruce. I rang you earlier for a chat but you didn't answer. My train has just pulled in so I've got to dash but I'll call you later."

And then she was gone. And Bruce was cursing himself for not being awake earlier. They had things to talk about. The documents they'd discovered in Milkman's filing cabinets, for a start. And what about her parting words after he'd dropped her off at Bristol Temple Meads railway station, which were accompanied by a kiss and an affectionate squeeze of his hand for emphasis, 'I'm afraid I might be getting a bit too fond of you Bruce,' she'd said. Just thinking about her saying those words brought a smile to his face. He couldn't remember when he'd last felt like this.

The unfamiliar feeling only lasted for another hour, ending, not coincidentally, when he arrived at the AMG office. Plum was first on the attack.

"What is the matter with you?" Plum said, thrusting today's Daily Hate in Bruce's face. "Do you have a death wish or something?"

The headline in the women's section read: 'Yes, porn DOES degrade women' and beneath it was the tagline: 'Industry spokesperson admits what everyone – except this government – has known all along'.

Bruce read the body copy. As he feared, the 'industry spokesperson' named in the article was him. Alex was sat at her desk, smiling to herself and skimming through this week's AMG, which hit subscribers today and would be on sale in retailers tomorrow. Its front page story, about Julian Gregan's group opposing BATA's application for a grant, was not just old news it was prehistoric. The debate, as the media was fond of saying, had moved on.

"I didn't actually say that..." Bruce said.

"No? Well you'll need the number of a lawyer who specialises in libel," Plum said, theatrically offering Bruce a telephone directory.

"They've taken it completely out of context and they've used what I said to fuel their own agenda." As he said this Bruce glanced across at the cover of AMG that Alex was holding, with its non-story that he had fabricated.

"This is still an embryonic industry," Plum said, glaring at Bruce. "And it wouldn't take many more pieces like this for the government to legislate it out of existence."

"Well maybe you shouldn't have given this Molly woman my number," Bruce said.

Nick raised his hand. "That was me, sorry."

Plum stared at Nick. "Why didn't you pass her on to Alex?" he said.

"Because she asked for Bruce, and it was his story after all," Nick said.

"Obviously I'd have handled it very differently," Alex said, getting to her feet with an extremely smug look on her face.

"Perhaps you would," Nick replied. "But you were out getting your hair cut when she rang."

The smug look left Alex and attached itself to Bruce's face. Thank you, Nick.

"In future, make sure all media requests go through me," Plum said to Nick. "Bruce is not a spokesperson for AMG."

Plum read the piece again. "Although it might not all be bad news," he mused. "She does describe AMG as the porn buyer's bible – that's got to be worth a few extra sales. Shame they've also quoted this bloody Gregan idiot though. That's not at all helpful."

Bruce put his lunchbox in the fridge, poured himself a water, sat at his desk and booted up his computer. Alex put aside the issue of AMG and wandered across to him.

"Well?" Alex said.

"Very well, thanks," Bruce replied, without looking up at his colleague. "Couldn't be better."

"What happened yesterday?" Alex persisted. "At the Love Shack open day?"

"It was uneventful," Bruce said.

"Did you talk to them about advertising?"

Bruce swivelled his chair towards Alex. "Advertising? I think you'll find that's one of the few functions here that has yet to be dumped at my door. Now, if you don't mind, I'd like to write up my report."

The only slight issue preventing him doing that was he had left behind the press pack. But he was confident he could toss off a thousand words from memory and he had some pictures to provide visual cues. No quotes though, as he hadn't got around to using the mini disc.

He banged out the first couple of paragraphs but was interrupted by his phone. Dee said it was someone called Zara from BATA and she didn't sound happy. No, she probably wasn't. Daily Hate had named him as an industry spokesperson and quoted him saying that porn degrades women. He should explain to Zara that he hadn't actually said that, and that his words had been twisted and there was no mention of the things he'd said defending the industry...

"I'm not in today," Bruce said to Dee. "Take a message and tell her I'll get back to her tomorrow."

"And what do you want me to do with any other calls – put them through to Alex?"

"That would be wonderful," he said, putting down the phone.

The first of those calls went through just seconds later. Alex was less than pleased to receive it. She shouted across the office: "Bruce, why am I getting your calls?"

"I'm busy."

Alex scowled and transferred the call to Bruce's phone anyway. The button he needed to press to accept it blinked red in an annoying fashion. He ignored it and looked around the office. Just within earshot, Alex was telling Dee she would make an official complaint about her if another one of Bruce's calls came through to her extension. Nick was wearing headphones connected to a mini disc player which was spitting heavy metal into his ears. And then there was Plum. The hypocrite was in his office boasting to one of his Rotary chums that AMG was mentioned in today's Daily Hate. Bruce sighed. What was he doing here? In this place, with these people? He pressed the blinking red button and accepted the call.

"Finally! You celebrities are so hard to get hold of!"

"Rachel!"

"Can you talk? Or have I got to go through your agent now?"

Bruce laughed. "I'll always try to find time for the little people."

Her tone changed. "Listen, I think Milkman might have done something to Honey Peach."

"He might be a lecherous old creep but I don't believe he would hurt anyone."

"He's got a motive, and it's the oldest one in the book."

"Love?"

"No you dummy – money."

Bruce chose his words carefully. "Rachel, if you think something has happened to your sister then you really should go to the police."

Bruce was more than a little concerned about Rachel's relaxed attitude towards taking the law into her own hands. The breaking and entering in Brighton was bad enough but yesterday she'd added theft of a mobile phone, impersonating a government official, misappropriating commercially sensitive documents... And he could be deemed to be complicit in some of those charges and a conspirator in others.

"Oh Bruce, you are naive. Do you really think they would give a rancid rat's rectum about the disappearance of someone who takes it up the arse for a living?"

Bruce felt obliged to point out that Legend of the Amazon Women only featured Honey Peach in girl-on-girl scenes, with no anal penetration.

"Oh okay, that makes a world of difference," Rachel said. "Trust me – the police are not interested. Listen, I've had a good look through the documents we photocopied and took away..."

The documents that you photocopied and took away...

"And your friend Milkman has basically been skint for the last few years – which is no great surprise, having seen his office – but Legend of the Amazon Women has done well in the UK and he could really hit the big time if he could sell it overseas. There's just one minor issue – the contract he's got with Honey Peach. It seems she drove a hard bargain and would only sign a release form if she got paid a royalty on sales. That isn't normal, is it Bruce?"

Bruce didn't think it was. His understanding was that British girls, particularly first-timers, were paid a relatively small one-off fee, unlike the very top performers in America who really did lead film-star lives.

"That's what I thought," Rachel said. "And in the contact is her royalty figure – one pound for every unit sold."

Bruce let out an appreciative whistle. "He obviously knew he had something special with her because that is a very high figure for an afternoon's filming."

"Some guy in America liked the film so much he wanted the worldwide rights to it, and he guaranteed he would sell at least 30,000 copies, but he didn't want to buy finished goods. Do you know what that means?"

Bruce explained that 'finished goods' referred to DVDs that had been duplicated and packaged ready to sell. Instead of paying for the manufacture and shipping of thousands of units, Milkman's buyer just wanted the DVD master disc. He could then duplicate the film locally, which would be far more cost effective. Plus, Bruce said, some scenes may need to be cut from the film to comply with legislation in other territories, and that could not be done with finished goods.

"That makes sense," Rachel said. "Unfortunately the royalty the American guy was offering was just five pence more than Milkman had already agreed to pay Honey Peach."

"Perhaps that royalty was just for the UK?"

She laughed. "The contract doesn't mention overseas sales at all. He obviously got it drawn up on the cheap. This American guy needs Milkman to confirm that no one else had any retention of title clauses or ownership claims on the product. So unless Milkman is happy making five pence a unit while Honey Peach makes a pound, he will need to get her to rescind the original contract and agree to a different deal. And why would she do that? I certainly wouldn't. Bruce, we've got to confront him about this."

"No, we can't do that," he hissed.

"I knew there was something shifty about him," Rachel said. "He was so evasive when I questioned him about the relationship he had with Honey Peach."

"When did you do that?"

"When you were changing your shirt."

"Bruce, who are you talking to?" Alex was standing over him, with a bigger scowl than usual.

"Why?"

"Because that bimbo downstairs wants you and she had the nerve to ask me to get you. I'm not your bloody PA, Bruce."

"Believe me, that is just as much a cause for celebration for me as it is for you," Bruce said, holding his hand over the phone's mouthpiece. "Can you just tell her I'm busy on a call?"

"I'm bloody busy too!" Alex snapped.

Bruce looked across at the magazine open on her desk. "A particularly challenging issue of Celebs & Scandals this week is it? Have they used some big words?"

"I'm putting her through so you'd better finish that call," Alex said, returning to her desk. "And then I'm going down there and having this out with her."

Bruce explained to Rachel that he would have to put her on hold while he dealt with Dee.

"No need – that was everything I had to tell you. I'll talk to you tomorrow," Rachel said, hanging up.

Bruce pressed the blinking red button to speak to Dee. "Yes Dee, what is it now?"

"I've got a Mr Jones for you," she said.

"Tell him I'm not in, will you?" Bruce said, suddenly feeling a little sick.

"I can't really tell him that," Dee said. "Because he's not on the phone, he's standing right in front of me here in reception."

***

As Bruce emerged into the reception area, he noticed that Dee was smiling and looking down at one of Milkman's business cards. She'd obviously just been asked if she was a model.

Milkman was sat on the sofa, jigging one of his long skinny legs. He had a leather man-bag on his lap and he was wearing the same clothes Bruce had seen him in yesterday. He stood up and walked towards Bruce.

"What happened to you yesterday?" Milkman said.

That's a good question. "What do you mean?"

"You left early," Milkman said. "Spaghetti was asking about you. You missed a cracking night. He certainly knows how to throw a party. Don't know if any of us will be welcome back at that hotel though. When they stopped serving drinks at three in the morning, Spaghetti went behind the bar and just helped himself. It was a right beanfeast."

"It sounds it," Bruce agreed. "I had to get back, unfortunately."

"I wouldn't have had to come here today if you'd hung about," Milkman said. "It's just as well that Bath is only over the Severn Bridge. And who was that bird you were with? I can't abide noisy women aggravating me. From one of the London papers, was she?"

"I think so."

"I thought as much. That's what they're like down there, isn't it? She kept banging on and on about Honey Peach."

"She was really disappointed Honey Peach wasn't there."

"Not as much as me, I can tell you," Milkman said. "Right, let's go somewhere quiet because I've got a bit of a scoop for you."

***

The cellar bar at Marelli's was quiet, with just the bored looking barmaid staring up at them as they clumped down the stairs.

"Shall I find us a table?" Bruce said, gesturing at the empty bar.

Milkman didn't notice Bruce's weak joke. He had other things on his mind. The usual things. "What's a lovely girl like you doing down here all on your own?" he smarmed to the barmaid.

She looked at him disdainfully but Milkman was well practiced.

"You've got beautiful eyes," he said to her. "I suppose everyone tells you that?"

Her face suggested that they didn't.

Still he continued. "You must be a model. Are you a model?"

Bruce couldn't listen to this again. "I've got to be back in the office soon," he shouted across the empty bar from what had become his favourite table.

Several minutes later, clutching one of his own business cards in his teeth, Milkman brought two pints of Guinness across to Bruce's table. Setting the drinks down, he removed the card from his mouth and looked at the number 'Anna' had written on it. "Can I borrow your phone? I just want to check that the number she's written down isn't fake. They do that sometimes, just to get shot of you."

"Sure," Bruce said, sliding his phone across the table.

"I lost my bugger yesterday," Milkman said, dialling the number.

The sound of a mobile ringing could be heard behind the bar.

"Hello again lovely," Milkman said, when Anna answered. "I'm just checking you wrote the number down correctly..."

She giggled.

Anna had been pouring Bruce's pints several times a week for almost a year and in all that time he had exchanged fewer pleasantries with her than Milkman had managed in three minutes. And Milkman had also found out her name. Sometimes you just have to doff your cap to a master craftsman at work.

Bruce tapped his wrist, pointing out that time was ticking away on his imaginary watch. "You said you had something to show me?"

"Right enough," Milkman said, handing the phone back and removing a laptop from his leather bag. "This will knock your bloody socks off."

Bruce stared at his companion while he placed the machine between them on the table and pressed the 'on' button.

"People are bored with today's porn," Milkman said. "No plots, no set ups, just bang, bang, bang. And don't get me started on the women's tattoos, fake tits and shaved minges! What's that all about?"

Bruce decided it was a rhetorical question.

When the laptop had run through its start-up sequence, Milkman removed a blank CD case from his bag. It contained a recordable disc with the word 'arse' scrawled on it in black felt tip pen. Milkman inserted it into the laptop's DVD drive and repositioned the screen so Bruce could see it.

The Windows icons were replaced by footage of a young woman walking through what appeared to be the garden of a stately home. She was dressed in a long black silk pelisse, adorned with gold braid, and a lacy veil hid her face. The camera followed her as she approached a nearby tree, where she stood under its branches. She slowly removed all her clothing and, with her back against the trunk, she slid down to the ground. After caressing her breasts for about a minute she parted her legs and revealed a mass of dark pubic hair to the camera.

"I know what you're thinking," said Milkman "You're thinking 'where the Dickens did he find this unspoiled girl?' Am I right? And that works on two levels because I'm going to pornalise the works of Charles Dickens."

Bruce savoured the Guinness and tried not to laugh.

"I'm starting with this one, Bleak Arse – instead of Bleak House – and I've already got plans for loads of others. I'm going to call them the Dick-Ins series. Do you get it? Dick-Ins?"

Bruce got it.

"It's going to bring the Sunday night historical drama crowd into porn," Milkman enthused.

Bruce pulled a sceptical face. "Isn't the dialogue going to be an issue for the performers? Are there any Dickens' works which feature the characters saying 'Yeah baby' a lot?"

"That's the brilliant thing – they're not going to say anything. The dialogue is going to be via subtitles only, which you can switch off when you just want to crack one out, and it's going to be in loads of different languages. DVD is bloody great isn't it, compared to VHS?"

"Do you actually know the story of Bleak House?" Bruce said. "The book does not, on the surface at least, instantly lend itself to porn."

"No one under fifty reads books anymore," Milkman said.

"I'm not sure if that's completely accurate," Bruce said. Gesturing to the screen, where two men dressed as grooms were watching the woman masturbate, he added: "This looks expensive – you must have made quite a bit out of Amazon Women?"

"I'm boning a bird who works in the BBC Wales wardrobe department," Milkman whispered, so that Anna didn't hear. "She can get me the actual clothes they wore in the real series, on the quiet like. She's got a face like a fry up but she's got a nice arse and you've got to empty your sacks somewhere, haven't you?"

"Is she in the film?"

"God no. The girl in the film is an East European bird called Katarina. She's completely natural – no tattoos, no piercings, and no implants – and as you can see, she's still got her bush. I'm going to name her Lady Victoria something-or-other."

"Actually, you might just have something here," Bruce admitted.

"I'm glad to hear you say that, because I need your help," Milkman said. "What I want you to do is make Bleak Arse your Movie of the Week."

"I'll certainly consider it if you want to leave me a copy," Bruce said.

Milkman popped the disc from the drive and handed it across, along with another disc which he took from his bag. "This one has got some stills from the shoot and the cover artwork. Is there anything else I need to give you?"

"The usual mechanical info – release date, retail price, running times, whether there are any extras on the DVD, that sort of thing…"

"I don't mean all that stuff," Milkman said, waggling his finger. "What do I have to give you?"

"Just a DVD that I think is better than any of the others." Bruce said.

"I'm not making myself clear," Milkman said, leaning closer. "What do I have to give to you, personally, for it to be Movie of the Week? Girls? Drugs? Money? To be honest I'd rather it wasn't money…"

Bruce finally understood. "That's not how things work," he said. "I'll look at it and, if it deserves to be Movie of the Week it will be. That's all I can say."

Milkman was disappointed. "You're missing a trick there. You could have a nice little sideline going."

"Have you ever considered releasing all your old stuff on DVD?" Bruce said, changing the subject.

Milkman took a deep gulp of Guinness. "To be honest, there's no point now. I couldn't afford the BBFC fees for a start."

UK legislation required every film, whether shown in a cinema or sold on VHS or DVD, to carry a rating issued by the British Board of Film

Classification. It cost £12 a minute for a BBFC examiner to scrutinise a film and it was a slow process, particularly if the regulatory body required cuts to the footage.

Milkman continued: "It's all been pirated to death anyway and the quality wasn't there in the first place – it was only filmed on VHS with a budget of two bob."

Bruce nodded in an understanding way then, after a pause of a few seconds, said: "Any news about Honey Peach?"

Milkman closed the laptop lid. "Sadly not, though I'm sure she'll turn up eventually."

"Aren't you worried about her?"

Milkman nodded his head. "Of course I am, but what can I do? She's vanished."

"Perhaps she's gone to America," Bruce said. "I would imagine the Americans would love her. Have you considered looking for a distributor for Amazon Women in the US?"

Milkman was staring at Bruce. "Can I borrow your phone again?" he said. "I haven't checked in with the office yet today."

Bruce nonchalantly slid the handset across the table to him again and watched as Milkman dialled the number. Had he gone too far? His last question about Honey Peach had definitely made Milkman uncomfortable. And during his phone conversation with Megan, Milkman's face grew gloomier by the second until his thin lips formed an upside down smile.

Milkman ended the call and handed the phone back. "I've got to go," he said. "The bloody VAT man paid me a visit yesterday. That's all I bloody need."

***

Back at the AMG office, Bruce filled a cup from the water cooler and sat down at his desk. His answerphone messages included one from a very agitated Zara, saying his comments in today's Daily Hate had set back BATA's cause several years. There were also messages from bright young things with names like Pippa and Sophie, from other newspapers. He deleted them all.

He opened the drawer of his desk and pulled out this week's film releases. There was the odd VHS tape but most were now DVD, which Bruce much preferred – not so much for the increased quality but because he could skip scenes much faster, which made reviewing a less painful process. There were almost thirty new releases to wade through, and he could tell just by looking at the boxes that many of them were going to be formless and gormless formulaic productions.

A UK publisher had bought the rights to a long running US series, called California Cum Whores, and had released the first six instalments simultaneously. Bruce looked at the collection of ugly people on the covers and decided that this was one series AMG was not going to showcase within its pages. He grabbed the six films and took them straight to the archive, the walk-in cupboard in which he stored all the video tapes and DVDs he had been sent for review.

The archive was about six feet deep and six feet wide and it was lined on all sides with shelving. The videos and DVDs were arranged in alphabetical order, with their spines facing out, so any title could be easily retrieved. Bruce filed the newcomers, still in their clear plastic wrapping, with all the others that began with the same letter. Once they had been jammed in he slowly looked around, taking in the hundreds and hundreds of pornography titles. The solid wooden door to the archive had warped over the years and it no longer closed properly. The gap was slightly less than two inches wide and Bruce peeped through it into the office. He could see the office's rear window and Alex's desk from here. She was on the phone, arranging a test drive with Reeves & Jeeves for a Mini. He sighed. What kind of life was this for a man of his age?

***

As Bruce approached Jan's bed her face lit up but she looked a little older than when he'd last seen her. When was that? Only two days ago? He smiled back and handed her a copy of the new issue of AMG and a small bunch of red and yellow chrysanthemums. "The florist said they are the best for hospital because the pollen is inside the flower, not exposed," Bruce explained.

The florist had actually recommended roses, for the same reason, but Bruce didn't want his gesture to be misconstrued. Roses were for Valentine's Day, not sick work colleagues.

"Oh Bruce, they are lovely," Jan said, wiping the corner of her eye. "Thank you."

"How are you?" he asked, feeling a little awkward.

"On the mend but it's going to be a slow old process. But never mind me, what about you? I nearly choked on my porridge this morning when I saw you quoted in the Daily Hate. How did that come about?"

Bruce pointed to the cover of AMG. He explained how he'd fabricated the original story and how Gregan had taken it to the tabloid. "There was even a debate on Radio 4 about it," he said.

"With you?"

He shook his head. He knew Jan would have been impressed if he'd appeared on her beloved Radio 4. "No, that was Zara, from the trade association, debating with Gregan."

"How did she do?"

"I don't know, I fell asleep."

She frowned at him, forming creases above the bridge of her nose.

"Don't look so disappointed, you know Radio 4 does that to me. All those soothing old fashioned accents and perfectly pronounced vowels."

"Well I hope someone heard it and has written it up as a news story."

This was why Jan was an editor and he wasn't. "Look what Alex has done with your Welcome page," he said, changing the subject.

Jan pulled a surprised expression but said nothing as she flicked through the issue, until she came to Bruce's report on Leathers, Tethers and Feathers. "Did you actually go to Brighton to cover this?"

Bruce nodded.

"That's not like you."

Should he tell her? After a long pause he explained everything. How Honey Peach had not shown up for Spaghetti's shop opening, how her sister had come looking for her, how the two of them had broken into Honey Peach's house and escaped over the gardens, how they had fraudulently gained entry to Milkman's office and made copies of some of his documents and how Rachel now suspected that Milkman may be involved in Honey Peach's disappearance.

Jan stared at him in amazement. Eventually she said: "Well, you know what you've got to do now."

"What I should have done in the beginning – make her go to the police."

"No, you idiot, get back down to Brighton and find out who that bloke in her house was. This is a real story Bruce, so go and be a real journalist."

CHAPTER NINE: THURSDAY 12TH JUNE 2003

The M4 motorway between Bristol and London is best avoided before nine in the morning as it becomes a battlefield for commuters, especially close to the junctions for Swindon, Reading and Slough. Bruce didn't care. He had the Mazda's roof up, allowing him to blast out the summer sounds of the Beach Boys. He turned the CD off after less than a minute though. Little Deuce Coupe was one of the last songs he'd heard when Rachel was in the passenger's seat and he didn't want to dilute the memory it evoked by playing it again so soon. He turned on the radio but, since his Mazda's aerial had been vandalised, the only channel he could pick up which didn't suffer from distortion was devoted to news and current affairs.

There was much talk about Prime Minister Tony Blair's Cabinet reshuffle but five minutes before the end of the programme the subject was changed quite dramatically. The presenter stumbled over the words 'hardcore pornography' as if he was saying them for the first time, which he might well have been. He then introduced Julian Gregan.

"So let me get this right, Mr Gregan, you're calling for a blanket ban on these films but on what grounds?" The presenter was famed for his combative style and he saw it as his role to always play devil's advocate with his guests.

"On what grounds? On the grounds that they are a blight on society. On the grounds that they corrupt. On the grounds that they degrade..."

"With respect Mr Gregan, those are purely subjective assessments..."

"On the grounds that they depict illegal acts..."

"Illegal acts? But these films have been through the BBFC process."

"Is living off immoral earnings legal in Britain?" Gregan said.

The presenter sighed. It was his job to do the haranguing, not the rent-a-quotes the producers dug up, eager for their fifteen minutes of fame.

"Of course it's not," Gregan answered his own question. "Yet that's what the people who make these depraved things are doing.."

"What they're doing is making adult entertainment..."

"Adult entertainment?" Gregan butted in. "I'm an adult and I can assure you that I don't find these films in the least bit entertaining – do you? All they are is essentially visual records of prostitution. The women are paid to have sex outside of a loving relationship. I'm sorry but whether there's a camera present or not, by any definition that is prostitution."

"But the law says these films are perfectly legal to buy and sell, as long as the buyer is over eighteen and the transaction takes place within the confines of a licensed sex shop…"

"Why are you defending this repugnant trade in misery?" Gregan said.

"Mr Gregan, you've made your moral position perfectly clear but do you have any evidence that these films cause harm? Pornography has been around since man first learned to draw on the walls of his cave…"

Gregan paused.

"Mr Gregan?" the presenter prompted, desperate to avoid dead air.

"I suppose I should have expected the BBC to side with the liberal left that has sold this country down the river," Gregan said.

"From that response I'll assume that you have no evidence that these films cause harm but you've certainly made your position clear and I'm sure none of our listeners are in any doubt about that. Thank you Mr Gregan, I'm afraid that's all we have time for…"

Bruce turned the radio off when the nine o'clock news started. He drove with just the sound of the wind roaring in through the Mazda's open windows but as he approached Reading the flow of the traffic began to slow. He lit a cigarette and picked up his mobile. Should he call Rachel and tell her what he was doing? He jumped as the phone suddenly burst into life. It was AMG.

"This is Bruce," he said, feigning the voice of someone important.

"Where the bloody hell are you?" Alex said.

"I'm not at my desk right now but if you'd like to leave a message I will get back to you as soon as I can. Beeep…"

"Stop pissing about Bruce, why aren't you in work?"

"I am in work, I'm just not in the office. I'm looking into something. I sent you a mail explaining that I might be out for most of today."

"That's why I'm ringing you," Alex said. "It's Thursday, you should be writing up the news."

"That's what I'm looking into, a news story."

"What time do you intend coming in?"

"Tomorrow," Bruce said, blowing smoke out of the open window and pressing the 'end call' button simultaneously.

Twenty minutes later the phone rang again. This time it was Plum demanding to know why he wasn't in the office. He told Plum the same thing as Alex, though more politely. Plum told Bruce that he wanted to see him in his office at nine in the morning.

As he approached the M25 the phone rang again.

"What now, Plum?"

"What now? I'll tell you what now – we've just had the partner of Roz, the organiser of that fetish fair, on the phone. He's seen your report in the latest issue and he's spitting bullets. Apparently the fair got broken up by the police because she didn't have the right permit or something, and in the resulting melee she was arrested and collapsed while she was in police custody."

"Well she was a belligerent old boot," Bruce said.

"What is wrong with you, Bruce? This woman has four children and she was doing this to put food on the table. We should be highlighting her plight but how can we, after the hatchet job you did on her? What I don't understand is that all this happened in the early afternoon and I spoke to you several hours later. Why did you not know about this?"

Bruce didn't answer. Dead air didn't bother him.

"We'll discuss this in detail tomorrow morning Bruce. Make sure you're not late."

Bruce didn't need to hang up – Plum had beaten him to it.

***

Bruce was able to park on the same street as Honey Peach's house, though several hundred yards away beneath a sign that stipulated his stay could be for no longer than an hour. As he locked the Mazda he realised he could have justified this excursion by profiling one of Brighton's many adult retailers while he was here. He could still do that, he decided, once he'd done what he came for. He didn't have the mini disc with him but he could buy a notebook and a disposable camera…

As he approached the house he thought back to his original motive for doing this. There was no point lying, it was because he had developed a bit of a crush on Rachel. But now he also wanted to prove to Jan that he could be a real journalist. But the way his insides did a gentle flip when he thought about Rachel suggested that his adolescent-like crush was the stronger motive. Thinking about her made him want to hear her voice again so he called her.

"Hello?"

"Hi Rachel, sorry about yesterday."

"Yesterday?" She sounded distracted and appeared to be in a noisy environment. Bruce could hear raised voices and occasional bursts of laughter in the background.

"When we were speaking on the phone and I had to hang up."

"Of course," she said. "Don't worry about it."

"You said we'd speak today. Well, you'll never guess where I am..."

"Bruce, this isn't a good time for me," she said. "I'm in the hospital with my mother. Her condition has deteriorated overnight and the doctors are not sure how long she's got."

"Oh no, I'm so sorry to hear that," Bruce said.

"We're not supposed to use mobile phones in here so I'm going to be incommunicado for a while. I'll ring you when I can, okay?"

"Okay but..." Bruce started to say before realising she had ended the call.

He stopped at Honey Peach's gate and surreptitiously looked around in every direction. The street was deserted so he walked up to the door and rattled the letterbox loudly. There was no response. He repeated the action and this time placed his ear to it. Silence. He whipped out his credit card and ran it down the edge of the door near the lock. He'd practiced the manoeuvre several times that morning on the door of his own flat and his efforts were rewarded with the delicate click of the lock relinquishing its charge.

The kitchen appeared pretty much unchanged from his previous visit, he discovered. The lounge contained little more than a television, hi-fi and large leather sofa while the dining room seemed to be a dumping ground. There were a few black bags of laundry, a vacuum cleaner, an ironing board and an exercise bike, along with some boxes of women's magazines.

As Bruce walked back into the hall he heard the distinctive creak of the gate. A figure could be seen outside, through the frosted glass of the front door. He froze. The figure opened the letterbox and posted through a flyer promoting a fast food outlet before moving on to the house next door. Bruce exhaled with relief and retrieved the flyer for Kalamazoo Fried Chicken from the doormat. The outlet referred to itself by its initials on the inside of the flyer. Very clever. Or very stupid.

Then a thought occurred to him: houses in this street must be inundated with junk mail. If there was no one living here there should be a mound of it behind the front door, yet there was just this lonely leaflet, with its grammatical errors and poorly laid out stock imagery. So that must mean that someone removes it all on a regular basis. His stomach lurched and he bounded up the stairs.

Upstairs consisted of two decent-sized bedrooms and a small bathroom. The first bedroom contained only a clothes rail, crammed with barely-there outfits which glistened in the sunlight, and a full length mirror. The master bedroom was dominated by a double bed, a dressing table littered with brightly coloured bottles and a built-in wardrobe with sliding mirrored doors that ran the length of the wall. She really did appear to live the simple life. He opened the drawers on the dressing table but they just contained underwear. He laughed out loud at the thought of her coming through the door now and catching him rifling through her knickers. Um, I can explain…

Sliding the wardrobe's doors open revealed a riot of coloured material, though the garments were more conventional than the stripper-like items in the other bedroom, as if she had compartmentalised the upstairs to match her life. In the other room was her porn life, here were her coats, jackets, blouses, skirts, dresses. The entire length of the floor area was packed with shoes, some of which were still in their boxes.

Two double plug sockets were located either side of the bed. Permanently plugged in, though switched off, on one side were a set of straighteners and a hairdryer. The sockets on the other side were connected to a radio/clock and a… the cable went under the bed. Bruce bent down to see what it was attached to – a laptop. He yanked the cable and dragged the laptop towards him. He flipped open the case, which was adorned with stickers of pink unicorns, and stabbed at the power button. It burst into life then, once the start-up sequence had run its course, the computer presented him with a dialogue box. It was password protected. Bugger.

He sat on the extremely soft and comfortable bed. The sun shone in through the window and he suddenly felt very tired from the early start and the journey. He had to resist the urge to pull back the duvet and climb beneath it. Being found asleep in her bed would look just as bad as being caught rummaging through her smalls. Still, he relaxed his shoulders and closed his eyes for a few seconds.

The piercing crash of breaking glass made him physically jump up from the bed. It was quickly followed by the sound of the front door being opened. Someone was breaking in, the old fashioned way. He looked around for an escape route. Only the tops of the bedroom windows appeared to open, and he wouldn't have fitted through them even if he was two stone lighter. There seemed no obvious way to get out to the front balcony so the only escape route was back down the stairs – and that wasn't his option of choice under the current circumstances.

The sound of the front door closing could be clearly heard upstairs. Like Bruce before him, the intruder quickly realised that the lounge and dining room held nothing of value and he headed into the kitchen. Cupboard doors were wrenched open and then banged closed. The drawers slid in and out on their runners and then there was silence. For a whole minute. Nothing. Then Bruce could hear footsteps on the stairs. They were getting louder. And closer.

He grabbed the laptop, leaving the power cable plugged into the wall socket, slid the mirrored door of the wardrobe open and dived inside between the evening gowns. By the time the intruder reached the upstairs landing, Bruce had managed to stealthily slide the door back into place.

Inside, the light from the laptop screen was more than sufficient for him to choose a heavy red velvet dress to hide behind. He closed the laptop's lid and was relieved to hear its fan stop as it put itself into hibernation mode. He was surprised to note that although his heart rate had increased he wasn't actually panicking. Quite the opposite – maybe it was his body's survival instinct taking over but he found himself wondering if being discovered in here would be worse than being found asleep in the bed.

The bedroom door opened. A floorboard under the thin carpet creaked. Whoever this person was he or she was just a couple of feet away. Bruce could hear them breathing. Deep breaths, almost wheezing. It sounded like a bloke. An unfit bloke.

Several times the intruder moved between the two bedrooms and the tiny bathroom but, like Bruce before him, he settled in the master bedroom. He was definitely looking for something. Was he going to open the wardrobe? Bruce started to perspire and wondered if it was due to the situation or the claustrophobic heat.

The sound of a key turning in the front door carried up the stairs. Bruce could feel his legs starting to tremble but the other occupant of the bedroom appeared to be even more disturbed by this development. He swore under his breath and gently slid open the other mirrored wardrobe door, clambering in and settling about six feet and thirty dresses from Bruce.

The front door slammed and footsteps echoed in the hall. This third person appeared to be heading for the kitchen. Bruce strained to hear what was happening downstairs but his fellow wardrobe dweller was having difficulty breathing, loudly gulping in the stale air and strenuously blowing it out again. Was Honey Peach downstairs?

"Can you put me through to the police please," a man's voice from downstairs said. "I'd like to report a break-in… It's the second time in less than a week… I don't know what time it took place, I've just come in and noticed the glass in the front door has been broken and the kitchen has been ransacked… No, I haven't checked upstairs… Well can you send someone round straight away?"

Bruce gasped as the other wardrobe door was suddenly wrenched open. The figure burst out and ran down the stairs. Bruce heard a shout, followed by the sound of a scuffle, then the loud clang of metal hitting something soft, and then there was silence.

Bruce felt sick but knew he had to get out. He extracted himself from the dresses, crept along the landing and peeked down the stairs – a balding middle-aged man lay face down in the hall with blood seeping from a wound on the back of his head. Next to him was a chrome kettle, leaking tepid water onto the hall's chequerboard tiles, seemingly in sympathy. A slight smudge of crimson could be seen on its base.

Bruce cautiously made his way down the stairs. Through the open front door he could hear someone screaming, suggesting that the prostrate body could be seen from outside. Still clutching the laptop under his arm, Bruce leapt over the man lying in the hallway, avoiding looking at him. Once outside, he could see a woman on the opposite site of the street, standing in her garden and pleading down her phone for the police to come. Bruce held up the laptop to shield his face from her and ran for his life back to his car.

***

"And this really happened?" Jan said, astonished.

"Of course it really happened," Bruce said.

"Are you sure it wasn't a dream you had after watching a Carry On film?" Jan adopted a cockney accent: "Oi mate, this wardrobe ain't big enough for the both of us – whoops, he's been bonked on the head with a kettle."

"It wasn't funny."

"That just makes it sound even more like a Carry On film."

"Luckily the wardrobe was actually big enough for the both of us but it was a heavy kettle – can you die from a kettle blow?"

"A kettle blow?" Jan said, suddenly laughing. "Have you searched the internet for the correct term for such an assault?"

"It's not funny," Bruce hissed.

"Oh it is," Jan replied, returning to her cockney accent: "Oi mate, have you seen my trousers? Fancy a bit of how's your father? Oh no, it's the vicar!"

Bruce waited for Jan's laughter to subside. "While I'm delighted to have brought some amusement into your life, what I was really looking for was a constructive suggestion or two."

"Did you call the police?"

Bruce shook his head. "You told me not to."

"That was yesterday," Jan said. "Don't tell me you just ran out of the house, leaving some poor bloke bleeding on the floor and casually drove back to Bath?"

Bruce nodded confirmation. "It wasn't casually though."

"What are you – a simpleton?"

Bruce shrugged, and then nodded again.

"Who runs away from a crime scene apart from the guilty?"

"There's another reason why I didn't call the police."

"Another reason? In addition to you breaking in and stealing a laptop? Have you considered, even for a moment, that you might have got the wrong house?"

"Oh I'm sure it was the right house."

"How can you be so sure?"

"Because I recognised the other burglar when he ran out of the wardrobe – it was Milkman."

CHAPTER TEN: FRIDAY 13TH JUNE 2003

Bruce awoke to the sound of a belligerent Radio 4 presenter jousting with a defiant Julian Gregan. Again. "But Mr Gregan, the government has released a statement which quite categorically says that it has no intention of subsidising 'the overseas jollies of pornographers' as you put it. You should be rejoicing. You've got what you wanted, you've won."

"How can I rejoice when there's a tide of filth washing over the country? How can we have won when there are people making money from filming young girls doing the most degrading acts?"

"Mr Gregan, we asked you on the programme to comment on the government statement, not to pursue a personal agenda..."

"And these films can be purchased over the counter, perfectly legally, in High Street shops up and down the country."

"You used the term 'perfectly legally' yourself there Mr Gregan – you as an individual might find it distasteful but it has been legal for people over eighteen to buy pornography in a licensed sex shop since the year 2000 and there are safeguards in place to prevent impressionable people under that age getting hold of these products."

"Do you think people stop being impressionable when they reach eighteen? In that case there would be no advertising industry..."

"That's rather besides the point..."

"You're right – the real point is that the girls in these films are being paid to have sex with strangers. Isn't that the definition of prostitution? So therefore it must follow that the people making these films are living off immoral earnings, which is a crime punishable by six months imprisonment when heard before a magistrate and seven years in a Crown Court. So why aren't we prosecuting these people? It surely cannot be due to lack of evidence – they've incriminated themselves by recording their crimes."

Bruce turned the radio off. Christ, what had he started with his fabricated story? He'd elevated Gregan into a national figure.

***

"I really don't know where to start," Plum said, handing Bruce two A4 sheets of paper, stapled together. "So I'll let you read this first."

Bruce looked at the charge sheet, which documented recent actions of his that were either against company policy, incompatible with what was expected of a senior member of staff or just plain and simple misconduct. They included lateness, insubordination, unauthorised absences and making threats. At the bottom of the document's second page was provision for two signatures. Plum had already signed and dated one of them.

"I am very unhappy with you Bruce," Plum said. "Not least because I had to consult an employment lawyer to ensure the company's disciplinary process adheres to current legislation, and they don't come cheap."

Bruce started to speak but Plum hushed him with a finger-on-lips gesture and continued: "I want you to consider this a formal warning because that's exactly what it is. I've clearly been too indulgent with you in the past but we are short staffed and need all hands to the pump. Do you have anything to say concerning your absence yesterday?"

Bruce decided, after some consideration, that he didn't. "It's a long and winding road of a story."

"Is it really? Well as I hope you are capable of understanding – and if you're not I have underlined the relevant passage – further indiscretions along the lines of any of the examples outlined in this document will result in a second formal written warning. And if you persist down this path then you'll soon be exploring alternative employment opportunities. Is that completely clear?"

It was. As his computer booted up it informed Bruce that today was not just deadline day, it was Friday the 13th – the unluckiest date in the calendar, according to the superstitious. Surely my life can't get any worse than this moment, Bruce thought, tossing the written warning onto his desk and trying to ignore the sound of Alex on the phone, complaining because her lunchtime appointment with a nail technician had been cancelled.

He had more pressing concerns, such the events of the previous day. Should he ring Rachel and tell her that her suspicions about Milkman might be correct? And who was that bloke that Milkman attacked with a kettle? From what he said on the phone to the police, he was the same bloke they escaped over the gardens from. Bruce needed to find out who he was, but he was hardly in a position, on either of the occasions he had met him, to make such an enquiry.

This was the sort of thing the internet should be used for, thought Bruce, but experimenting with search terms just resulted in dead ends. If only he'd found a utility bill while he was in there...

Nick wheeled his chair across from his own desk to Bruce's. Pointing to Plum's office, he said: "How did it go in there?"

"Great," said Bruce. "He's given me a pay rise and made me Employee of the Week."

"I thought as much," Nick said. Looking at Bruce's monitor, he added: "What are you working on?"

"It's a long and winding road of a story."

Nick gestured at Alex, who was still on the phone. "Mate, I hope it was worth it because she was calling for your head yesterday. But you were right about her. She sent through some copy and it was riddled with errors. I didn't actually realise this before but she can't bloody write. I had to correct it."

Bruce stroked his chin and furrowed his brow, miming deep thought, then he said in a fruity voice which sounded uncannily like Plum's: "Let's see now, AMG needs an acting editor but rather than give it to the person who does most of the actual writing I'm going to give it to the bit of totty who sells the ads."

Nick laughed. "Mate, it does sound a bit nuts when you think about it."

Bruce gazed across at Alex and shook his head. "I try my best not to think about it."

"So, come on then, what have you been up to?"

Bruce stared at Nick and said quietly: "If I tell you, you've got to keep it to yourself."

Nick raised his eyebrows in expectation. "You're finally coming out as gay?"

"This is just between the two of us, right?"

"I'm probably supposed to say that I had no idea but that would be a lie. I've always suspected it. Everybody has."

Bruce turned his chair away from Nick.

"Alright," Nick protested, grabbing Bruce's chair and pulling him back. "Anything you say will remain confidential. You big gaylord."

"I think something might have happened to Honey Peach," Bruce said.

"Honey Peach the porn star?"

"No, Honey Peach the Secretary-General of the United Nations."

Nick's muscular arm mimed the 'wanker' gesture at Bruce. "What sort of thing?"

"She's disappeared. Her sister asked me to help her find her, because her mother is ill, but no one knows where she is."

"She's probably on holiday," Nick suggested. "It is the summer, after all. She's probably been whisked off to the Algarve by a Premier League footballer. They tend to go for girls who look like that. Is this why you weren't in work yesterday?"

Bruce gestured at Alex and hissed: "Will you keep it down? I don't want Her Royal Highness to know."

Alex finished her call and approached Bruce's desk. "Where were you yesterday?" she said.

"I was petitioning the council to have a statue of you erected at the entrance to Vicky Park," he said. "For your outstanding services to journalism. So far I've got one signature but I'm not convinced it's genuine."

"You'd better pull your finger out Bruce," she said. "You left us up Shit Creek without a paddle yesterday. You were supposed to do the news but the first eight pages of next week's issue are currently blank."

"I'm planning to run last week's stories again," Bruce replied. "We can jiggle them around a bit so they're in different places though, just in case anyone is paying attention."

Alex suddenly became very serious. "That's not funny Bruce. The news pages are the lifeblood of a magazine."

"They may be in Celebs & Scandals," Bruce replied. "But no one buys AMG for the news pages. To be fair though, ours don't feature pictures of soap stars with no makeup or singers with sweat patches under their arms."

Picking up a copy of the Daily Hate, Alex said: "That should have been our story."

"It was," Bruce said.

"I want AMG to have all the news first," Alex continued. "I want other people quoting our news and crediting us with it, not beating us to publication with it."

"That's a truly noble aim," Bruce replied. "But we don't own the news anymore. Anything that's important goes around the world in seconds. It's called the internet – if it was up to me, and there was a big red button to turn the bloody thing off, I would press it. But we appear to be stuck with it for the foreseeable future."

"Well you're just going to have to work harder then, aren't you?" Alex said. "Or we'll start looking for someone else who will."

As she flounced off, Bruce was tempted to say something very rude but he thought better of it. That was probably what she wanted, following the issuing of his written warning.

"Talking of the news, any idea of what we are going with on the front page, mate?" Nick said. "I should crack on with the layout so if you can give me a clue about the word count…"

"He hasn't got a clue, full stop," said Alex.

"Oh shut up, you useless bitch," snapped Bruce.

Alex stared at Bruce for a few seconds and then marched off to Plum's office with a look of triumph on her face.

"Mate, you're really not helping yourself," Nick said. "You can't speak to her like that."

"Hardly slander though, was it?" Bruce said. "Returning to your question, I thought we'd lead with something about Dick-Ins from Milkman. Allow for about 400 words."

"Okay. Any images?"

"I've got a disc with some stills here," Bruce said, attempting to open his desk drawer. It wouldn't budge. Then Plum and Alex were looming over him.

"A word, Bruce," said Plum. "My office, now."

"Hang on," Bruce said. "I can't get my drawer open. It looks like it's locked."

"Well unlock it then, Einstein," said Alex.

"I never lock it," Bruce replied. "I don't even have a key for it."

"Bruce…" Plum said, in a louder voice.

"You do have a key mate," said Nick quietly.

"No I do not," Bruce snapped.

"You do," Nick persisted. "It's on your keyring."

Alex grabbed Bruce's keys, which he always kept on his desk as a paperweight. "What's this then, dickhead?" she said.

Bruce snatched them from her. Along with the keys to his flat and the Mazda there was a small metal one that looked like it would fit the lock. His hands seemed to tremble and a cold sensation passed across his forehead. He tried the key in the lock and the drawer slid obediently open.

"Is this it?" Nick asked, removing a blank CD which had the words 'Arse pix' scrawled on it in black felt pen.

Bruce nodded, his forehead prickling with perspiration.

"Are you alright, Bruce?" Plum said, with what could have passed for genuine concern. "You look dreadful."

"Let's hope it's nothing fatal," said Alex.

"I'm fine," Bruce said, standing and ushering his colleagues away. "I just need a cigarette."

Alex refused to move out of his path. "You're not going anywhere…"

"Let him go," Plum said, gently holding her back. "I'll deal with him later."

***

When Bruce returned from his smoke in the courtyard, he approached Nick's desk a little unsteadily. "Were those images alright?"

"They're fine," Nick replied. "But you'll need to tell me what the story is going to be about before I choose which ones I use. And any thoughts on the headline?"

"Something like 'New BBC costume drama porn unveiled'," Bruce said.

Nick stared at Bruce. "The BBC is doing porn?"

"A bit of an exclusive, wouldn't you say?" Bruce said. Then, impersonating Alex's northern accent, he added: "I want AMG to have all the news first. I want other people quoting our news and crediting us with it."

"That's a pretty good impression," Nick said, laughing. "The BBC is not really doing porn though, is it?"

"Just make sure you use inverted commas in the headline," said Bruce.

Nick shrugged. "Okay, it won't be me who gets sued."

"No one will get sued," Bruce replied, rubbing the side of his head.

"Is that still bothering you?" Nick said. "Did you ask them to give you a scan while you were down the hospital?"

"If you're going to tell me that incident with the desk drawer is somehow connected…"

"Mate, you claimed you didn't have a key to your drawer. But I've seen you use it loads of times."

Bruce changed the subject. "In your former life as an IT expert, what would you do if someone said they'd forgotten the password for their laptop?"

"You haven't, have you?"

"It's an old one and I can't remember what I typed."

"Mate, you really should get that bang on the head checked out. You're forgetting passwords, denying you had a key to your desk, and then there was that episode with the news last week… I told you, even slight injuries can lead to brain damage."

"Tell me again, when did you graduate from medical school?"

"Is it this one?" Nick said, getting up and walking across to Bruce's desk.

"What?"

"Is this the laptop you've forgotten the password to?" Nick said, holding it up.

"Yes."

"I've got a similar model," he said, pointing to the machine on his desk. "I use it to download mails when my main machine is rendering graphics. I must say, the pink unicorn stickers don't look at all gay. Which version of Windows is it running?"

"I don't know."

"How can you not know?"

"I just don't," Bruce said. "Now can you stop turning this into a Broadway production and tell me if you can do anything about it?"

"I've got an Emergency Boot CD at home that will allow me to get in and change the password, even the administrator's password. Did you set up an administrator account on it?"

"I can't remember."

"I'll take it home tonight and sort it for you," Nick said.

"No," Bruce said, snatching the laptop back. "Bring the disc in and sort it out here."

"Alright Mr Grumpy," Nick said. "Scared of me seeing your internet history?"

"I am a bit," Bruce said. "I keep being drawn to sites which have pictures of your mother with a cock up her arse."

"You sick bastard, my mother's dead."

"Oh I am sorry – was it too much cock?"

Nick threw a plastic cup containing an inch of water at Bruce. "I'm telling Plum," he said, feigning indignation.

Returning to his desk, Bruce typed up the story about Milkman making 'BBC-style' costume drama porn and sent it to Nick. He then scoured his emails for company announcements which could be turned into other news stories. After rapidly processing these he realised he still had a gap for a supporting front page story.

As was customary, Plum had wandered across to approve the front page. "Nick, you really do believe in gilding the lily, don't you?" he said. "I honestly think you would keep adding elements to the layout ad infinitum if we let you."

He instructed Nick to remove one of the pull quotes and to make the boxout for the second story bigger, before shouting across to Bruce: "Fair play Bruce, that's a bloody good piece."

"Thanks," said Bruce.

"Have you got anything juicy to support it?"

Bruce shrugged.

"What about our friend Roz?" suggested Plum. "Have there been any developments down there? Have the Brighton Old Bill charged her with anything?"

Bruce didn't know.

"Trawl the local media's websites," Plum suggested as he walked back from Nick's desk to his office. "There's bound to be something about it. Hopefully our readers won't remember the hatchet job you did on her last week. This time our position will be fully supporting Roz the martyr, our dear colleague and industry friend."

It took Bruce less than a few minutes to find the website of Brighton's most popular newspaper – and just a few seconds to realise that, in its lead story, he perfectly matched the description of a suspect police were looking for in connection with a burglary and assault. Although the name and address of the victim was withheld, a picture of a very familiar street accompanied the story.

Bruce felt physically sick. "I don't feel well," he said to Nick. "I'm going to lunch."

***

"Well now you're going to have to tell someone," Jan said to Bruce. "If you don't, and they find you, you will be in real trouble."

"Don't say 'if they find you', that suggests I'm on the run," Bruce said.

"Well you are a bit," Jan said.

"And keep your voice down," he added. "The old biddy next to you is listening."

"She's away with the fairies," Jan said. "She probably thinks she's at a Lyon's Tea Shop enjoying a slice of cake with a suitor during a break from the doodlebugs."

"What?"

"Her mind has gone, poor dear."

"I'm starting to know how she feels," Bruce said, thinking of the desk drawer lock.

"Are you?"

"It's a long and winding road of a story."

"How enigmatic," Jan sniffed.

"How can I go the police and tell them what Milkman did?" Bruce said. "I can't exactly say 'I know it was him because I was in the wardrobe too – oh and by the way, it was me who stole the laptop'."

"What about your friend?" Jan asked, saying the words 'your friend' in a rather disapproving tone. "Or should I say your co-conspirator?"

"I'd rather not bother her. Her mother is ill."

"But you said she took away copies of some of Milkman's paperwork."

"She did. We weren't able to access his computer because it was password protected and…" Bruce stopped in mid-sentence, deep in thought.

"What are you thinking?"

"I'm thinking what Rachel would do."

Jan looked blank.

Taking a phone out of his pocket, Bruce dialled a number and handed it to Jan. "When it answers, ask to speak to Mr Jones," he said.

"Who the hell is that?" Jan said, panicking a little at her sudden involvement.

"That's Milkman's real name. Just ask to speak to him."

"Oh hello," Jan said into Bruce's phone. "Can I speak to Mr Jones please?"

Jan mouthed the words 'what shall I say?' at Bruce.

"Just tell him you're from the VAT office and see what he says," Bruce whispered.

"Oh isn't he? That's a shame."

"Where is he?" Bruce whispered.

"He's gone away for the weekend," Jan whispered back.

A smile spread across Bruce's face.

"My name?" Jan looked around her bed in a panic, before picking up this week's copy of Celebs & Scandals. "Just tell him that Miss Aniston called, from the VAT office."

Jan handed Bruce's phone back to him. "Don't ever ask me to do that again," she said, wiping her face with a tissue. "I feel like a criminal now."

Bruce smirked, placing the phone on Jan's bedside cabinet and pouring her a plastic beaker of water. "Here, drink this and call me in the morning."

They were interrupted by the shrill sound of a ringtone. But it wasn't coming from the mobile on the cabinet – it was coming from Bruce's pocket. He took the phone out and examined the caller display. Before Jan could ask why he had two mobiles, Bruce answered, in a Welsh accent: "Hello? Who's this?"

Even though she sounded much tinnier through the speaker, Jan could tell instantly who it was. She'd just been speaking to her.

"Oh hello Megan..." Bruce said.

Jan shook her head slowly and downed her water.

"What's that? The VAT people just rung? Oh, I meant to tell you about that – they're coming back this afternoon," Bruce continued, maintaining the accent. "Yes, I know you finish early on a Friday... I'm sure they won't be long... I know, they're a pain, but what can you do?"

Jan stared at him as he ended the call. "You're not thinking of..."

"I must dash," he replied, collecting his things. "I've got some inspecting to do."

***

"I was saying to Mr Jones, I hope you won't be long because I finish early on a Friday," Megan said. Then, as she looked Bruce up and down, she added: "I'm amazed at how casual you people are. I would have thought you'd have to wear a suit."

He declined the offer of a hot beverage and went straight to Milkman's computer. "I suppose this has a password, does it Megan?"

She nodded, cautiously.

"What is it?"

"I can't tell you that, Mr Jones would have my guts for garters."

"Megan, I can easily go back to the car and get my Emergency Boot CD to circumvent the password screen," Bruce said. "But I don't want to do that because I'm parked several streets away. And that will mean that we will both be here a lot longer than we'd like. In addition to you not finishing early, I will of course have to put in my report that you wilfully obstructed my investigation."

The corners of Megan's mouth turned downwards. "But I have to meet my granddaughter from school on a Friday."

"Have you ever seen the inside of a jail cell, Megan?" Bruce said in a softer voice.

She slowly shook her head.

"You wouldn't like prison," Bruce continued. "Though I think you'd be popular with the lesbians."

Bruce gently took Megan's hand and held it up in front of him. "Yes, those nice soft hands of yours would be put to some pretty extraordinary uses, I can tell you. You'll be dancing to the four-fingered foxtrot in no time."

"Big tits," Megan said quietly.

"Two words, no space between them?"

***

It was slightly after five when Bruce eventually returned to the AMG office. Alex had finished for the day but Nick was still playing with the front page, with Plum stood over his shoulder.

"The wanderer finally returns," Plum said, without looking at Bruce.

"Sorry, I wasn't feeling well," Bruce said.

"All better now?" Plum said with a look of concern which may or may not have been sincere. "While we appreciate you rising from your sick bed to finish what you started five hours ago, I hope you won't be too disappointed to learn that we finalised the front page in your absence."

Bruce walked across to Nick's desk. The box on the front page displayed an ad, rather than a second story. Parodying the Lord Kitchener World War One recruitment poster, a finger pointed out of the page at the reader and the headline read: 'AMG wants YOU! Adult Movie Guide is expanding its editorial team and we are looking for fresh, new writing talent. If you'd like to join our staff please submit a sample film review of no more than 500 words along with a copy of your CV and tell us why you are the person we need.'

"It's time we had one or two new faces around here," Plum said. "And don't think I've forgotten what you said to Alex – immediately after you'd been given a written warning about your behaviour. We'll talk about this once we've put the issue to bed."

If Plum was expecting Bruce to react, he was disappointed. Instead Bruce walked slowly back to his desk, slumped in the chair and woke his computer from its hibernation. His monitor still displayed the story about the Brighton burglary and assault. That was careless. Though, in mitigation, Plum had told him to look at local media websites.

Nick walked across and pointed to the laptop on Bruce's desk. "I sorted that out for you," he said.

Bruce stared at the laptop. "You've done what?"

"I popped home and got the Emergency Boot CD during my lunch break. You'll find you can access it again now."

Bruce felt his stomach lurch.

Nick continued: "I don't know why you bothered setting up a password though, there is absolutely nothing on it. It's as clean as the day it left the factory. What did you use it for?"

"It's not actually mine," Bruce said. "It was left at my place by an ex."

Nick burst out laughing. "You had an ex? Don't make me laugh! That would suggest that you once had a relationship."

***

It was almost seven when Bruce trudged into Jan's ward. She was watching the evening news on a coin-slot operated television trolley.

"I gave in," Jan said, gesturing at the console. "It's an exorbitant cost but Dolly and I finally ran out of conversation."

"I've brought you some chocolate," Bruce said, slumping into the chair set out for visitors.

"Thank you, but would you mind just sitting there and shutting up? We're watching this, and you should too."

"What is it?" Bruce asked, tearing the wrapper from the chocolate.

"Banging The Drum, it gives people with an agenda a platform to air their views…"

Bruce threw a large chunk into his mouth. "I haven't come here to watch…"

"Shush a minute," Jan said, slapping his arm. "I'm paying a premium price for this."

A man who looked to be in his early sixties, balding with large owl glasses, was discussing hardcore pornography with a genial looking-host of a similar age. The latter boasted a luxuriant mane of silver hair.

"I'm not blaming the girls," the balding man said. "I am calling for the girls to be rescued. By their families, by their friends, but most of all by the government, the people we elect to make laws on our behalf."

"Oh come on now Mr Gregan, it's not the government who is encouraging these girls into pornography…"

Bruce stood up. "That's Julian Gregan?"

"Shush, will you?" Jan said, pulling him back down into the chair.

"No, but the government has created a market for the films, with its 'anything goes and hang the consequences' attitude. We need to outlaw the making of these films and we need to outlaw the selling of them. Do you know there are thousands of shops around the country where they can be bought?"

"Are you calling for restrictions on their numbers?" the host asked.

"They are already restricted," Bruce shouted. "And there's hundreds, not thousands. Do your research."

"Restrictions?" Gregan said. "I don't want them restricted. I want them closed down altogether…"

"I think you'll find that prohibition has been proven not to work," the host said.

"And I think you'll find that there is growing support for CRSP," Gregan replied. "The number of letters, emails and telephone calls of support we've had over the last few days has been overwhelming. But it's not only support we're receiving, it's pledges of donations, and I've even been contacted by a Member of Parliament who has offered to sponsor a Private Member's Bill…"

"Wow," said Jan. "That's some genie you've let out of the bottle, Bruce."

Bruce held up his hands in a gesture of surrender. "If the British Empire and its Commonwealth last for a thousand years, men will still say, this was my finest hour."

"How did you get on at Milkman's this afternoon?"

"I got into his computer," Bruce said proudly.

"Ladies and gentlemen, Mr Carl Bernstein," Jan said theatrically. "And…?"

"And I found an email from Honey Peach, in which she said she was not prepared to accept a lower royalty fee for overseas sales of her film."

"If anything has happened to her, it sounds like you have a prime suspect."

"You'd think so," Bruce said. "But Spaghetti is bringing out a range of sex toys for men based on parts of Honey Peach's anatomy…"

"I think I can guess which ones."

"I'm sure you can – and part of the deal Spaghetti had with her, through Milkman, was that she had to do so many personal appearances to support the launch of the range. Well after she didn't show up at his shop opening, I found an email from Spaghetti warning Milkman that he was going to sort Honey Peach out."

"That doesn't sound good."

"After what happened in Brighton, I was convinced Milkman was behind Honey Peach's disappearance but now I'm wondering if Spaghetti may have 'sorted her out' for letting him down. He probably invested a fair bit into the sex toys project and he was counting on her to promote it."

"Can you have two prime suspects?"

"I don't know," Bruce said. "I'm going to have to do some more digging."

"Well it was certainly a worthwhile trip," said Jan. "And please tell me you made a note of Honey Peach's email address…"

Bruce nodded.

"Are you going to mail her tonight?"

"I'll do it in the morning," Bruce said. "Tonight I'm just going to get pissed."

"I think if she replies and says she's on holiday or something, you'll be really disappointed," Jan said. "Because you're having the time of your life in this little caper, aren't you?"

Bruce shrugged.

"And I can see why – it's because until recently there's been no drama in your life."

"It's not just drama," Bruce said. "I've been lacking all the genres – action, comedy, thrillers, romance, sex…"

"You never know, she might have just had enough of it all and bought a Volkswagen camper van to go bumming around Europe."

Bruce shook his head. "You don't go bumming around Europe in a camper van when you look like Honey Peach."

The smile left Jan's face.

"Sorry, I didn't mean…"

"I know what you meant Bruce," Jan said, turning away from him. "You'd better be going now, there are half a dozen pints of Guinness in Marelli's craving your company."

CHAPTER ELEVEN: MONDAY 16TH JUNE 2003

Monday morning at AMG means going through the proofs of the previous week's issue before going to press. After the proofing comes the Previous Issue Post Mortem, when everyone says what they liked and didn't like about the issue.

Plum had grumbled about the cost of bringing in a freelancer to cover for Bruce's 'extra-curricular activities' but he couldn't complain about the report on the Love Life event and he had to concede that the front page lead was one of AMG's best. 'BBC costume drama porn – Sunday nights will never be the same' was the rather misleading headline, though the copy was careful to only refer to the Dick-Ins series as 'BBC-style' costume drama porn. It was sure to be picked up by other media outlets, particularly given the current heightened interest in the subject, largely thanks to Gregan.

"But let's leave any further discussion about Mr Gregan to this afternoon's planning meeting," Plum said. "I have some thoughts on this subject and what our next move should be. We'll adjourn until then. And remember, I want to hear new feature suggestions from you all this afternoon. Bring your best ideas to the table."

After the post mortem had broken up, Alex sat at her desk reading Celebs & Scandals. She was wearing a funky new set of earphones which were connected to her MP3 player. Nick was stood by the water cooler, seemingly deep in thought.

Bruce had a lot to think about too. Discovering there was nothing at all on Honey Peach's computer had been a huge disappointment. He'd checked, and Nick had been right. Now, without its power supply unit – which had been left plugged in at Honey Peach's house – the laptop lay lifeless on his desk, its battery discharged. He could buy a replacement but there seemed no point when there wasn't even an internet history to investigate. But she must have used it for something – it had been left plugged in.

Bruce smiled to himself. He was starting to think like an investigative reporter. He had spent much of the weekend researching criminal detection techniques on the internet. In murder cases, police would prioritise suspects with the means, motive and opportunity, he'd learned. Milkman clearly had a motive but so did Spaghetti. Honey Peach had caused him to lose face twice. And Bruce had seen first-hand why, like the junction, it was best not to cross him. He had sent

Honey Peach an email, asking how she was, but he had not received a reply.

"Fair play mate, that BBC story was a corker," Nick said, bringing him back to reality. "How are you going to top that?"

Bruce stared at Nick. Should he tell him? "I'm working on something."

"Give me a clue?" Nick said, taking a sip of water from his plastic cup.

"It's too soon," Bruce said.

"Oh come on, you big tease," Nick said, ruffling Bruce's hair.

"You might want to try paginating the words 'one of our porn stars is missing' across the masthead for a future issue," Bruce said.

"Say again?"

"I told you last week that I'm looking into the disappearance of Honey Peach…"

Nick guffawed. "That's your next big exclusive?"

"Keep your voice down," Bruce hissed. "I don't want Alex to know about this."

"Don't worry about her," Nick said. "She's listening to a demo from some boy band one of her mates is managing. Don't be surprised if the mag has a new music section next week."

"Nothing at AMG surprises me anymore," Bruce said.

"Honey Peach is probably just taking some time out," Nick said.

"I don't think so," Bruce replied.

"You seriously think something has happened to her?"

Bruce nodded.

"Have you been to the police?"

Bruce shook his head. "I did suggest it to her sister but she didn't think there was much point. Besides, she's got other stuff going on."

"More important than the disappearance of her sister?"

"Her mother is ill. That's why she's trying to find Honey Peach."

"Have you got a suspect?" Nick asked, finishing his cup of water.

"I'm currently torn between Milkman and Spaghetti."

A jet of water spurted out of Nick's mouth onto Bruce's desk, attracting the attention of Alex, who glared at them.

"Mate, I strongly suggest you forget about this," Nick said. "Implying the BBC is moving into porn is one thing but if you say that someone like Spaghetti is responsible for Honey Peach disappearing you're not going to get sued, you're going to get your legs broken."

"I never said I was going to name anyone," Bruce hissed. "You asked me if I had any suspects."

"Well before you flag up the Honey Peach thing, you'd better have some pretty convincing evidence," Nick said, ambling back to his own desk. "Plum and Alex will hang you out to dry otherwise."

Nick was right. The clock on Bruce's computer told him it was just after eleven o'clock – he had a few spare hours before this afternoon's planning meeting so decided to put them to good use. The first thing he did was to use his mobile to send Rachel a text message informing her that he had discovered Honey Peach's email address. He was sure she would appreciate being kept informed of his progress. Then he emailed Honey Peach again, asking her to get in touch with him as a matter of urgency, just in case she had been on holiday.

What else could he do? Within inverted commas, to narrow the focus of the results, he typed the name 'Gerardo Sachetti' into his favourite search engine. The outcome was a half-dozen or so regional newspaper articles about his shops applying for licences.

Bruce frowned. He thought for a minute and then removed the inverted commas from the name. There were far more matches, though most appeared to be of either one name or the other. But there was one result for 'Gerardo Antonio Demetrio Sachetti' from a regional newspaper.

The report was several years old and it referred to charges of assault being dropped against Mr Sachetti due to lack of evidence. The brief article explained that Sachetti had allegedly confronted and then assaulted a member of staff who he suspected of stealing from him. The victim later changed his story and told police that the attack had left him in a confused state and that he had incorrectly identified Sachetti as his assailant. The story concluded by quoting from local government licensing guidelines which state that a criminal conviction will disqualify any person from applying for a sex shop licence.

You didn't need to be Miss Marple to figure out the real story there, Bruce decided, but he already knew Spaghetti could be a nasty piece of work. What was it Honey Peach had said? He couldn't make an omelette without breaking legs? He saved the information to his hard drive and sent a copy to the laser printer that all AMG's computers were connected to.

The printer was notoriously slow so, while he was waiting for the document to be processed, he went down to the courtyard to smoke and consider his next move. He thought about his two suspects,

Milkman and Spaghetti. He really needed to narrow his focus down to one of them. What would Rachel do? That was easy – she would confront them. He thought about this for a few minutes and gradually a possible solution presented itself to him.

Bruce finished his cigarette and walked back in to Legal House. He passed through reception and slowly made his way up the stairs into One East, where he sat at his desk and dialled the Love Shack head office number. When the receptionist answered, he asked to be put through to Gina.

"Hey Bruce, how are you?" Gina said. "It was great to see you last week. We were so sorry you had to leave early."

After a few more exchanges of pleasantries Bruce got to the point. "What is the best number to call if I want to speak to Mr Sachetti?"

"I can help you with anything you need."

"I appreciate that, but I just wanted to get a quote from him, about last week."

"Didn't you take away the press pack?"

He hadn't. "Of course I did but..."

"There are some great quotes in there."

"I know, but they are the same ones everyone else has and I want something unique."

"Haven't you guys already gone to press with this?"

Damn. She wasn't just a pretty face. She knew AMG's deadlines. "Er, yes, we have, but we're also doing a follow-up piece in next week's issue, about the porn star body parts."

"The Signature Series? There's a lot of great stuff in the press pack and I can get you anything else you want..."

"I would like to speak to Mr Sachetti myself, so the quotes have a more natural flow and I can ask him follow-up questions."

Bruce could tell Gina was pouting as she replied. "Well okay but you've got to promise me that you'll run the story by me before you go to press."

"That's not our policy..."

"He can be a bit old school in some of the things he says. He was in this business before it was mainstream..."

Before it was mainstream? Christ it isn't that now, Bruce thought. She must mean before it was legal.

"And we're making great strides in presenting Love Shack as a contemporary brand for women and couples, and I don't want anything he might say to be taken out of context. I mean, you know what the media are like these days – you were in the press yourself this week."

Bruce metaphorically tipped his hat to Gina's astuteness. "Of course," he said. "I promise I will give you copy approval before we go to print."

Satisfied, Gina gave Bruce Spaghetti's mobile number. Bruce went for another smoke, this time at the front of the building so he could see when Alex and Nick left for lunch. He was part-way through his second cigarette when they eventually emerged, separately. Alex was first. She ignored him but Nick did ask if he was okay and if he wanted anything from the newsagent.

"No, I'm fine," Bruce replied then, gesturing at Nick's sports holdall, added: "Are you going to the gym on a hot day like this?"

Nick looked down at his bag. "Best time. You really build a sweat up. You should try it some time. You might lose some of that gut."

As soon as Nick headed off towards the city centre, Bruce scrambled up the stairs to the office. Tapping in 141 to block AMG's number, he dialled Spaghetti's mobile.

The building's cleaner chose that moment to enter the office. "Alright if I put the Hoover around?" he asked. "I didn't get chance this morning because someone had been sick outside and Muggins here had to clean it up."

Bruce ended the call immediately. "It's not exactly convenient," he said. "I was about to make a very important phone call."

"Well you'll have to make it in twenty minutes or so when I've finished," he said.

"Go on then, I'll make the call outside," Bruce sighed, picking up the note with Spaghetti's number on and taking his mobile from his pocket.

***

Alone in the tranquillity of the courtyard, he lit a cigarette and dialled Spaghetti's number again, remembering to preface it with 141.

"Hello?" Spaghetti answered straight away. Bruce wasn't prepared for that.

"Hey you," Bruce said in an attempt at a Glasgow accent. "I'd like a word with you."

"Who the fuck's this?" Spaghetti snarled.

"Never you mind who this is," Bruce said, trying to sound like a threatening version of Billy Connolly. "You just listen to me. I know about you and Honey Peach."

Spaghetti fell silent.

"Are you still there?" Bruce asked.

"What do you want?" Spaghetti said in a very quiet voice.

Bugger. Bruce realised he should have planned this conversation a little better in advance, including a few if/then scenarios. "What do I want? I want money," he said, unable to think of anything more appropriate.

"How much?"

How much? How much? Think of a number…"I want £30,000," Bruce blurted out, thinking of the Jaguar he'd admired on the forecourt of Reeves & Jeeves. "In cash, in non-sequential used notes."

"Where and when?" Spaghetti said, through what sounded like gritted teeth.

"I'll call tomorrow with the details," Bruce said, hanging up.

Bruce stood up. Both his armpits were weeping perspiration. Fingers trembling, he fumbled for his cigarettes. His hands were shaking so much he dropped his box of matches, spilling the contents all over the floor.

Two cigarettes later Bruce returned to the office, his clothes heavy with sweat. It was an exceptionally hot day but it wasn't the weather that was responsible for his sweat glands working overtime, it was his blackmailing of one of the most powerful men in the UK adult industry. He wiped his forehead with his sleeve. Who needs to go to the gym to build up a sweat, Nick?

Just as that thought crossed his mind, Nick walked into the office eating a peach, and not sweating at all.

"Changed your mind, did you?" Bruce asked.

"Huh?"

"About going to the gym."

"Why do we let the council run the leisure centre?" Nick grumbled. "The air conditioning is broken so the gym was closed."

Bruce wasn't listening. He was psyching himself up to ring Spaghetti again. This time he was going to be playing himself and he regretted that he hadn't made this genuine call first. But he couldn't find the scrap of paper with the number on – perhaps he'd left it in the courtyard in all the excitement? It wasn't an issue though as he could easily retrieve the number from the 'last calls made' section of his mobile. As it was in his phone, and he had nothing to hide this time, he used his mobile to call Spaghetti, who answered almost immediately.

"Hello Mr Sachetti," Bruce said, in an overly exaggerated English accent. "My name is Bruce Baker, from AMG magazine and…"

"Bruce Baker?"

"That's right, from AMG magazine."

"Weren't you up at our event last week?" Spaghetti sounded calm. Was that a good thing?

"I was and that's why I'm calling really…"

"Why did you shoot off so suddenly? I wanted a little chat with you."

More sweat gushed out of Bruce's armpits. "I'm afraid I had a bit of a family emergency and…" Bruce's accent was getting more and more Hugh Grant-ish. All he needed was a stutter now…

"Pity," Spaghetti said. "What can I do for you?"

"Well, um, well, um…" Oh great, here it comes.

"What?"

"Well, um, I was hoping to ask you some questions about the launch of the porn star products."

"The Signature Series? What sort of questions?"

"Well, you know…"

"No, I don't know. If I did I wouldn't be asking you."

"Which consumer demographic they are aimed at…"

"Let me stop you there," Spaghetti said. "You need to speak to Gina about all that kind of stuff."

"But I'd also like to include you in the piece," Bruce said. "So you can talk about the heritage of the Love Shack brand…"

"That's Gina's department as well…"

"And we'd like you to tell our readers how the industry has changed over the last decade," Bruce said, in an attempt to come up with a question that Gina couldn't answer. "And where, with all your vast experience, you think it's going over the next few years."

"Tell you what," Spaghetti said. "How about you ring Gina and set something up? She knows all my movements and will make an appointment for you to come and see us at head office."

"That would be great," Bruce said, then attempting to distance himself from the Billy Connolly caller he added: "I will do that. And in case you were wondering, it was Gina who gave me your number. She gave it to me a few minutes ago. I was just speaking to her."

As soon as the call was over, another one came through.

"Bruce, it's Milkman it is," a familiar voice said. "I'm in a bit of bother I am. The VAT man has been here and taken some of my stuff away."

"They do do that," Bruce said, almost lapsing into a Welsh accent himself.

"But when I rang them no one knew anything about it. There's something very bloody fishy about this," Milkman said with emphasis. "And I need some legal advice. Do you know any good solicitors?"

"I can't say I do," Bruce said. "I'm sure the trade association could help with that."

"I'm not a member," Milkman said. "I won't pay the subs."

"Have you spoken to Spaghetti?"

"Why would I speak to him? He's not a bloody solicitor."

"I know, but he's sure to know a good one, given his past," Bruce said.

"Given his past?"

"Well, he must have made loads of licence applications over the years."

"I suppose he must have but I'm not really in his good books at the moment, what with Honey Peach letting him down and everything."

"Spoken to him recently, have you?"

"Aye."

"How well do you know him?"

"He's my best customer. He's most suppliers' best customer."

"I met him for the first time last week and he seemed a bit… short tempered."

"He's as good as gold," Milkman said. "As long as you don't cross him."

"That's what I've heard," Bruce said. "But what happens if you do?"

"You don't, not if you want to keep your business."

"But if you did, what would he do?"

"You haven't wound him up, have you?"

***

Nick brought a tray of coffees into the Next Issue Planning Meeting and placed hot steaming cups in front of Plum, Alex and Bruce. Only Bruce thanked him.

"This coffee's shit," said Alex, reading the funky brand name on the cup. "I only drink Starbucks. This is the most bitterest coffee I've ever had."

Bruce looked at Plum. "Did you hear that Plum?" Bruce said. "This is the most bitterest coffee she's ever had. That's your editor speaking. Your editor."

"Before we go into the nuts and bolts of the next issue, let's discuss new feature ideas," said Plum, ignoring Bruce's comments.

Alex said: "I think we should introduce a 'spice up your sex life' section."

Bruce inadvertently spat some of his coffee across the table. "That's as relevant to our readers as Jethro Tull," he said. "And I don't mean the prog rock band."

"Who is Jethro Tull?" asked Alex

"What's a prog rock band?" asked Nick.

"It doesn't matter," Bruce said. "The point is, we write about porn films. Our readers don't have sex lives, they have masturbation lives."

"Speak for yourself," Alex said.

"I think it's an excellent idea Alex," Plum said. "Especially if we could feature porn stars passing on their tips on how to make love better."

"Porn stars don't make love," Bruce protested. "Not in the way normal people do. They act out a hideous, exaggerated version of sex for the consumption of others."

"And we could open it up to the readership," Plum added. "Offer a prize for the best sex tip of the month. Excellent suggestion, Alex. Let's give that the green light. Next?"

"I've got an idea," Nick said. "And it's sort of related to what Bruce said about our readers being big masturbators, and about his report on the Love Shack event in the last issue. Why don't we regularly feature sex toys for blokes too?"

Plum thumped the table. "Another excellent idea! Why should the women have all the fun? What do you think, Bruce?"

Bruce thought it was a good idea.

Plum said to Nick: "How would you like to take responsibility for that? Bruce has already got quite a wide remit."

Nick looked at Bruce and Alex. "Are you two okay with that?"

Both nodded.

"Splendid," Plum said. "From this day forward, Nick is in charge of our new sex toys for men section."

"It could also be good for income," Nick said. "As it means Alex will be able to approach a whole new selection of advertisers who haven't used AMG before."

Plum beamed. Nick was talking his language.

"And I've thought of the perfect way to kick it off," Nick said. "A beauty contest of inflatable dolls. We pick a dozen dolls and photograph them on a beach and give them marks for, I don't know, sex appeal, personality, ease of use…"

Plum thumped the table for a second time. "That is absolutely inspired Nick! We could ask the readers to vote for their favourite too. Get on to it straight away. Now, what have you brought to the table, Bruce?"

"One of my features for the next issue is going to be on the launch of Love Shack's anatomical toys – heads, vaginas and hands."

"Hands?" Plum said.

"For the best handjob you've ever had," Bruce replied, remembering the tagline on the box he had seen. "They have been moulded from the actual body parts of three porn stars and…"

Plum held up his hand to stop Bruce. "We've all just agreed that this sort of thing is Nick's responsibility now, so pass the details on to him. And didn't we already cover this in the Love Shack piece anyway?"

"We mentioned it but I was going to go into more detail…"

"Let Nick do that now," Plum said. "I've got other plans for you."

Plum pulled a copy of today's Daily Hate out of his briefcase. "One of the Monday regulars is a column called 'What is the World Coming to?' and today's is written by our friend Julian Gregan."

Plum looked down at some marks he had made on the paper. "He's becoming more evangelical by the day. Now he's saying that it is morally right to rescue and rehabilitate porn stars, by force if necessary, as they are under the influence of, and I quote, 'predatory men who persuade them to engage in activities designed to kill their souls'. But not only that, he also wants to close down the shops. That's dangerous stuff, for us and for the whole industry. What is the trade association doing about this?"

Bruce shrugged. He wasn't really on the best of terms with BATA.

"They should be all over this," Plum said. "Every trade body needs a cause, particularly if there's a threat attached to it."

"I can make enquires," Bruce said.

"I want this to be your priority now," Plum said. "Your absolute raison d'etre. You've always fancied yourself as an attack dog well this is your opportunity. I want you to channel all that bitterness and put it to work for us, for once. That man is very bad for business. Dig into his past, find out his pleasures, his peccadilloes, his perversions... I want him destroyed, or at the very least discredited. This is your opportunity to prove your worth, Bruce."

"You want me to drop everything else?"

"What was your front page going to be?"

"Well, um, it was going to be about these new body parts from Love Shack."

Plum pulled a sour face. "That's a bit weak, Bruce," he said.

"That's funny, because I heard you were working on a piece about the disappearance of a porn star," Alex said. "Honey Peach, wasn't it?"

Bruce glared at her. She smiled sweetly back at him.

"Can someone please explain?" Plum said, looking at Alex and Bruce in turn.

"Her sister asked for my help a couple of weeks ago," Bruce said. "She hasn't been seen since she came to Bath and went out with us."

"And?" Plum said.

"Her mother is ill and..."

"We're not Social bloody Services," Plum said. "If someone vanishes you report them as a missing person. End of story."

"You haven't heard the best of it, Plum," Alex said. "Bruce thinks the bloke who owns Love Shack – who I would do absolutely anything to get as an advertiser – has bumped her off."

"What the hell is wrong with you?" Plum said to Bruce. "A private word in my office please. Right now."

Bruce dutifully followed Plum from the boardroom into his office. Plum closed the door and sat behind his desk.

"Is this the reason behind the unauthorised absences?" Plum asked. "Because if it is I think we've got a problem. You've already got that incident with Alex pending."

Bruce slumped into Plum's guest chair, uninvited. "You've got to admit it will make a great story. I wasn't going to say anything until I was sure of everything."

"And are you sure of everything now?"

"No."

"So how does Alex know so much about this?"

"I was telling Nick about it earlier, when she had her earphones in," Bruce said. "She must have been able to hear what I was saying."

Plum stared at Bruce. "You might find this difficult to believe but I do hold you in some affection, Bruce. You're a complete pain in the arse at times but you showed faith in me and my idea for Adult Movie Guide when you left a reasonably well-paid job, in an industry where you had built up a reputation, to start again from scratch. I can't forget that."

"Yes but..."

"Bruce, I'm offering you an olive branch here. Take it. Let's forget about the incident with Alex, your unauthorised absences and any porn stars who may or may not have gone astray and let's just concentrate on fighting Gregan."

"Okay," Bruce replied.

"Good - now go and shaft the bastard."

CHAPTER TWELVE: TUESDAY 17TH JUNE 2003

Nick was on his fifth blag call of the morning and, Bruce had to admit, he was doing it rather well: "Hey, how are you guys? Nick from AMG magazine here, we're huge fans of your stuff. Listen, we're doing a product focus on inflatable dolls in our next issue and we'd love you to be a part of it..."

Plum had been right about Julian Gregan being bad for business. After the previous day's propaganda for his cause, this morning's Daily Hate featured another piece about him vowing to bring a private prosecution against a producer of pornography for living off immoral earnings.

In the piece Gregan was quoted as saying: 'We fully accept that these unfortunate women are victims and we are urging them to contact us, in complete confidence. CRSP will bring a test case against an individual pornographer and once a precedent has been set in a court of law we will do everything in our power to encourage the authorities to take up the cudgels.'

Nick put down his phone triumphantly and walked over to Bruce's desk. Picking up the newspaper, he pointed to the picture of Gregan and said: "Now there's a bloke having the time of his life. And he owes it all to you."

"Do you mind?" Bruce went to snatch the newspaper from Nick but he deftly avoided his lunge.

"Too slow old man," Nick laughed. "Hey listen to this: 'The word pornography is derived from the Greek 'porne' which means 'prostitute' and 'graphos' which means 'writing' so 'pornographos' was quite literally 'writing about prostitutes'. Did you know that?"

"Don't stop him from working," Alex said to Nick as she approached them. "He's on special assignment, remember?"

"What shall I do with this then?" Nick said, brandishing an A4 piece of paper. "It's a press release about the opening of a brand new spanking club in Leeds."

"Don't you mean a brand spanking new club?" Alex said, frowning.

"I'm afraid not," Nick replied. "This is where you go when you've been naughty."

"I don't understand these people," Alex said, shaking her head as she returned to her desk.

Nick lowered his head to be closer to Bruce's and whispered: "She's looking rather naughty today, don't you think?"

Bruce grimaced.

"Oh come on," Nick said. "You'd have it if it was on a plate for you, wouldn't you?"

"Not even if I was on death row," Bruce replied. "In fact I would put in a request to be moved further up the queue rather than engage in sexual activity with her. Now, if you don't mind, I have things I need to crack on with."

"Okay, catch you later, masturbator," Nick said, ruffling Bruce's hair.

He is becoming a bit of a cock, Bruce thought, as he watched Nick make another blagging call. He's going to end up in ad sales at this rate.

Bruce's online research into Julian Gregan had failed to unearth any skeletons so far. He appeared to have been a pretty normal bloke for most of his life, though admittedly this account came from the About Us section of the CRSP website. A former civil servant, he took early retirement after the death of his wife. The quiet life was evidently not for him as he formed CRSP the same year. Typing his name into a search engine brought up thousands of matches but, frustratingly, they all appeared to be as a result of his recent activities.

Bruce sighed. If he was a real reporter he would carry out a thorough background check, accessing court records and the electoral roll and even digging into Gregan's finances, but he didn't know where to start. Maybe he should sub-contract this out to a private investigator? But how much would that cost? Would Plum allow him to put it on expenses? And if he did, what would that say about Bruce as a journalist? That he wasn't up to the job?

Bruce concluded he might be able to dig a little deeper if he knew more about Gregan, so he bit the bullet and called him.

"Is that Mr Gregan? You might not remember me but I'm Bruce Baker, the person who, in a way, bought your ticket for this rollercoaster you're currently riding."

"I remember you very well," Gregan replied. "And I also remember thinking at the time that you were trying to goad me, and that you didn't take my concerns seriously."

"Well, everyone is taking you seriously now…"

"Yes, what was it Iain Duncan Smith said about not underestimating the determination of a quiet man?"

"No one would call you quiet now either, which is why I am ringing. Do you know much about AMG magazine?"

"I can't say I do."

"Our focus is something you're opposed to – pornography – and I wondered how you'd feel about talking to us."

"I'm talking to you now."

"I mean sit down and talk face-to-face, on the record, where you can explain your views to our readership."

"No thanks," Gregan said. "I don't need to speak to you. Every newspaper in Fleet Street wants to hear my views."

"But our readers are all buyers of pornography," Bruce said. "If you're really intent on changing the system, you need to address the consumers of the product."

Gregan was silent for a few seconds. "You're obviously going to do a hatchet job on me, aren't you Bruce?"

"Not at all..."

"I'm not interested, but thank you for asking."

"What about if I offer you copy approval?" Bruce said, trying to hold on to his customer. "If you don't like the feature we write based on the interview, we'll just drop it."

Gregan paused for a second. "Okay then, on that basis," he said.

Bruce sighed. That was twice in a week he's offered subjects copy approval – also known as That Which Shall Never Be Offered Under Any Circumstances, according to the Book of Plum. "Could we sort something out for next week?"

"Out of the question, I'm afraid," Gregan said, over the sound of rustling diary pages. "How does early September sound?"

"Not ideal," Bruce replied. "Can you do something sooner? You choose the time and place and I'll fall in with your plans."

"Well I could fit you in tomorrow afternoon..."

"I can do tomorrow," Bruce said.

"There's a car coming for me at three to take me to the House where I'm due to brief a parliamentary committee, so how about two o'clock?"

"That will be great," Bruce sighed with relief. "Where can we meet?"

"I live in Brighton," Gregan said. "Do you know it?"

"A little," Bruce replied, wondering if Sussex Police were still looking for him. "What's the address?"

Bruce's heart skipped a beat as he scrawled the address on his notepad. It was the same street as Honey Peach's house.

"Will you need directions?" Gregan asked.

"I'm sure I'll find it okay," Bruce replied. I might need a disguise, but not directions.

***

Plum was delighted to hear that Bruce had been granted an audience with Gregan so quickly: "That's excellent news Bruce," he said. "I want him crucified. Use every weapon in the journalistic armoury against him. Gain his confidence, suck up to him, praise his achievements… And for goodness sake make sure you record the whole thing with more than one mini disc. Take the video camera as well. Get him to talk off the record if you have to – if he says something incriminating we can always edit out the bit where you say it's off the record. That's one of the benefits digital recordings have over analogue."

This did not seem to be the ideal time to inform Plum that he'd offered Gregan copy approval, so Bruce just smiled and nodded. He stood up and told Plum that he was just popping down to the courtyard for a smoke while he made some calls.

The courtyard was deserted so he pulled out his mobile and rang Spaghetti: "Hey you," Bruce rasped, channelling the spirit of an angry Scotsman again. "I want the money brought to Brighton tomorrow. You got that?"

"Yeah, I've got that."

"And you've got the money?"

"Yeah, I've got it – non-sequential used notes."

"I'll call you at noon tomorrow with your instructions. Don't fuck it up," Bruce cringed as he was saying it. He should practice these accents a few times before attempting to use them in the real world, and he should also consider writing a script.

When he returned to the office, he collapsed into his chair and wondered what the hell he was doing.

"Bruce, answer your bloody phone, will you?" Alex said, derailing his train of thought.

"Oh sorry," Bruce replied. "I was miles away there."

"I wish you bloody were," she said.

"That's funny because I was just thinking what a loss to the world it would be if you died, and how the crowds would be lining the route of your funeral procession like Princess Diana's."

"Just answer it, will you?" she said wearily.

"At once, Your Vagesty."

Bruce picked up the phone and his stomach did a gentle flip when he recognised Rachel's voice.

"How is your mother?" he asked.

"She's not good Bruce," Rachel said. "It's nearly the end."

"I'm so sorry."

"You left me a message saying you had Honey Peach's email address."

"That's right."

"You darling," she trilled. "How did you get that?"

"It's a long and winding road of a story."

"Hey!" Rachel scolded him. "You can't steal my catchphrases! Seriously, tell me."

Bruce explained that he'd visited Megan at Randy Milkman Enterprises again and this time he'd persuaded her to give him Milkman's password so he could access his emails.

Rachel praised him for his ingenuity but said she thought Milkman might be a red herring.

"You wouldn't have said that if you'd been hiding in Honey Peach's wardrobe when he broke in the house," Bruce said.

"What?"

"Nor if you'd seen him hide in the same wardrobe when someone else came in through the front door."

"What?" Rachel said again, considerably louder this time.

"Nor if you'd witnessed him knock this other bloke out with a kettle as he escaped, leaving me to run off through the streets of Brighton with her laptop."

"What?" This time it was a scream.

"But enough about me," Bruce said.

"You've got Honey Peach's laptop?"

"Indeed, but…"

"Can you courier it to me? Actually, I'll come and get it…"

"As I was about to say, don't get your hopes up. There's nothing on it."

"There must be something – pictures, letters…"

"There's nothing at all."

"That's ridiculous. Who has a computer with nothing on it?"

"She does, apparently."

"Who was the victim of the kettle assault?"

"I don't know…"

"Oh come on Bruce, you're supposed to be a journalist," she said, a little impatiently.

"I just review porn films," Bruce protested. "This is all new to me."

"Did you search the body?"

"He wasn't a body, he was just a bloke who'd been hit on the head by a kettle. And there was a screaming woman phoning the police."

"What a missed opportunity," Rachel tutted. "I suppose you've already tried to email her, have you?"

"Of course," Bruce replied, a little hurt by Rachel's attitude.

"And there was no response?"

"If there had been I would have told you," Bruce said. "It might still be worthwhile you emailing her though. If she is okay, she is more likely to respond to you than me, as you're her sister."

"Maybe. Listen, what do you know about Julian Gregan?"

"Not much," he said, remembering his fruitless internet searches. "Why?"

"What would you say if I told you I think he's involved in the disappearance of Honey Peach?"

"After all I've just told you about Milkman?" Bruce said. "I'd say you're barking up the wrong tree. Gregan is just a publicity-hungry campaigner who likes seeing his name in the papers."

"But have you heard some of the things he has been saying? That these women need rescuing and that it's morally right to take direct action and remove them from their surroundings, by force if necessary? He might have done that with Honey Peach."

"He'd be crazy to do that," Bruce said.

Rachel lowered her voice. "What if he is crazy? And what if I told you he lives on the same street as Honey Peach?"

"I know, it's quite a coincidence, but I'm following another line of enquiry. Have I told you about Spaghetti?"

"Hang on - you know? And you think it's 'quite a coincidence' that someone who advocates the snatching of porn stars lives just a few doors away from a porn star who has disappeared?" There was a definite tone of irritation in Rachel's voice as she said this. "And how do you know his address? He's not on the electoral roll and it's taken me ages to find out where he lives…"

Bruce also felt a little frustrated at the way the conversation had gone. "Rachel, the longer this goes on the more I think you should involve the police," he said.

"I've already told you, the police aren't interested," Rachel snapped. "Do you know how many people go missing every year? Almost a quarter of a million. Most of them turn up again so, unless it's a child or someone particularly vulnerable, the police have other priorities."

"Well I'll make sure I ask Gregan about Honey Peach tomorrow but…"

"You're seeing Gregan tomorrow?"

"I'm interviewing him at his house which is, as you mentioned, just a few doors away from Honey Peach's, at two o'clock."

"Wow," she said.

"How did you discover where he lives?" Bruce asked her.

After repeating the question Bruce realised that Rachel was no longer there. He called her back but her phone went straight to voicemail.

***

Bruce took a padded envelope from the pile on his desk and ripped it open. It contained a single DVD and a With Compliments slip. He tore open the plastic wrapping, popped open the case and inserted the disc into his computer's drive. Tomorrow was shaping up to be quite a day, especially with the Spaghetti situation. He hadn't even told Rachel about the blackmailing.

Spaghetti had to be his prime suspect – why else would he agree to pay £30,000 to a blackmailer? But he still couldn't rule out Milkman, with his huge financial motive, breaking and entering, hiding in a wardrobe, common assault with a kettle…

"What are you watching, Bruce?" Plum said, bringing him back into the office.

"Oh, um, Meating Place," Bruce replied, looking at the DVD case. "The heart-warming story of a boy, a girl and a giant salami. Filmed on location in an East London kebab shop."

"I don't want you doing any more film reviews," Plum said.

"Our readers won't toss themselves off," Bruce said. "Well, they will, but they need guidance and pointing in the right direction."

"I don't want Bruce doing any more reviews," Plum shouted across the office to Alex.

She looked up, mystified.

"Get a freelancer in to cover all Bruce's work over the next couple of days," Plum said. "I want him devoting all his resources to bringing down Gregan."

As Plum marched back to his office, Alex shot Bruce a dirty look. Bruce shrugged in response, stood up and took his jacket off the back of his chair.

"I'm finishing early today," Bruce told her. "I'm going to the library to do a little research. It's what Plum wants. Then I am going to visit Jan."

***

Even though it was only a few days since Bruce had last seen her, Jan appeared to have aged a little more. Her eyes were puffy, like she had been crying. Bruce had brought her a bag of sunflower seeds from a health food shop. When she asked him to open the bag for her, he dropped some of the contents at his feet.

"Oh no, I'm spilled my seed on the floor," he said, expecting an appreciative laugh in response.

Jan smiled, weakly. "You're perky tonight," she said.

"I suppose I am," Bruce said, helping himself to a beaker of Jan's water.

"Life treating you well, is it?"

"It's a long and winding road of a story," he said.

"Been talking to Rachel again?"

He nodded.

"She really has made quite an impression on you, hasn't she?"

He shrugged in response.

"I can see why," she said. "At your age, you're like a customer in a cake shop at five o'clock in the afternoon, when everything left on the shelf is either damaged or stale."

Bruce picked up the three paperbacks which were on Jan's bedside cabinet. "What have you been reading?" he said, scanning their titles.

Jan continued: "But then you spot this tart topped with delicious ripe strawberries and fresh cream. Of course you're going to be attracted to it, rather than all the fingered choux buns and the grubby éclairs."

"What a delightful analogy," Bruce said. "Are you the choux or the éclair?"

Jan stared at him.

"I'm beginning to think that particular cake is out of my price range," he said. "And I've got other things going on."

"Oh?" Jan said, pouring some of the sunflower seeds into the palm of her hand.

Bruce told her about his special assignment to bring down Gregan, how Rachel now thought he was behind Honey Peach's disappearance, and how he was blackmailing Spaghetti.

Eventually Jan sat up in bed. "That's enough, Bruce," she said, reaching for a tissue and dabbing her eyes.

"Are you okay?" Bruce asked. He'd never seen Jan cry before.

"Never better," she sobbed. "Would you mind if I get some rest now?"

"What did I say?"

A passing nurse stopped to comfort Jan and, seeing Bruce's look of helpless confusion, gestured at a copy of today's local newspaper which lay folded at the bottom of the bed. Bruce was amazed to see a picture of Jan on the front page. The headline read: 'Crash woman to be charged with drink-driving'.

Bruce picked up the paper and read the report as he walked out the ward: 'A woman has been charged with drink-driving following a crash which took place on Marlborough Lane on the evening of Monday 2nd June. Jan Jenner, 44, is currently a patient in Bath's Royal United Hospital with injuries sustained as a result of the crash, in which no other vehicles were involved. Jenner will appear at Bath Magistrates' Court on August 2nd. She is among 26 people who have been charged as part of Avon and Somerset Constabulary's summer crackdown on drink-driving.'

***

Bruce was annoyed to see that his Mazda was blocked in. Space is a precious commodity in hospital car parks, so drivers of large vehicles are invariably at a disadvantage, but this Lexus RX300 wasn't partly blocking him in, it was completely blocking him in. It was almost as if it had been parked there deliberately to prevent him from leaving.

Perhaps the driver was bringing in an emergency patient and simply did not have time to park properly, Bruce thought, as he approached the jet black 4x4. The side windows had been so darkly tinted that they matched the paintwork, giving the vehicle the appearance of a van from a distance.

Bruce wondered how long the driver would be, and was considering going back inside to see Jan, when his phone rang. The number in the caller display looked familiar.

"Hello Bruce, how are you, son?"

It took a second or two for Bruce to recognise the voice because the call was so unexpected. "Mr Sachetti?"

"That's right son," Spaghetti said. "Have you rung Gina yet to fix up a date to come down to see us?"

Bruce relaxed. "No, I'm working on something else at the moment and so I've had to put that feature on hold."

"Oh that's a shame," Spaghetti said. "Short of a few bob, are you?"

"No, it's nothing like that, I'm writing a different piece which is more time-sensitive so we'll have to reschedule it for a future issue."

Suddenly the driver and passenger doors of the Lexus burst open and Spaghetti, still holding his phone to his head, emerged with one of the man mountains Bruce had encountered at the Love Shack event.

"Get in the back," Spaghetti snarled, grabbing Bruce roughly by the arm and leading him to the dark cavernous space in the rear of the vehicle. He was pulled in by the other bouncer from the event, making Bruce the filling in a bodybuilding sandwich as the first giant climbed in besides him and slammed the door.

"Guys, I think you're overreacting a bit here," Bruce protested. "I didn't say we were going to cancel the feature, I said we'd have to reschedule it."

Spaghetti got in the front of the car, which was large enough for him to kneel on the driver's seat, spin around and face Bruce in the rear. "I'll ask you again," Spaghetti said. "Short of a few bob, are you?"

"Well, um, I could always do with more," Bruce said, wondering what the correct reaction to such a question should be.

"Is that why you're trying to extort thirty grand out of me?"

Bruce's insides did a full flip, and it was nothing to do with Rachel this time.

"Did you think I wouldn't find out it was you?" Spaghetti demanded.

"Was it the accent?" Bruce wondered.

"No, you fucking idiot, it was your number. The accent was pretty convincing."

Bruce suddenly realised what had happened. "Ah, I forgot to type 141 before I called you today, didn't I? Damn."

"So, do you want to tell me what this is all about?"

"Well, um, well, um, to cut a very long story very short, Honey Peach has disappeared, I'm trying to help her sister find her and I heard you had a reputation for sorting out those who crossed you – I saw what happened at the hotel…"

"That toerag was stealing from me, I couldn't be seen to let that happen."

"And I knew Honey Peach had let you down twice and so I wondered if you had her bumped off – is that the right expression?"

Spaghetti leaned further into the back of the car so his face was just inches from Bruce. "How dare you!" he shouted. "I have never had anyone bumped off in my life."

Bruce was surprised. "Haven't you? Oh well, um, is that good news for me?"

"Not yet I haven't anyway," Spaghetti said. "But then I've never met anyone stupid enough to try to blackmail me. Do continue."

"Right, well, this is going to sound a bit stupid but you were one of two people who I suspected, and I was trying to think of a way of quickly establishing if you were actually involved or not. So I wondered how you would react if someone said they knew about you and Honey Peach. If you'd laughed at me then I would have crossed you off my list and moved on. But you didn't, and your response suggested that…"

"Did you really think you were going to get thirty grand out of me?"

"That was the first figure I thought of – I wasn't prepared…"

"Why thirty grand?"

"There's an XK8 convertible at a dealer that I pass on my way to work every morning, and that's how much he's asking for it."

"What colour is it?"

"Red, but not an unpleasant brash red, like you see on city traders' Porsches, this is a deep maroon, a bit like Aston Villa's shirts."

"Sounds sweet," Spaghetti nodded. "What's the mileage?"

"I haven't looked into it that closely," Bruce said. "I don't have that sort of cash and I probably wouldn't be able to afford to run it."

"You say that, but prestige cars don't cost as much to keep as many people think," Spaghetti said. "Especially if you have them serviced at an independent specialist rather than a franchised dealer. Have you asked them how much they would give you for your Mazda?"

Bruce shook his head.

"You should, you might be pleasantly surprised, and it's never been cheaper to take out an unsecured loan if you decide to finance it."

"That's good to know," Bruce said. "Thanks for the advice."

"So why do you want me to take the cash to Brighton?"

"I thought if I asked you to bring it to Bath you might put two and two together."

Spaghetti nodded. "It's always best to shit where you don't eat, but why Brighton?"

"I'm going there to interview Julian Gregan and…"

"That prick! Fuck me, I'd pay someone thirty grand to get rid of him right now."

The two men in the back looked at each other.

"It's just a figure of speech boys," Spaghetti said to them. "Don't get no ideas."

Bruce continued: "I wasn't going to take the cash – I've seen enough films to know there's always a tail on the money – but I just wanted to see if you were prepared to bring it. If you were, then you clearly had something to do with her disappearance."

"I can see the logic," Spaghetti conceded. "It's misguided and it could have got you killed with someone less amenable than me, but I can understand what you were trying to do."

Addressing the men either side of Bruce, Spaghetti said: "Guys, why don't you two wander over to the cafeteria and get yourselves something to eat? We've got a long drive back and I've got this situation under control."

Spaghetti handed one of the men a twenty pound note. "And get a receipt," he emphasised. Turning to Bruce, he explained: "Always get a receipt for everything you buy. You'd be amazed at what you can claim for these days."

The men left and Bruce was able to fully appreciate the soft leather upholstery for the first time.

"The thing is, when you called me originally you said you knew about me and Honey Peach," Spaghetti said in a quiet voice. "And I panicked."

"You panicked?"

"Yeah, well between you and me, I did have a little dabble there, when we were taking casts of her for the Signature Series. We went to see this artist who lived in the middle of Wales and me and the three girls were staying in a hotel. We'd been out for a meal and had a few bottles of wine and in the middle of the night I hear this knocking on my door. It was Honey Peach and, well, I was hardly going to turn her down, was I?"

"Probably not," Bruce said, remembering how Honey Peach had dazzled the clientele at Marelli's.

"The thing is, if the wife ever gets to hear about it she will go ballistic. All her mates are divorced and they all live like the Queen of Sheba. She'll have the house, the villa in Spain, the cars… she'll even have half my pension, so you can see why I would like that particular indiscretion of mine to remain private."

Bruce nodded in agreement.

"It was a one-time thing. No one else knows about it, except Ben and Jerry."

Bruce looked puzzled.

"The boys who look after me," Spaghetti gestured in the direction of the two titans walking towards the hospital. "And I know they'd never breathe a word to anyone. So I thought I'd got away with it, but then I get Rab C Nesbit on the blower giving it the 'I know about you and Honey Peach' thing – well, I practically shit myself."

"Do you mind if I have a smoke?" Bruce asked. "This has all been a bit…"

"You're not smoking in here," Spaghetti said. "If you burn those seats my wife would garrotte you. Not literally, of course, she's a lovely gentle woman. Go outside."

Bruce did, and Spaghetti joined him, accepting one of his cigarettes.

"It's eight months since I last had one," Spaghetti said, lighting his from Bruce's. "So I'm probably going to be tripping."

They smoked in silence for a minute and then Spaghetti said: "Bruce, I swear to you that I have had nothing to do with Honey Peach's disappearance. Do you know how much I've invested in moulds of her? Shitloads. Wherever she's gone, I want her back. I know I've got this reputation for being a nasty piece of work…"

"I have been told you got your nickname from the Birmingham junction…"

"That's what everyone thinks," Spaghetti said, giving Bruce's shoulder a squeeze. "It was the kids at school who called me Spaghetti because they couldn't pronounce my surname. It was me who started the rumour that I was called it because you never want to cross me. This is a dog eat dog industry full of chancers, and if someone can take your trousers down they will, so a reputation for being a violent sociopath goes a long way when it comes to getting your bills paid."

Bruce smiled. "I must admit, this meeting went very differently to how I imagined it would go when you pulled me into the back of your car – which is really lovely, by the way."

"You can't beat the Japanese for reliability and generosity of standard equipment," Spaghetti beamed. "You can keep your Mercedes and Audis and BMWs – overpriced and overrated."

Bruce nodded. "I wouldn't know..."

Spaghetti took a deep drag on the cigarette and continued: "You have been a great help to me, Bruce, over the last couple of years. I was going to tell you this when I saw you at the hotel and when you came down to see me. My buyers wouldn't know a good porn film if it sneaked up behind them and fucked them up the arse."

Bruce nodded again.

"So I tell the buyers to only order big numbers of the films you recommend. You've made me a fair bit of money, and you've saved me a fair bit too, because we don't get stuck with all the rubbish anymore. So let's put this little misunderstanding behind us, shall we?"

"Gladly," Bruce said.

Spaghetti gave Bruce one of his business cards and they shook hands. "And it goes without saying, if I can do anything for you sometime then give me a call. You've got my number."

Bruce thanked him and said he would.

Spaghetti climbed in the Lexus cabin and opened the driver's side window. "But don't expect me to give you thirty fucking grand to buy a Jag," he laughed.

"Okay, the Jag is off the table," Bruce said.

"Why are you trying to find out what happened to Honey Peach anyway? What's your connection with her?"

"Her sister came to see me..."

"And you had the hots for her?"

Bruce looked embarrassed.

"I knew it," Spaghetti laughed.

"Well okay, there was a bit of that..."

"It's always about a woman," Spaghetti said, playfully punching him in the arm.

Was it? Bruce thought it was about more than that. And that punch hurt.

"Who's your other suspect, as a matter of interest?"

Bruce wondered if he should tell him.

"Would it help for Ben and Jerry to have a word?" Spaghetti said. "They're good at getting people to open up to them – they should be fucking therapists!"

Bruce was confident he could deal with Milkman. "I'd really rather not say at this stage," he said. "Just in case I'm wrong and I make another fool of myself."

"Okay, I can respect that, but before you go," Spaghetti said, as he moved the car so Bruce could extricate his Mazda. "If you breathe a word of anything I have told you tonight to another living soul then the lads will hunt you down, cut your cock off and shove it up your arse."

CHAPTER THIRTEEN: WEDNESDAY 18TH JUNE 2003

"What are you doing in the office?" Alex said from behind her copy of last week's Celebs & Scandals magazine. "Aren't you supposed to be having a day out at the seaside on special assignment?"

Bruce went to his desk, opened his drawer and rummaged through it, picking out assorted cables and plugs. "Belt and braces - I'm taking two mini disc recorders with me," he explained. "And I can't find the power supply unit for the old one."

Eventually he was successful and he added the cable to his shoulder bag and checked off his list. "Right, that's two recorders, two PSUs, two cameras, spare batteries, pre-prepared questions..."

Satisfied, he fired up his computer and wandered across to the water cooler, attracting the attention of Plum, who emerged from his office wearing a frown.

"Why are you here?" Plum demanded to know.

"I ask myself that very question every day," Bruce replied.

"Shouldn't you be making tracks?"

"I've got plenty of time," Bruce said. "I just want to check my emails before I set off."

"Well make sure you're on the road before ten," Plum said, pointing a chubby index finger in the direction of the office clock.

Bruce slouched in his chair and, with computer booted, began downloading the morning's emails. He skipped through the release schedules, press releases and requests for information on the size of the market from real-world journalists. There was nothing from Honey Peach.

Hang on, how could she reply to his mail, when he had her laptop on his desk? But there was no dedicated email programme – or indeed anything – installed on there, so either she used an online email client, leaving no trace on the laptop, and regularly expunged her browsing history, or this wasn't her main computer...

Her email address – Hello@honeypeach – suggested she was in the process of setting up her own web presence but trying to reach it directly just led to a 'this address has been reserved for one of our clients' message from the hosts. Perhaps he would contact them, when he had more time, and find out who was paying the bills...

Bruce wondered if something bad had happened to Honey Peach or if she had just decided to walk away from her life in porn and all its associated obligations to people like Spaghetti. Even though he had turned out to be a surprisingly decent bloke.

Bruce knew from experience that when an email account is not accessed regularly, the mailbox fills to capacity and additional messages are denied entry – with the sender receiving an automated non-delivery notification, also known as a bounce-back. When Bruce took a few days off, his mailbox rapidly reached its limit as he was frequently sent mails with large attachments.

Bruce thought that a good way to determine if Honey Peach's mailbox was being accessed on a regular basis would be to do the same to her – if the mails bounce back, her mailbox is full. If they don't, it is being emptied. He looked in his 'current issue' folder for a few large files to send and decided to import them into an image manipulation program and increase their size even further. He chose the cover of Meating Place and a less than flattering image of porn star Wanda Wette.

While the images were being resized, a courier wandered into the office and asked Bruce if there was anyone who could help him unload as Legal House had no lift. "I've got ten cartons for you," the courier explained, waving a delivery note.

"For me?" Bruce looked at the name on the document. "Ah, these are for Nick. He's the one with the muscles over there. He plays rugby and goes to the gym so don't let him weasel out of giving you a hand. I'd love to help but I've got to be in Brighton in a couple of hours."

After the packages had been carried up the stairs, Nick stacked them against the back wall of the office. "Thanks for all your help," he said, his clothes soaked in sweat.

"Look on the bright side," Bruce replied, as he sent four emails to Honey Peach, each with a 10MB graphic attachment. "At least you won't need to go to the gym this lunchtime."

Nick went to the water cooler and poured two full cups over his head. He then approached Bruce. "I need a hug after that, Bruce," he said.

"Stay away from me, you sweaty oik," Bruce knocked over his chair in an attempt to escape Nick's outstretched arms. "I've got a meeting this afternoon and I can't turn up wearing Eau de Twat."

The kerfuffle attracted the attention of Plum. "What the hell is going on? And what are all those boxes doing here?"

"They're the dolls," Nick explained. "For the Blowup Babe Beauty Parade feature."

"But they're huge," Plum said. "I thought they'd be like lilos."

"The cheap ones are," Nick said. "But the upmarket ones come with moulded heads, hands and feet. I've even got an inflatable Honey Peach doll for Bruce."

"They can't stay here," Plum said. "The cleaner will have a heart attack."

"I'm going to hire a van and take them to Weston-super-Mare for a photo shoot," Nick said. "Can you imagine how cool that will look, with all the dolls queuing up to get on the pier?"

"I can imagine you getting arrested," Plum said. "You do know that Weston is a family resort?"

"I'm going to do it at sunrise tomorrow, when no one is about," Nick said. "I've checked the times of the tides and I'll be able to drive the van straight onto the beach and get all the shots I need. I might even take them in for a paddle."

"I hope you've got a good pump," Bruce said. "And if you're driving on the beach you'd be better off with a 4x4 than a van."

"I don't want people to see what I'm carrying in the back," Nick said.

Bruce shrugged as he lifted his shoulder bag of equipment and checked his jacket pockets for his keys, wallet and cigarettes. "Makes sense. Well have fun, I'm hitting the road."

"Don't forget Bruce," Plum said, miming a frantic hammer and chisel action. "Nail the bastard."

***

Although Gregan's house was located only five doors further along from Honey Peach's, it was a world away from her new century minimalism. A neatly trimmed hedge towered above the wall separating Gregan's property from the pavement, and tubs of flowering shrubs lined the edges of the short path leading up to the handsome oak front door.

Bruce rang the bell and Gregan opened the door within seconds, despite having only one arm free, the other clasping a hands-free landline to his ear. He ushered Bruce in but continued his conversation, in a hushed voice. Bruce was being led towards the kitchen he noticed, being something of an expert on the layout of these houses now. As he passed the lounge he spotted a garish brown and orange carpet, set off by a plethora of chintz on the walls and a log-effect electric fire.

Gregan's kitchen was much longer than Honey Peach's, with the oak cabinets either side matching the round table and chairs. The table was located close to the patio doors, presumably so that breakfast could be enjoyed in the sunshine.

Gregan finished his call, slipped the phone in his trouser pocket and offered his hand to Bruce. "Pleased to meet you at last," he said.

"How do you do?" Bruce responded, adding as he approached the table: "Did you put this extension in?"

"Yes, we had it done a few years' ago," Gregan replied. "It's ate into the garden space unfortunately, but I don't miss the weeding."

Bruce smiled and nodded.

"You found it alright then?"

"Yes, no problem," Bruce said.

"And how was your journey?"

"Uneventful."

"That's the best type," Gregan said. "Would you like some tea?"

"That would be fab," Bruce said.

Did all crucifixions begin with such banal small talk?

"While you're doing that, shall I set up the recording equipment on this table?" Bruce asked.

"Yes of course, here let me move all those papers out of the way. If you need an electrical socket there are two low down on the wall. Just pull out the plug that's already in, it's only for the dehumidifier."

Formalities out of the way, tea brewed and poured and recording equipment set up and tested, Bruce's opening gambit concerned Gregan's background. "What set you on this particular road? Out of all the causes to campaign against, why choose this one?"

"It started three years' ago," Gregan said. "There have always been seedy shops where you could buy 'under the counter' videos but, as I'm sure you're aware, that was when it became legal to sell hardcore pornography on every street corner."

"Not on every street corner, only in licensed sex shops," Bruce pointed out.

Gregan waved a finger in disagreement. "My wife and I were in a newsagent and they were openly on sale, on the racks with the magazines, where young children could see them."

Bruce shook his head. "That should never happen."

"Of course it shouldn't," Gregan said. "I complained, as anyone would, but it was only when I made a test purchase in an attempt to encourage the local authorities to clamp down on it that I realised what I was dealing with."

"Did you watch the film?"

"I watched some of it but I had to turn it off before I was physically sick."

"So you bought a porn film 'for research purposes' and..."

"That's exactly what it was," Gregan interrupted. "So don't go implying in a snide way that it was for anything else. Anyway, the council finally responded to my complaint and said the newsagent wasn't breaking the law."

Bruce pulled a puzzled face.

"I was shocked too. I was telling a friend of mine about it and he suggested I visit a licensed sex shop to see the full extent of the situation. I did, and it was like entering the gates of hell. Even the titles were abhorrent. I could not believe any decent society would allow such vile things to exist, let alone to be openly sold."

"Did you buy any more films, for research purposes?" Bruce asked, hoping it sounded like an innocent question.

"I did, I bought four," Gregan said. "And they were far, far worse than I expected. Far worse than the film from the newsagent. They had actual sex acts – not simulated – and they took degradation to a level I never knew existed."

"Can I just clarify something?" Bruce asked. "So the first film you bought, the one in the newsagent, what rating symbol did it have? Was it a conventional BBFC 18, like you'd find on a horror film?"

"That's right."

"But the ones from the sex shop had a blue R18 logo?"

Gregan nodded.

"In that case the newsagent was doing nothing wrong."

"Nothing wrong?"

"Newsagents have traditionally used the top shelf of their magazine racks for adult entertainment products. You might find it distasteful..."

Gregan's cup clattered into its saucer. "Distasteful? It was nauseating..."

"So nauseating that you bought four much more explicit films," Bruce said, confident he had scored a point. "Can I ask, what did your wife think of these films you kept buying?"

"Excuse me?"

"Did you watch them with her or did you wait for her to go to bed and watch them alone?"

Gregan glared at Bruce. "Don't you dare bring my wife into this," he said, removing his glasses and wiping the lens. "Or this interview will be terminated."

"I'm sorry," Bruce said. "I have to ask these questions."

"My wife was gravely ill at the time, and if you're suggesting that I… that I…"

Bruce held up both his hands. "Let's move on to CRSP. Am I right in assuming that because you didn't think your local authorities were taking your complaints seriously, you thought you would stand a better chance of getting your point across if it came from an organisation rather than an individual?"

"No," Gregan shook his head as he sat back down at the table. "I founded CRSP because so many people, at the bowling club, at Rotary and at church, were giving me their support and wanted to make donations. I obviously couldn't accept them as an individual."

Bruce consulted his sheet of pre-prepared questions. "I was going to come on to this later," he said. "How much have you earned from CRSP? Do you take a salary?"

"I have never taken a penny," Gregan said. "And the books are open to anyone who would like to inspect them, as long as they have a legitimate reason for doing so."

"Can we move on to your organisation's objectives?" Bruce said. "Would it be fair to say that you would like the judgement of 2000, which legalised the sale of pornography in licensed sex shops, to be repealed?"

Gregan nodded in confirmation. "And in the meantime, we want to prosecute those who are profiting from the commercialisation of sex. If you can tell me the difference between prostitution and pornography I'd like to hear it."

"I'm aware of the word's origins," Bruce said, remembering yesterday's lesson in ancient Greek. "But one is a strict commercial transaction and the other is a form of entertainment – even though I fully accept that not everybody will find the end product entertaining per se. And while prostitutes are being paid to have sex, porn performers are being paid to appear in a film, and they are not being paid by the person they are having sex with…"

"As far as differences go, those are so insignificant as to be…"

"But they are important distinctions in law," Bruce said. "And, for the record, let's not forget that both prostitution and pornography are legal, within certain constraints."

Gregan appraised Bruce. "Are you familiar with the term procuring, or pandering?"

Bruce appraised Gregan. Was he trying to trap the trapper?

"If so then you'll know that it is illegal to profit from the earnings of prostitution – or the commercialisation of sex – and yet isn't that exactly what the people who make these films do?"

Mindful that his allocated time was ticking away, Bruce moved on. "How do you feel about the women who appear in porn films?"

"My heart breaks for them," Gregan said. "They are victims. I'm not saying that prostitutes are not victims either – some of them endure unimaginable horrors – but the women who appear in these films have no comprehension that their actions have been recorded for all eternity. They don't realise that their children, their grandchildren and their great grandchildren will be able to witness their degradation..."

"You're projecting your morals onto them," Bruce countered. "Surely it's their decision."

"Some of these girls are barely eighteen, according to the labels – do you think they are capable of understanding the potential consequences of what they are doing? They don't even know their own minds at that age. Everyone makes bad choices occasionally, particularly when they are young, but imagine if there was someone filming every bad choice you made."

"Would it be fair to say then, Mr Gregan, that you are trying to save these women from themselves?"

"That sounds a little pompous but..."

Consulting his questions, Bruce asked: "Do you think they should have to undergo a psychological test of some kind, which I understand is what happens on reality TV shows, before they are given a licence to perform? And would you be happier if there was a minimum age limit for performers? If so, what would you deem acceptable? Twenty-five? Thirty?"

Gregan considered Bruce's questions but said nothing for a few minutes. Instead he shifted in his seat, turned away from Bruce and stared into the garden. Bruce noticed that the back of Gregan's balding head had a wound that had recently been stitched.

"Mr Gregan?" Bruce knew that Gregan was trapped by these questions, which addressed his principal objections. If he approved of the suggestions Bruce had put forward, he would essentially be condoning pornography, albeit in a slightly modified format.

Eventually he responded. "Do you have children, Bruce? If so, I assume you would be happy for your daughter to pursue a career in pornography?"

It was Bruce's turn to feel trapped by a question he couldn't answer. He considered responding in the same manner as Gregan – with an unrelated question of his own – and was choosing the best way to phrase 'Are you aware that one of your own neighbours is a porn star?' when his phone rang. Bugger, that was unprofessional. He should have turned it off at the start of the interview, and requested Gregan do the same.

"You had better answer your phone," Gregan said. "Otherwise it will ruin the recording."

Embarrassed, Bruce said: "I really am sorry about this."

Retrieving the handset from his jacket pocket he looked at the caller display – it was Rachel. "Hi, can I ring you back?" Bruce said. "I'm in the middle of something at the moment."

"Open the door," she said.

"What?"

"Open the door and let me in."

"You're here? In Brighton?"

Gregan could hear every word of Bruce's conversation and his frown indicated he didn't like what he was hearing. "Who are you talking to?" Gregan said.

"It's my photographer," Bruce said to Gregan, loud enough for Rachel to hear.

"We never discussed photographs..." Gregan mumbled. "Did she say she was outside?"

"Yes, shall I let her in?"

"I'll do it," Gregan said, tutting.

As he opened the door to Rachel, Gregan asked if she would like some tea. She stared at Bruce but said nothing to him, declining the offer of tea with a request to use the loo instead.

"Where were we?" Gregan said, sitting back at the table as Rachel went upstairs.

Joining him, Bruce consulted his questions. "Well, um, I asked you if you would prefer porn performers to be above a certain age..."

"And I asked you if you would be happy for your daughter to appear in these films," Gregan retorted.

They sat in silence, neither choosing to answer the other's question.

After a minute had passed Gregan looked at his watch and said: "Well it looks like we've reached a stalemate. I am going to have to go soon anyway so perhaps we should end it there and do the photographs – which I didn't agree to, by the way."

While Bruce was considering his reply, Rachel clumped down the stairs and marched into the kitchen, adjusting her blouse and ferreting in her handbag.

"Shall I wait in the lounge until you have finished?" she asked Gregan.

"There's no need," Gregan said. "I think we're just about done. Do you want me with my jacket on or more casual?"

"Actually before we move on to that, and if Bruce has finished, I've got a few supplementary questions I'd like to ask," Rachel said.

"Supplementary questions?" Gregan looked at Bruce.

Bruce avoided his gaze. He didn't know what to say.

"Please do sit back down Mr Gregan," Rachel said. "It will only take a minute."

Gregan sat down, leaving Rachel standing over him. Bruce wondered if he should offer her his chair. He carried on drinking his tea, with an awkward, apologetic grin. Where was she going with this?

"Are you attracted to young girls, Mr Gregan?" Rachel asked. "I assume Bruce didn't ask you that?"

Gregan's face reddened. "Of course not."

Bruce inadvertently made a comically loud swallowing sound.

"Of course he didn't ask you or of course you're not attracted to them?"

"I'm not attracted to them," Gregan said slowly.

"Do you prefer young boys then?" Rachel asked.

"I'm not going to dignify that with an answer," Gregan said, standing in outrage.

"Do you have sexual fantasies in which you wield power over young girls?"

"No."

"Have you ever paid for sex?"

"Since when do photographers ask questions like this?" Gregan said to Bruce.

Bruce shrugged helplessly.

"And where is your camera, anyway?" Gregan said to Rachel.

"Do you mind explaining why you have a photograph of this woman in your bedroom?" Rachel asked, taking an A5 sized framed portrait of

Honey Peach out of her handbag. She appeared to be several years younger and she was wearing much less makeup in the picture but it was definitely Honey Peach.

"That was by the side of my bed!" Gregan shouted.

Bruce knocked his cup over, unleashing a tide of brown tea on his recording equipment. He quickly picked up the mini disc recorders and placed them on clear parts of the table. Should be get a cloth and wipe it up?

"For the record, yes it was," Rachel agreed. "Is it normal for men of your age to have pictures of porn stars – who, incidentally, live just a few doors away – on their bedside cabinets? Especially when they are spearheading an anti-porn campaign?"

Gregan turned away from her and her hostile questioning.

"Well?" she said.

Gregan said nothing.

"Do you have pictures of other young girls or did you just single her out?" Rachel persisted.

Gregan still said nothing.

"Was she special in some way?"

Gregan finally turned around to face her, his eyes filled with tears. "She's my daughter," he said.

Rachel was visibly shocked. "Your daughter?"

After a few moments of silence, Bruce said: "But how can you…"

Rachel interrupted him: "Your daughter?"

Bruce finally got the words out: "How can you campaign against pornography if your own daughter is one of its biggest stars?"

"You bloody imbecile, she's the reason why I'm campaigning so much," Gregan sobbed.

"I don't believe you," Rachel said. "Prove it."

Gregan walked into the lounge and came back with a photo album. He handed it to Rachel. "See for yourself," he said. "Her name is Emily."

Rachel took the album and quickly flicked through the pages, which recorded significant moments in the young Honey Peach's life: as the star of a fifth birthday party with an enormous cake; paddling in a blue sea with a bucket and spade; sat on a pony, with her father holding her upright; in her smart new uniform for her first day of secondary school…

"Honey Peach's real name is Emily Gregan?" Bruce said.

Gregan nodded. "Emily was distraught after her mother died and said she couldn't live in this house anymore. Which is why I pay the rent on the property where she is living now."

"She is still living there?"

"She was," Gregan said, handing Bruce a tea towel. "I haven't seen her for several weeks."

"Do you know where she is?" Bruce asked, as he mopped up the tea.

Gregan shook his head. "I go in every day and water the plants and keep it clean and pray that she has come back, that she will be sat there watching television or reading in bed, but…"

"I had no idea," Bruce said, suddenly realising the significance of the wound on the back of Gregan's head.

"She was always quite a delicate child," Gregan said, wiping the tears from his face with a monogrammed handkerchief. "And she has a heart condition, so obviously I am very concerned about her safety."

"Have you been to the police?" Bruce said.

Gregan nodded. "I've filed a missing persons report but I didn't tell them about her… other life. I couldn't. We've been estranged ever since she was manipulated by that evil man."

"Jones the Milkman?" Bruce ventured.

"I won't say his name in case the words choke me," Gregan said. "My daughter was working on the makeup counter in a department store in town, a perfectly respectable concern, and he targeted her. He kept coming into the shop, badgering her, trying to tempt her with promises of making her rich and famous."

That certainly sounds like Milkman, Bruce thought. And no doubt it started with 'Are you a model?'

"We obviously fell out about it," Gregan said. "I was already campaigning against it and suddenly my own daughter tells me she's going to be doing it. How do you think that made me feel?"

Bruce shook his head. This was not the time for a 'like dancing?' response.

Gregan looked at his reflection in the mirrored surface of the cooker. "Look at the state of me, there's a car coming for me in five minutes. We're going to have to call this a day."

Bruce stood up and turned off the mini discs. "Of course."

Rachel was still looking through the family album, examining every picture.

"Everything from when your photographer – if she is a photographer – intervened is obviously off the record," Gregan said. "And don't forget, I only agreed to this interview because you offered me sign-off on the article, so I don't expect to see any 'My daughter the porn star' headlines."

"You won't," Bruce said. "Though it will come out at some time. You know that, don't you?"

"I dare say it will," Gregan replied. "And when it does I hope people will understand why I do what I do. But I don't want it to get out while she is missing."

"Do you think she might have just run away?" Bruce asked.

"From me? It's possible, of course it is, and part of me hopes that is what has happened. That she is off somewhere now, alive and well and hating my guts for trying to stop her living this life. That's a million times better than the alternative. I pray every night that she will come back to me."

Bruce felt like putting a comforting arm around Gregan but wasn't sure if it was appropriate.

"Now, I really will have to show you out so I can get changed," Gregan said.

"Can I give you a word of advice?" Bruce said to Gregan as he wiped tea off his recording equipment and stuffed it into his bag. "If a journalist offers you copy approval in future, make sure you get it in writing before you speak to them."

As they emerged onto the street, Bruce said to Rachel: "I don't know about you but I need a drink after that."

He opened the Mazda's passenger door and she climbed in.

"Shall we go to Da Vinci's again?" Bruce said, walking around to the driver's side. "It's not far from here."

Rachel spent the whole of the short journey texting on her phone, and this continued when they were shown to a table.

"Well, I think you can rule Gregan out as a suspect," Bruce said, as he looked at the menu.

"Do you think?" Rachel said, her voice dripping in sarcasm.

"There's a few things I don't understand though," Bruce said.

"Just a few?" she snapped.

"You said you and she had the same mother – but Gregan said his wife is dead. And how did you not know that Gregan was her father?"

"How did you not recognise Gregan when you jumped over his prostrate body?" Rachel countered.

"He was laying face-down at the time," Bruce said. "And I was trying to hide my face from a woman phoning the police."

Getting out of her seat, she said: "If you'll excuse me, I need to use the loo."

During her absence Bruce thought about Milkman and his pick-up techniques. Why had no one knocked him out? He felt like doing it now, on Gregan's behalf and on behalf of every woman who had been made to feel uncomfortable from Milkman's unwanted advances. And if everything Spaghetti had said the previous night was true, then Milkman was once again the prime suspect in the disappearance of Honey Peach. With her out of the way he wouldn't have to pay any royalties, which was probably how he could afford to finance the Dick-Ins series. That line he had spun about him having access to the BBC Wales costume department was probably a load of rubbish. He had played Bruce. Exploited him. Just as if he had approached him on the street, given him a business card and asked if he was a model. The bastard.

Rachel returned, wearing a large pair of sunglasses that covered most of her face.

"Well that leaves us with Milkman," Bruce said. "I'm convinced of it…"

"Can you just hold off a minute," she said, holding up her hand and looking down at her phone. "Let me get my thoughts together."

They sat in silence for the next few minutes and then a waiter approached Rachel. "Excuse me madam," he said. "There is a telephone call for you."

"For me?" she appeared surprised.

"Who knows you are here?" Bruce asked.

"It's probably my sales director," Rachel replied. "I sent her a text telling her where I was as I had to cancel an appointment with a customer to come here."

"Why didn't she ring your mobile?"

Rachel looked at her phone. "Flat battery," she said. Then, turning to the waiter, she asked: "Where is your phone?"

"It's in the manager's office, madam, just behind the bar at the rear."

"See you soon," Rachel said to Bruce, following the waiter through the restaurant.

After five minutes had passed, Bruce signalled to the waiter.

"Yes sir, are you ready to order?"

"No, I'm waiting for my friend to come back. Is she still on the phone?"

The waiter gave Bruce a pitying look. "Sorry mate, she's legged it out of the back door."

"What?"

"When she came out of the ladies' she gave me a tenner and told me to come over to the table and call her away."

"She asked you to do that?" Bruce was shocked. "Why?"

The waiter shrugged. "She said she was on the blind date from hell and needed to escape."

CHAPTER FOURTEEN: THURSDAY 19TH JUNE 2003

"Have you seen this?" Plum demanded, thrusting a copy of today's Daily Hate in front of Bruce's face. "He's actually going to do it."

Bruce paused the mini disc and removed his earphones. "What did you say?"

"Gregan has announced that he is bringing a private prosecution against that Welsh bloke, Jones the Milkman, for deriving financial gain from the prostitution of another," Plum explained. "Did Gregan say anything about this yesterday?"

"Not exactly, but I can't say I'm surprised that he's chosen Milkman to be his test case."

"Did you get something we can use to hang him out to dry with?"

"I'm doing the transcribing now," Bruce said, pointing to the mini disc.

"Well be as quick as you can," Plum urged. "I don't want events to overtake us again."

"I came in before nine," Bruce said. "And I've been at it non-stop since."

"Nine? That's the middle of the bloody day mate," said Nick, waltzing casually into the office. "Some of us were up at four this morning."

"I hope you've got some good shots," Plum said. "You do realise that the cost of hiring a van has made this our most expensive photo shoot ever?"

"Ah, the glamour of magazine publishing," Nick said. "How are we all today?"

"Just hurry up, will you?" Alex snapped. "I'm the only one taking calls this morning."

"What's the problem?"

Alex gestured in Bruce's direction. "His lead story is making some people go mental."

"Ah, of course, the new issue hits the newsstands today," Nick said. "Who is making a fuss about it?"

"The BBC for one," Alex snapped. "And plenty of other media outlets."

"Dear God, are people really that stupid?" Nick said. "The piece said that BBC-style costume drama porn was being made, not that the BBC was making porn."

"The headline did not make that distinction," Alex said, through gritted teeth. "I can't believe Plum approved that cover."

The phone on Nick's desk burst into life. He stared at it. "What are we supposed to say?"

"You can either explain that they've got the wrong end of the stick and to read the copy," Alex said. "Or they can ring back after four when they speak to the author of the piece."

"Why can't they speak to him now?" Nick said, pointing at Bruce. "He's right there."

Alex rolled her eyes. "Plum's orders – he's got to be left alone to write up his interview with Julian Gregan."

Bruce was not at his most productive this morning. After Rachel had walked out on him the long drive back to Bath had been exhausting due to an accident on the M25 and roadworks on the M4. And even after he arrived home he had been unable to sleep, his thoughts dancing awkwardly between Gregan, Milkman and Rachel.

If he wanted to, he had enough ammunition to completely destroy Gregan and his organisation. Yes there were moral ambiguities – notably around the copy approval offer and the 'off the record' revelations – but once the story appeared, the damage would have been done. Bruce would not just be elevated to industry hero status, breaking this story would make him a name in mainstream journalism, particularly in anti-censorship left-leaning circles.

What should he do about Milkman? Bruce and Rachel were the only ones who knew Milkman's motive for wanting Honey Peach out of the way. But what was going on with Rachel? He understood she was emotionally vulnerable from coping with her seriously ill mother, but was that an excuse to run out on him? And she said her mother was also Honey Peach's mother, but that couldn't be the case – unless one of them was adopted?

"Bloody hell," Nick muttered from his desk, interrupting Bruce's thought process. "I've just booted up the laptop and some dick is sending me a huge email attachment and the server keeps falling over."

"Why do you use a laptop for mail when you've already got a desktop machine?" Alex asked.

"Because Plum is too mean to buy me a decent Apple Mac workstation," Nick replied, pointing to his desktop computer. "This antique can take minutes to render a full page image. That means I'm twiddling my thumbs every time I adjust the levels or add a drop shadow. Take now, for instance, I'm opening all the images I took on the digital camera this morning. It's going to be another five minutes at least…"

Bruce could hear the conversation even through his earphones – just like Alex had overhead him talking with Nick – and he noticed for the first time that Nick's laptop was the same brand as Honey Peach's. Perhaps Nick's power supply unit would fit and he could get someone else to have a look at it. Maybe there were some hidden files tucked away?

"You can man the phones while you're waiting then," Alex said. "So that I can get on with my own work. Hey, the BBC website has just been updated and one of its top stories is about us."

Plum shot out of his office. "What does it say?"

Alex peered intently at her monitor. "Hang on… 'A BBC spokesperson has strenuously denied reports that it intends moving into the production of pornography. The corporation criticised a "disingenuous" and "misleading" article in a specialist interest publication, which also alleged its costume department allowed its resources to be used by third party pornography makers, and said it would make no further comment until it had taken legal advice on the matter. An internal investigation has also been launched.'"

Plum was crestfallen. "They didn't even name us?"

Alex shook her head. "They also say that they will take action against any other publication or media source which repeats the allegation."

"Bastards," Plum said. "They knew only too well that we were desperate for them to name us, which was why they didn't. What a pity, eh Bruce?"

Bruce shrugged and pulled his earphones out. That story was, quite literally, old news as far as he was concerned. "I'm taking a break for a smoke," he announced. "I need to think."

"Don't be long," Plum said to him. "I'm going out for lunch in a minute and I'd like to see the first draft of your Julian Gregan crucifixion by the time I come back."

When Bruce returned to the office he unplugged the mini disc, wound the cable up and dumped the device into his drawer.

"What are you doing?" Alex said. "Plum said…"

"Fuck Plum," Bruce replied, making a call on his mobile. "I've got something more important to do."

Alex said nothing but Bruce noticed that she made some notes on a pad, after checking the time on the wall clock. That will be additional information to be included in the next written warning, he concluded.

"Randy Milkman Enterprises," a familiar voice answered.

"Can you put me through to Mr Jones please, Megan?" Bruce said. "It's Bruce Baker from AMG magazine."

Bruce could hear Megan's muffled voice asking Milkman if he wanted to speak to him – he did – and then he heard her ask Milkman how Bruce knew her name.

"Bruce?" Milkman said.

"How are you?" Bruce said.

"I've been better," Milkman said. "I suppose you've heard what that nutter is doing, have you?"

"The private prosecution? Yes, why do you think he has singled you out?"

"Because he's a nutter?"

"On the plus side though, you're on the cover of AMG today."

"I saw that – thanks a lot. That should be a big help."

"And did you notice that Bleak Arse was Movie of the Week? That's going to mean a big order from Spaghetti."

"Oh, you know about that, do you?" Milkman said, a little sheepishly.

"Now I understand why you were so keen to offer me an incentive," Bruce said. "Spaghetti told me he bases his buying decisions on my recommendations."

"When did you speak to him?"

"I need you to do something for me now," Bruce said. "I want you to come to the office for a follow-up piece."

"No problem… I'll be happy to do that anytime."

"Good, because I need you to do it now."

"Now?"

"This minute. We've got a four-page feature to fill in the next issue and I thought it would be perfect for you."

"Four pages?" Milkman said. "Too bloody right. The only thing is, I had a few beers with the boys down the club last night and it turned into a bit of a session, so I don't know if I can drive."

"Catch a train," Bruce suggested.

"I'm not catching a bloody train to Bath in the middle of summer," Milkman said. "I would have to change at Newport, which is in the opposite direction. I suppose I could get Megan to drive me across…"

"Megan?" Bruce did not want to see Megan.

"The woman who answers my phone," Milkman said. "She said you knew her name. How's that then?"

"You mentioned it."

"Did I? I don't know if I'm coming or going this morning. She can do a bit of shopping while she's waiting for me."

With an assurance from Milkman that he would be in Bath within the hour, traffic permitting, Bruce rang Zara at BATA. After a few slightly awkward pleasantries, he got to the point: "Will the association be supporting Milkman, if Gregan's private prosecution reaches court?"

"That's something we are going to have to discuss at our next committee meeting," Zara said. "On the one hand, issues like this are what trade associations are for. It's obviously in our interests for the case to fail, because if it succeeds it will have a devastating impact on our members and the industry as a whole."

"There is a 'but' though, isn't there?"

"But on the other hand Milkman is such an odious creep – that's obviously off the record. He's even come on to me, with his ridiculous spiel…"

"Are you a model?" Bruce said, in his best Welsh accent.

"That's the one," Zara said. "Also, he is not one of our members. I've tried to get him to join several times but he thinks he's too successful to need our support – so part of me wants to see the prick suffer."

"I can understand that," Bruce said.

"I've even told him that our biggest supporter is the company that needs us the least."

"Who's that?" Bruce asked.

"Love Shack – Spaghetti practically bankrolls BATA."

"Because when you're promoting the industry as a whole, you're also promoting its biggest players," Bruce said. Thinking of CRSP, he added: "And an organisation will always be taken more seriously than an individual."

"That's obviously true," Zara said. "But Spaghetti also supports a number of charities and youth organisations. And he doesn't do it for the publicity – you won't see an under-nines football team with 'Visit Love Shack, your friendly neighbourhood sex shop' on their shirts – he does it quietly and anonymously."

***

Bruce took Milkman through to the AMG boardroom, where two mini disc recorders were set up on the table, and he ushered him into a chair. After switching the recorders on and checking the levels Bruce began by asking Milkman about his future plans for the Dick-Ins brand.

Milkman had very ambitious plans for Dick-Ins, he said, and he hoped to release the second title in the series in September, subject to BBFC approval. The initial reaction had been overwhelming, he added, with retailers throughout the UK placing re-orders before their first deliveries had even arrived. He concluded by saying that he had great expectations for September's Great XXXpectations and that The Thick Dick Capers would be available by the end of the year – and he was confident they would both be AMG Movies of the Week.

Bruce moved on to the current debate about porn in the media, with the agenda being set by Julian Gregan and CRSP, and Milkman said that while he respected Gregan's opinion he obviously did not agree with it. "It's not the responsibility of the state, the government or any self-appointed moral guardian to determine what consenting adults may or may not do in the privacy of their own homes, providing it does not affect anyone else," he read from a piece of paper he retrieved from his pocket.

"Did you write that?" Bruce asked.

"Yes, of course I did," Milkman said loudly into the mini disc microphone while vigorously shaking his head. Picking up a copy of today's Daily Hate which had been left on the boardroom table, he added: "But as someone a lot more brainy than me once said, there's only one thing worse than being talked about…"

"Before we wrap the interview up," Bruce said. "What can you tell me about Honey Peach?"

Milkman stared at Bruce and pulled a disagreeable face. "What do you want to know?"

"Do you have any plans for any more Honey Peach films?"

"It's difficult to say…"

"But I understand Legend of the Amazon Women did very well for you – that was also an AMG Movie of the Week, wasn't it?"

"It was," Milkman said. "When she returns from her holiday…"

"She's on holiday? You've heard from her?"

"No, but I can only assume…"

"How did you meet her? Did you advertise? Did you go through an agency?"

"I can't honestly remember now…"

"Or did you just waltz up to her and use your 'Are you a model?' chat-up line?"

Milkman stared at Bruce. "What's that got to do with anything?"

"That actually works, does it?" Bruce asked, with a disarming smile.

"Off the record, it's a numbers game. Nine out of ten will blow you away but the ones who don't make it all worthwhile."

"Have you considered what effect your recruitment technique might have on those other nine, who perhaps are uncomfortable being approached in this way?"

Milkman shrugged.

"You'd be happy for your daughter to be spoken to like this, in her place of work, by a man old enough to be her grandfather, would you?"

"I don't have a daughter," Milkman smirked. "Not that I know of anyway."

Bruce wanted to punch the smirk off Milkman's face. "Going back to Legend of the Amazon Women, that's been quite a hit here in the UK but are there any plans to release it overseas? I can imagine it doing very well in America…"

"There have been some discussions," Milkman said. "But there are territorial complications and I'd really like to concentrate on the Dick-Ins series."

"What are you waiting for?" Bruce asked. "I would have thought now would be the perfect time to release her film in America."

"Why?"

"Before her body is found."

"What do you mean?"

"Won't buyers be put off buying the film, once they know she is dead? Or are you going to tell me the necrophilia sector is particularly vibrant these days?"

Milkman stood up. "I don't know what's going on here…"

"You killed Honey Peach on the night of Monday the second of June, that's what's going on," Bruce said, as casually as he could. "You met her off the train, took her back to your place and… please fill in the blanks for me. Did you get into a fight with her when you tried to get her into your bed?"

Milkman stared at Bruce. "Have you gone off your trolley?"

"Are you saying you know nothing about her disappearance?"

Milkman tried to walk around Bruce to get to the door. "Yes, I am, now get out of the way before I…"

Bruce blocked Milkman's exit. "Before you what? Hit me over the head with a kettle?"

The colour drained from Milkman's face.

"Or do you only do that to old men after you've broken into their daughter's house and hid in the wardrobe?"

Both of Milkman's scrawny legs began trembling.

"Yes, that was Honey Peach's father," Bruce continued. "He doesn't know it was you who attacked him – at least not yet – but he will."

Milkman tried to push Bruce out of his way but Bruce pushed him back into the room.

"The door is locked," Bruce said, holding up a key which he flamboyantly placed in his jeans pocket. "And you're not getting out of here until you tell me what you did to Honey Peach."

Milkman tried to grab Bruce's arm but Bruce once again pushed him back into the room, more forcefully this time. He fell, tripping over the mini disc power lead and knocking over a chair. The rumpus attracted the attention of Alex and Nick, who were staring in amazement through the glass door. After a few seconds they were joined by an even more amazed Plum, just back from lunch.

"And you still don't realise the connection between Honey Peach's father and the moral guardian who will be pursuing you through the courts, do you?" Bruce said to the prostrate Milkman, who was frantically trying to scuttle under the boardroom table.

"Let me out of here," Milkman yelled, his voice shaking with fear.

Plum banged on the glass door. "Bruce, open this door," he shouted.

Bruce retrieved the mini disc recorder that Milkman had tripped over. "You've pulled the power supply out of the wall, you clumsy oaf," Bruce said. "It's stopped recording. Luckily we have a belt and braces policy here at AMG magazine."

"Nick, run down to reception and get the spare key for the inner offices," Plum said, as he continued banging on the door.

"Shall I ring the police?" Alex asked, picking up her phone.

"I don't know anything about Honey Peach going missing," Milkman wailed.

"I don't want to hear anymore of your lies," Bruce shouted, throwing the mini disc recorder at the cowering Milkman's head. "You killed her because she's worth more to you dead than alive, isn't she?"

Milkman emerged from under the boardroom table on the other side of the room. His hands were shaking as he tried to lift the five foot tall potted Ficus tree that Plum had been cultivating for almost a decade. He hurled it at Bruce but it fell short, landing on the boardroom table, where the terracotta pot shattered. Bruce grabbed the plant stalk and brandished it at Milkman, roots first, like a club.

"With her out of the way you could sell Amazon Women all over the world without paying a penny in royalties, couldn't you?" Bruce snarled, swinging the plant at Milkman. Every swipe resulted in a shower of soil flying off the plant's roots and filling the air. "You just needed to find her copy of her contract, so you could destroy it, which is why you broke into her house by smashing the glass in the front door."

Dodging the swings of the plant stalk, the terrified Milkman picked up two of the larger pot fragments and hurled them at Bruce. The first one missed him and knocked a print of Ye Olde Streets of Bath off the wall, the thin wooden frame splintering as it fell to the ground. The second pot fragment caught Bruce on the side of the head. He staggered backwards, raising his hand in an attempt to stem the blood that was flowing down his face, and then everything went black.

***

Bruce's head was throbbing and he couldn't decide if the ice-cold water running down his face was making the pain worse or better. He opened his eyes and saw Nick looming over him, wet towel in his hand. The white material was streaked with red. Bruce looked around him. He was sat in Plum's guest chair. He tried to stand.

"Hey, relax Bruce," said Nick. "You've had a nasty blow to your head. You're going to be a bit disorientated for a while."

"Where's Milkman?"

"Don't worry about him."

Bruce raised his head to peer through Plum's door into the office. Alex was the only one there, talking excitedly on the phone to one of her friends. "And then he attacked him with a plant!" she squealed.

"Here, have a drink," Nick said, offering Bruce a plastic cup of water, which he gratefully accepted.

"I need to speak to Plum," Bruce said.

"Oh don't worry mate, you will," Nick said, still dabbing Bruce's head. After a few seconds he said: "Well, that's the bleeding stopped, but if I was you I would get that checked out by a doctor."

Bruce slowly stood up. "I will," he said. "Where is the mini disc?"

"I put it in your drawer," Nick said. "After I wiped all the soil off it. That stuff gets everywhere. You're not going to be popular with the cleaner once he sees the boardroom."

Bruce tentatively made his way to his desk where he crashed down into his chair. Alex stared at him, shaking her head but with a huge grin on her face. She had the look of someone who had unexpectedly won something.

Nick left the towel on Plum's desk and followed Bruce. "Seriously mate, you really do need to go to A&E this time," he said.

Bruce closed his eyes and wallowed in the throbbing in his head. Vivid colours flashed on and off, even when he covered his face with his hands.

"Has he come around?" Plum said.

Bruce opened his eyes and stared at Plum to confirm that he had indeed come around.

"Bruce, I may have used the words 'you've gone too bloody far this time' on a number of occasions in the past but I can assure you that they have never been more true than today," Plum said.

Nick said: "Hang on Plum, it's not his fault."

"Not his fault? Whose is it?" Plum spluttered.

"He had a knock on the head the night that Jan crashed her car," Nick said. "He should have had medical attention."

"Are you defending him?" Plum spat.

"He needs help," Nick said. "He doesn't need you shouting at him."

"You do know what took place here today, do you?"

"He's been behaving a little oddly ever since that night," Nick said. "You've seen some of it – like when he claimed he didn't have a key to his desk drawer and it was on his keyring – but there have been other instances. A week or so ago he said he'd written the news and transferred it across to me but there was nothing there. And he's been coming out with all these conspiracy theories – today he accused Milkman of being involved in Honey Peach's disappearance but earlier this week he reckoned that Spaghetti was behind it..."

"Where is Milkman?" Bruce asked.

"He's downstairs in reception," Plum replied. "Waiting for his assistant to get his car from Charlotte Street. He's talking solicitors, damages... this could close AMG down."

Bruce yanked open his desk drawer to retrieve the mini disc recorder that Nick said he'd put there. As he grabbed it he noticed something glistening in the corner. He reached for it. It was a gold chain and on it were two charms – a pot of honey and a peach.

Bruce vomited onto his desk, covering his keyboard and splashing his monitor. Plum and Nick instinctively recoiled in horror.

Wiping his mouth with his jacket sleeve, Bruce slammed his desk drawer shut, secreting the jewellery in his clenched fist. "I need a smoke," he said.

Bruce carefully made his way down the staircase to the ground floor, followed by Plum and Nick who were arguing over what to do next. Instead of going towards the back of the building and the courtyard Bruce went to the front and the reception area. Milkman was sat, pathetically, on one of the chairs, staring at him.

"You keep him away from me," Milkman said, panic in his voice. "I'm an old man."

"He's come to apologise, haven't you Bruce?" Nick said. "He's been under a lot of stress lately."

Bruce took a cigarette from the pack in his jacket and lit it, his hands trembling.

"You can't smoke in here!" shrieked Dee, from behind the reception counter.

Plum shushed her and turned to Milkman. "If Bruce apologises, can we sort something out and draw a line under this?"

"He attacked me," Milkman shouted.

"With a plant," Plum replied. "But you assaulted him with an item of pottery, which is capable of doing far more damage than vegetation."

"And look at this jacket!" Milkman cried. "That's pure cotton that is and now it's got all earth rubbed into it."

Plum reached into his jacket pocket for his wallet and pulled out a number of twenty-pound notes. He offered them to Milkman: "We'll obviously pay for the cleaning," he said. "Is this enough?"

Milkman took the money and counted it. "Eighty quid?"

"Look, whatever it costs, send me the bill," Plum said. Gesturing at the money, he added: "And keep that too, obviously. Give it to a charity of your choice if you want to. And AMG will give you a free page of advertising as well."

"Every week?" Milkman said, after a long pause.

"Every week," Plum said, after an equally long pause. "For a month. Do we have a deal?"

Two men in suits were coming down the staircase, heading towards reception with concerned looks on their faces. "It smells like someone is smoking in here," one said to the other.

"Alright," Milkman said to Plum. "A free page of advertising every week for a month."

They shook hands.

"Look at him," Plum said, gesturing at Bruce. "You can see he's a bidet short of a bathroom suite."

The main entrance door to Legal House opened and in walked Megan. "The car's outside," she said to Milkman. "But I'm parked on double yellows and they tell me the wardens are red hot around here."

"I'm coming now," Milkman said.

Staring at Bruce, Megan said to Milkman: "Why is the VAT man here?"

CHAPTER FIFTEEN: FRIDAY 20TH JUNE 2003

Bruce shielded his eyes from the reflection of the early morning sun glinting on the Mazda's chrome. As he approached the car he noticed the boot was ajar. He rarely used it, as its capacity was so limited, and he quickly concluded that it had been broken into. Sure enough, the lock had been butchered. Bruce was unconcerned about any valuables going missing as there was never anything left in the boot, but considering whether the offence would be classed as robbery, as nothing has been taken, or just vandalism occupied his thoughts for a few seconds, which he was grateful for as it meant he didn't have to think of other, more worrying, things.

He didn't even get particularly angry when he noticed that the Mazda's canvas roof had been slashed with a sharp object in a number of places. He climbed into the car's cabin, released the clips which attached the roof to the windscreen surround, and yanked the structure backwards. He was going to drive the short distance to work in style today.

Unfortunately the Mazda refused to start. It appeared to have a flat battery, probably caused by the boot light trickling the charge away during the night. Well at least he wouldn't be bored this weekend, as he'd be charging the battery, repairing the roof and buying and fitting a new boot lock.

Bruce started walking. Should he ring ahead to tell them he would be late? Probably, but he didn't really want to speak to any of them, not after the events of the previous day.

As he passed the forecourt of Reeves & Jeeves he noticed the Jaguar XK8 was no longer in the coveted 'Car of the Week' slot and a 1973 Volkswagen Camper Van was now the dealer's choice. Bruce stopped and stared at it. Jan would like that. Fifteen grand was a bit steep for a thirty-year-old vehicle though.

His apparent interest in the merchandise attracted the attention of a hungry salesman. "Are you looking for anything in particular?" he asked Bruce.

"You had a Jaguar XK8 for sale a few days ago..."

"Ah, they don't hang around," the salesman said, shaking his head. "I've got a very clean BMW if you're looking for open top motoring though. Fully loaded..."

"The Jaguar wasn't bought by a guy named Sachetti was it?" Bruce asked.

"Vicar's wife from Chippenham," the salesman said. "She part-exchanged a Saxo."

Damn. If this had been a Richard Curtis film Spaghetti would have bought the car for Bruce as a token of his appreciation and gratitude. And wrapped it up with a big red ribbon and bow. And offered him a job. On double what he was earning now.

"Or, if you're shopping on a budget, have you considered a Mazda MX-5?" the salesman continued. "We've got a classic model just in, with the pop-up headlights and everything…"

Bruce walked away.

***

"Good morning," Bruce said to Dee.

She glared at him.

How rude. Wasn't it in her contract that she had to be civil to all Legal House tenants? If it wasn't, it should be. Didn't we pay her wages?

The reception from Alex was equally as chilly. And not in a good way, like Honey Peach tried to get the word to mean. Plum, on the phone in his office, noticed Bruce arrive but chose not to acknowledge him in any way, continuing his conversation.

Only Nick appeared pleased to see him. "Bruce, mate, how are you feeling?" he said. "Did you go to A&E last night?"

"Yes," Bruce lied. "They said I was suffering from under-appreciation. It was the worst case they've ever seen. What are you doing on Jan's computer?"

"We've got a new girl starting on Monday," Nick explained. "And she's going to be using Jan's machine. I'm making a partition on the drive so she has her own space and can't access Jan's stuff, such as her emails and any personal files, until Plum decides what to do with it. Apparently you can't just wipe personal data when someone leaves, not if there's the possibility of a court case anyway."

"But Jan hasn't left."

"Well…" Nick replied, reluctant to finish the sentence. "Do you fancy a coffee? I'm just about to pop out and get myself one."

"No thanks," Bruce said, retrieving the mini disc from his drawer. "I've got to finish transcribing the Gregan interview."

Ten minutes in, Nick waved at Bruce.

"What?" Bruce snapped.

"I think you'd better take a look at this," Nick said, beckoning him over.

Grumbling, Bruce removed his earphones and wheeled his chair across the office to Jan's desk.

"Since she's been off, Jan's emails have been forwarded to Alex," Nick explained. "But Plum asked me to set up an auto-response this morning, so the sender gets a message saying 'I am no longer employed at AMG magazine – please contact Alex for editorial or advertising opportunities in future issues'."

"But Jan might be coming back…"

"I'm sorry mate, but I don't think so," Nick said, shaking his head slowly. "After she appeared on the front page of the paper this week, Plum made some discreet enquiries with one of his Rotary chums on the force. Seems she was so far over the limit that they reckon the magistrates will make an example of her and impose a custodial sentence."

"Christ…"

"So I'm no longer 'acting' editor," eavesdropping Alex said as she sashayed past. "As I'm sure Plum will confirm when he comes off the phone."

Nick lowered his voice so Alex couldn't hear. "Anyway, while I've been in Jan's mailbox I couldn't help but notice an email she received from Honey Peach a couple of days before she came across for the interview."

Bruce perked up. "What does it say?"

"I think you'd better read it yourself, mate," Nick replied, clicking on the message and then moving backwards so Bruce could get closer to the monitor.

Bruce read the message aloud: "Hi Jan, looking forward to seeing you on Monday the 2nd for the interview…"

"Keep your voice down," Nick urged. "Or Alex will hear you."

Bruce continued, at a much lower volume: "But please don't leave me alone with Bruce. I think he's obsessed with me! Last time I was over he gave me a pendant with a pot of honey and a peach on it and he asked me to wear it every day. It's kind of sweet but it's also a bit creepy as he's older than my dad!"

"I'm sorry mate, but I thought you should see it," Nick said.

"That's bullshit!" Bruce whispered. "I'm a lot younger than her dad."

"Perhaps he's a trendy dresser…"

"I can assure you he's not," Bruce said. "And I did not give her that pendant!"

Nick closed the message and the program. "Well you do appear to have been a bit obsessed with her lately, and I just thought you should see it," he said.

Despite the warmth of the day, Bruce suddenly felt very cold indeed as he repeated the message back to himself. His hands began to tremble, his throat tightened and he had difficulty swallowing. He could feel his heartbeat racing and he had that 'butterflies in the stomach' sensation. Was he going to be sick again?

Plum chose that moment to emerge from his office. His face looked sad rather than angry. He approached Jan's desk, where Bruce and Nick were sat. "Bruce you look dreadful," Plum said. "And I don't think what I'm about to say will bring you any comfort. I've just got off the phone to Milkman's solicitor who is adamant that his client is pressing charges against you. Obviously there's the assault and the false imprisonment yesterday, when you locked him in the boardroom…"

"He agreed to forget about that in return for free advertising," Nick said.

"Well it's back on the table now," Plum said. "Because there is also the accusation that you impersonated a HMCE officer – that is a serious criminal offence, and you could go to prison for up to two years."

Alex said something but Bruce couldn't hear her. He suddenly had a piercing ringing sound in his ears. His chest felt tight and he had difficulty breathing. He couldn't decide if he was going to die or faint.

"Here, drink this," Nick said, offering him a cup of water.

Bruce gulped it down. "Thanks," he said.

"My mother used to say to drink sweet tea after a shock," Alex said. "Do you want me to get you one from the shop, Bruce?"

Bruce stared at her. He wasn't used to acts of kindness from Alex.

"I was going to get myself a Caramel Mocha anyway," Alex explained.

As Bruce put his hand into his jeans pocket to get some cash for Alex his fingers closed around the pendant he had found in his desk yesterday. His whole body shivered. How could he have forgotten about it? And how did it get in his desk? His other hand formed a fist and he punched himself in the face. Then he vomited on Jan's computer.

"Oh bloody hell Bruce!" Plum yelled. "Why always the keyboards?"

***

If pressed to recall what happened during the next fifteen minutes, Bruce would not be a reliable witness. Someone cleaned up the vomit, someone washed his face with a cold flannel and someone told Dee to hold all calls as the office was having a bit of a crisis, but Bruce was unaware of all these things taking place around him. He was just picturing a vicar's wife, roaring along the A4 back to Chippenham in her claret Jaguar convertible, with the roof down and her silver hair billowing in her slipstream.

There was an air of calm in the office when Alex returned, but she soon changed that. "We've been beaten to the Gregan story," she said, depositing the coffees on Jan's desk and holding up a new issue of Celebs & Scandals.

"This has just hit the newsstands," Alex said. "It's not due until Monday but the newsagent said it had been fast-tracked for early release, and that it's expected to be the biggest-selling issue they've ever printed."

The cover of Celebs & Scandals featured a grainy interior shot of a restaurant, with the focus on an old man deep in discussion with a blonde haired young woman. They were instantly recognisable to Bruce, Plum and Nick. The headline read: 'My daughter, the porn star!' followed by the tagline: 'Shock revelation! It seems PORN runs in the family for morality campaigner Julian Gregan who we can EXCLUSIVELY reveal is the father of Britain's biggest PORN STAR, Honey Peach! Inside, KT Green – the queen of the gossip scene – gives you the handle on the scandal that EVERYBODY will be talking about!'

Celebs & Scandals had devoted six pages to the story. In addition to publicity photographs of the two subjects, there was a series of snatched images from the restaurant, which culminated in her leaving the table. There was also a pre-porn photograph of a fresh faced Honey Peach, in which she wore a school uniform, and an aerial shot of the Brighton street, with arrows highlighting Honey Peach's and Gregan's houses.

The magazine was known more for its images of famous people looking rough than for the quality of its prose and the article itself said little more than what had been included on the cover, though there were boxouts devoted to Honey Peach's porn career and a selection of quotes from Gregan which, the magazine said, demonstrated what a hypocrite he was.

Plum eventually said: "Well, they beat us to it and fair play to them – they unearthed a story that we didn't have a clue about."

"KT Green is awesome," Alex said. "She's always doing exclusives."

"She must have got to him much earlier than us," Plum said, flicking through the exclamation mark-splattered pages and handing the magazine to Bruce. "I don't suppose he gave you any hint of this bombshell when you saw him, did he Bruce?"

Bruce quickly read the brief article inside. "It did crop up," he said.

Plum shouted: "It cropped up?"

Bruce nodded.

"And you didn't say anything?" Plum's face reddened. "You didn't have the common courtesy to inform us that you were sitting on the biggest fucking story that has ever come across our desks?"

Nick said to Plum: "Well, to be fair, you did say you wanted him to crucify Gregan and I'm sure Bruce was going to lead with it in his article – he hasn't finished transcribing his interview yet, what with one thing and another..."

Plum seemed to begrudgingly accept this. "Even so, if you'd come to me with this straight away Bruce, we could have done a deal with one of the tabloids. We could have licensed the piece to them, and used it to flag our next issue to their readers. For the full story, see the next issue of AMG etc."

"Well, I've got things I should be getting on with," Nick said, returning to his desk. "Are you sure you're alright now, Bruce?"

"AMG could have been all over that story," Plum grumbled.

"I wasn't going to use it anyway," Bruce said. "Like I said, it cropped up but Gregan told me it was off the record, and I was going to respect that."

A look of contempt took over Plum's face. "You are pathetic," he said.

"He's a father concerned about his daughter," Bruce said. "She is still missing and Milkman has..."

Plum clamped his pudgy hand over Bruce's mouth. "Let me stop you right there," he said. "I don't care if Milkman has killed her, sliced her, diced her, sautéed her in garlic butter and served her to his sheep with a leafy green salad on the side."

Nick looked up from his monitor. "The first online reports are starting to appear and they are all emphasising the fact that her current whereabouts are unknown," he said.

Bruce flicked through the pages of Celebs & Scandals and asked Alex: "Is there a picture of KT Green anywhere?"

"I've never seen one," Alex replied. "Why?"

"No reason," Bruce said, stopping on the magazine's flannel panel and picking up his phone.

"Who are you ringing?" Plum demanded to know. "At least finish the story before…"

"Before what, Plum?" Bruce looked up at him defiantly.

"Before…" Plum hesitated.

"Can you put me through to KT Green please?" Bruce said to his phone. After a pause of a few seconds he added: "Yes, I'm sure she is very much in demand but I'm equally sure she will want to speak to me. Tell her it's Bruce Baker."

Alex laughed. "Do you think she'll speak to you? She's important, she is."

Nick walked across the office and turned on the television, which normally only got pressed into service during World Cups, when England matches were televised during office hours. It showed a live news report, coming direct from a Brighton street which Bruce had come to know rather well over the last few weeks.

"There has been no sign of Mr Gregan since the story broke in a well-known gossip magazine," an earnest young reporter was saying to camera, while a scrum of other media representatives jostled for position behind her. "But we understand that he will be making a statement at some point today. Already commentators are saying that Mr Gregan's position as head of CRSP has become untenable and some are going even further and suggesting that by failing to disclose that his daughter was an adult entertainment actress he has undermined the credibility of the whole organisation…"

An adult entertainment actress – Gregan would hate to hear her being described in those terms, thought Bruce.

With Plum, Alex and Nick all engrossed in the broadcast, the reporter continued: "Mr Gregan's supporters appear to be distancing themselves from him, CRSP and the whole anti-porn campaign. One MP, who asked not to be named, said that he was previously one of CRSP's most enthusiastic advocates but with the stench of hypocrisy now beginning to engulf the movement it was impossible for it to be taken seriously anymore…"

"Well, you've got your crucifixion," Bruce said to Plum. "Does it matter who hammers in the nails?"

The live broadcast ended and back in the studio the anchor said: "You're watching the lunchtime news and we're delighted to be joined by a representative from the trade body of the British adult entertainment industry.

"It's called BATA," Zara said. "It stands for the British Adult Trade Association."

"You must be rejoicing at this news?" the anchor said.

"We are," Zara said. "Julian Gregan thought he could single-handedly destroy an entire industry and it's wonderful to see him get his comeuppance in such a public way…"

The rest of the discussion was inaudible to Bruce as KT Green finally came to the phone. "Hello?" she said.

"Hello Rachel," Bruce said.

"You've seen it then?"

"I have."

"Have you got a television in your office?"

"We're watching it now," Bruce said. "Are there enough pitchforks and torches for you?"

"Funnily enough, it's not the story I wanted," Rachel said. "I was chasing 'head of anti-porn group has affair with porn star' scandal, which would have been much better, but you can only work with what you've got."

"What's the story behind the cover picture?"

"That's what started it all. My fiancé and I were eating in a Brighton restaurant – we have a second home down there – and they were on the next table. I didn't know who they were but they were having a right argument. They looked so incongruous together so I took a few sneaky pictures of them…"

"You take pictures of strangers in restaurants?"

"If they look interesting," she said. "That's where we get many of our best pictures from – chance meetings – and there was something about them that made me think there was a story there."

Bruce sighed.

She continued: "A couple of weeks' later we received a press release from his organisation and it came with a photograph of him. I was thinking gossip column material at this stage. You know - who was the mystery blonde seen dining with anti-porn campaigner Julian Gregan? But not long after, James showed me that copy of AMG which had her picture in it. Suddenly we had a real story."

"So she's not your long lost sister after all?"

Rachel laughed. "Can you imagine it?"

"You'll be telling me next you're not actually a sales rep."

Rachel laughed. "You are funny, Bruce, I do like that about you. Anyway, I had an 'anti-porn campaigner shares intimate meal and rows with porn star' story, which was pretty cool and right up our street, but it was clear they knew each other well. The obvious conclusion was that he was bonking her, and I wanted the full details – every cover splash earns the writer extra cash. Before I confronted him, I wanted her side of the story so I tried to find contact details for her online – and there was nothing…"

"I discovered that too," Bruce said.

"And obviously I didn't know anyone in the industry so I thought it might be worth getting in touch with you – you guys obviously had some kind of relationship with her."

"So you were using me all along?"

"It's a dog eat dog world out there."

"So it seems."

"Oh come on Bruce, did you think we were going to be a couple, dashing around the country solving mysteries together like something out of Scooby Doo?"

"I assume you had a recorder of your own when we were in his house, because you've got everything he said, word for word."

"It's a sneaky one that fits in my pocket," Rachel said. "The microphone clips onto my bra. That was why I kept adjusting my blouse."

"I didn't notice."

"That's because you are such a gentleman."

"And when you used the loo…"

"I was going through his things upstairs, yeah…"

"You do know you've destroyed Gregan, don't you?"

"Don't be sore just because I beat you to it."

"You didn't beat me to it. I wasn't going to mention the connection between them. He asked for all that to be off the record…"

"Well you're an idiot then," she said. "And you have no right to call yourself a journalist."

"No, I probably don't," he said. "What about Honey Peach? She is still missing."

"That's a shame but, come on, who cares? The story is done now, let's move on."

"Let's find a new victim eh?"

"Look, I genuinely enjoyed spending time with you, you're a decent guy, but I'm going to have to go now," Rachel said, a little irritation creeping into her voice. "As I'm sure you can appreciate, things are pretty hectic here this morning and I'm not going to have someone who reviews porn films for a living lecture me about morality."

Turning the pages of Celebs & Scandals Bruce stopped on the page that featured the Secret Diner column. "Well, at least we'll always have Da Vinci's," he said, reading the write-up from their first visit. It scored two out of ten.

Rachel laughed. "I know, I'm shameless! But every review is worth three hundred quid and I don't even have to provide a receipt."

Bruce hung up the phone and turned his attention back to the television.

"And we're joined now by someone called Milkman who claims to be Honey Peach's manager," the anchor said, as the background image segued from Julian Gregan to a vintage photograph of Benny Hill.

"I should point out to any viewers who might be confused," the anchor said. "That this is a stock photograph of a milkman, not the Milkman I am currently talking to down the line…"

He paused briefly and then added: "I'm sorry, I've now been told that is not the case and that it is in fact a picture of British comedian Benny Hill, who had a number one hit in 1971 with Ernie The Fastest Milkman in the West, which some of our older viewers may remember… Anyway, Mr Milkman, I understand that you're Honey Peach's manager?"

"Manager, mentor, trusted advisor, friend…" Milkman's crackly voice replied.

"How is this going to go down with her? Is her father just as much an embarrassment to her as she must be to her father?"

"I don't know about that but I can confirm that Honey Peach's film, Legend of the Amazon Women, is currently flying off the shelves of licensed sex shops up and down the country…"

"Hey, come on, you can't…"

"We will have duplication plants working throughout the night to keep up with the expected demand and Legend of the Amazon Women, published by Randy Milkman Enterprises, is set to be the UK's biggest selling porn video of all ti…"

"That was Honey Peach's manager apparently," the anchor said as the feed was cut. "Or maybe we should start calling her Emily Gregan. Anyway, we're going back to Brighton now. Have there been any new developments, Kirsty?"

There hadn't.

"What's your honest opinion, Bruce?" Nick asked, adjusting the volume of the television downwards. "Do you think she'll surface with all this fuss?"

Bruce shrugged.

"If she's got any sense, she will," Plum said. "This exposure will make her a fortune. How long are you going to be with the story, Bruce?"

"I've still got some transcribing to do…"

Plum considered. "I'm not sure what our angle is going to be now the cat is out of the bag. Were there any other revelations during the interview?"

"One or two," Bruce said. "Though obviously that was the biggie."

"Give me the bullet points," Plum demanded.

"We talked about what got him started – believe it or not it was seeing a softcore video in a newsagent."

Plum harrumphed. "Anything else?"

"He has actually bought porn films himself – for research purposes."

"Did you get the titles?"

Bruce shook his head.

"Make them up," Plum said. "Go into the archive and pick out the most embarrassing sounding ones. Throw a gay one in too."

"I'm not doing that," Bruce said.

"Why not? What's he going to do, sue us? Bruce, it's open season on him now, and it won't only be us attacking him. The wolves have scented blood and they will have their kill. Someone answer that bloody phone, will you?"

Alex and Nick looked bemused.

"It's not me," Alex said. "I wouldn't be caught dead with a Britney Spears song as a ringtone."

"My phone is always on silent," Nick said.

The tinny tune continued. It appeared to be coming from somewhere in the vicinity of Bruce.

"It's you, Bruce," Alex said.

Bruce removed his phone from his jacket pocket and held it up to demonstrate its mute state, but he suddenly felt very afraid. The sound was coming from his desk drawer.

"Why have you got two phones?" Alex said.

Bruce yanked open his desk drawer and there, among the cables, cigarette packets and office detritus, was a distinctive gold case with the initials HP etched into it. He removed it, hands trembling, and dropped it onto his desk.

"That's Honey Peach's phone!" Nick shouted. "She had it when we were in Marelli's. Bruce, what's going on?"

Bruce stared at the device. "This is impossible," he said, in a quivering voice. "Its battery wouldn't have lasted nearly three weeks."

"It might if it hasn't been used," Alex said.

"But I've tried to call her," Bruce said. "Loads of people have. It's never rung before."

"Did you store it somewhere else though?" Alex said.

"I haven't stored it anywhere," Bruce cried. "I promise you, I have not seen that phone since she used it in Marelli's."

"Who's calling it?" Alex wanted to know.

Bruce picked it up to look.

"Drop it Bruce," Plum commanded. "If something has happened to her then this is evidence. And I have to say, evidence that appears to be somewhat incriminating for you."

The four of them looked at each other in stunned silence for almost a minute and then Plum went into his office and grabbed his phone. "Police please," he said into the receiver.

Bruce bolted out of the office and ran down the staircase, almost knocking over an architect carrying a stack of technical drawings. As he emerged from Legal House his head was thumping, his heart was racing, his armpits were streaming. For the first time in almost thirty years, he felt like he was going to cry, out of sheer despair, as he made his way through the busy city centre streets.

Seeing his bank, he had enough presence of mind to recognise that whatever his next move would be he would need money – and there might not be a better opportunity to get it.

He tried to appear normal inside the branch as he approached the counter and handed over his debit card to the cashier. His wages were paid directly into his account in the fourth week of every month, and by the third week he usually had very little left.

"Are you okay?" the cashier asked, a look of concern on her face. "You look a bit…"

"Yes, I'm fine," he said. "Can I withdraw some cash please?"

She swiped his card through her terminal, tapped some keys and said: "How much would you like, Mr Baker?"

Bruce cringed inside as he made his request. "Can I have £100? Is there enough there?"

She laughed. "I'll say! Have you considered opening a savings account? Balances of this size really should be working for you and earning interest."

"How big is my balance?" he asked.

"Just over £12,000," she replied. "Your transfer cleared this morning."

"What transfer?"

She clicked more keys and then wrenched her monitor around so he could see the details she was pointing at. "£12,000 was transferred into your account a few days ago," she said. "The only reference I can see are the words 'honey' and 'peach' – does that mean anything to you?"

CHAPTER SIXTEEN: SATURDAY 21ST JUNE 2003

The sound of the traffic woke him from a dream in which he was being chased by rats. Relieved to escape their clutches, Bruce opened his eyes and took in his unfamiliar surroundings: anodyne wallpaper with framed prints of flowers; an antique-looking desk, with headed notepaper and complimentary branded pen; a small screen television; and an easy chair and glass coffee table near the window. People pay almost £200 a night to sleep here?

He filled his tiny kettle from the en-suite sink and turned on the television. Flicking through the channels – most of which appeared to feature people in garish clothes gurning to the camera – he eventually found a rolling news channel. The kettle boiled and Bruce drank a black coffee through an extended report about Manchester United midfielder David Beckham's transfer to Spanish team Real Madrid.

The escapism of football gave way to the harsh reality of Bruce's situation, with the next story focusing on the resignation of Julian Gregan from CRSP. The organisation faced an uncertain future, the newsreader said, following the revelation that its founder had a daughter in the adult entertainment industry. He added: "The whereabouts of Miss Gregan are currently unknown, and police are becoming increasingly concerned for her safety. They are particularly keen to speak to Bruce Baker, a former journalist from Bath, as they believe he may have information which could prove useful to their investigation. They are urging him to come forward…"

A 'former' journalist from Bath? He opened the window, which increased the volume of the traffic noise, and lay back on the king size bed. Glaring contemptuously at the No Smoking sign, he lit a cigarette and wondered what to do.

***

Bruce approached Jan's bed, his face partly hidden by a huge bouquet of flowers.

"Hello stranger," she said, surprised and delighted. "I barely recognised you without your hair. That's a bit drastic, isn't it?"

"I've taken up competitive swimming," Bruce said, rubbing his newly shaved head with his left hand. "And I was advised that this would reduce drag. Not sure it's going to go down too well with the chicks though."

"I'm sure you won't get any fewer chicks than you did before," she said.

"Is it fewer or less chicks? Anyway, these are for you," he said, handing the bouquet to her.

"Oh Bruce, they are lovely," Jan said, sitting up in bed. "I'd better ask for a vase. To what do I owe this pleasure?"

"You have obviously heard the news?"

"About our friend Mr Gregan? Impossible to avoid it. The British media love to report on the bursting of a balloon, especially if they are the ones who inflated it."

"And have you also heard that the police are 'particularly keen' to speak to me?"

"I did – Bruce Baker, the vital witness in the story that everybody is talking about. You might be able to get a book deal out of this. Let me know if you need a ghost writer."

"You're more cheerful today than Tuesday," he said, drawing the curtain around her bed in an attempt to stay out of the sight of the other patients.

"Que sera sera," she shrugged, then pointing at the curtain, added: "Are you about to examine me?"

"Sh!" he replied, putting a finger to his lips.

"Were the police impressed with all your investigative work into the disappearance of Honey Peach?"

"I haven't spoken to them yet."

"Why not?" Jan said.

"That's a long and winding road of a story."

Jan gestured at her surroundings. "I'm not going anywhere."

"Neither am I now they've towed my car away."

"Who has towed your car away?"

"For reasons that I'd rather not go into, I caught a taxi home yesterday and when I arrived at my flat the police were already inside, turning the place over, and they were also loading the Mazda onto a tow truck."

"Don't tell me you're a suspect?" Jan said, a look of concern on her face.

"That would appear to be the case."

Jan stared at him. "Are you joking?"

He shook his head as he pulled the visitor's chair closer to her bed. "I wish I was."

"Oh Bruce, that's ridiculous," Jan said.

"That's what I would have said a couple of days ago too."

Jan continued to stare at him. "What did you do, when you arrived at your flat?"

"I told the taxi driver that I'd forgotten something in the office and to take me back into town. I bought a pair of clippers for my hair and booked myself into the Hicks Hotel, under a false name."

"The Hicks Hotel? Won the lottery, have you?"

"Believe me, money is currently the least of my worries," Bruce said, and went on to explain about the bank transfer.

Jan looked worried.

"There's more," Bruce said. "Her phone was found in my desk, and everybody saw it."

"Oh Bruce…"

"And I also found her pendant," he said, removing the item of jewellery from his pocket and showing it to her.

Jan took it from him and examined it. "It might not be the same one – these charms can be bought anywhere – but it certainly looks like hers. Where did you find it?"

"That was also in my desk, though nobody saw me take it out."

"You've got to tell the police about all this," Jan said, gently clasping his arm.

"I can't," he said. "Because I might have done it."

"Done what?"

"I don't know – whatever has been done to her. Remember I said I woke up on the street the next morning, after we all went out?"

"Yes but…"

"I can't account for my actions," he said, rubbing the wound on the side of his head.

Jan peered at Bruce's injury. "This is a fresh cut," she said. "When did this happen?"

"Do you remember getting an email from Honey Peach a couple of days before she came across on the Monday for the interview?"

Jan pouted as she thought. "It doesn't ring a bell. But I don't remember much at all about what happened before the accident. That's normal, apparently."

"I might be having some kind of breakdown," he said, rubbing his eyes.

"What did this email say?"

"She told you that she was afraid of being left alone with me because she thought I was obsessed with her."

Jan looked mystified. "I can't believe she would have said that."

"She did," Bruce said, holding his head in his hands. "I've read the mail on your machine. And yes, I checked the date stamp."

Jan reached across to her bedside table to press the button that summoned the nurse. "I'd better get a vase for these flowers," she said. As she stretched across, the baggy hospital gown flapped open, revealing a glimpse of the flesh at the top of her arm.

"I didn't know you had a tattoo," he said.

Embarrassed, she retracted her arm. "Now you know why I always wear long-sleeved tops."

"What is it?"

"Does it matter? When I told my husband I was thinking about getting a tattoo he said he'd never go near me again if I did – so that sealed the deal."

"You're married?" Bruce gasped, the shock momentarily making him forget his own situation.

"I was. Very briefly. We didn't stay together long."

Bruce stared at Jan. "I know so little about you."

The curtain was suddenly swooshed aside by a sour-faced nurse. "You can't be here outside visiting hours," she barked at Bruce.

***

Bruce kept his finger pressed on the bell continuously. Eventually he was rewarded when Nick, dressed in just a pair of boxer shorts, opened the door.

"You've already missed half the day," Bruce said, brushing past him and slamming the front door behind him.

"Do come in," Nick said, but Bruce had already cleared the narrow hall, clambering around a bright orange rubber dinghy that was leaning against the wall, and dashed into the ground floor flat's tiny lounge.

"Mate, what the hell have you done to your hair?" Nick said. "You look like a convict. You're not on the run from the police are you?"

Bruce said nothing, staring at Nick with a frightened look in his eyes.

"Oh mate, that was a joke," Nick said. "I didn't for one minute think you actually were…"

"Can you help me?" Bruce said. "I've got no one else to turn to who I can trust. Even Jan…"

"Jan?"

"I went to see her this morning and told her where I was staying…"

"Where are you staying?"

"At a hotel in the city centre – or I was. She was the only person I told, and by the time I walked back into town the police were waiting in the lobby. Jan was the only person who knew I was there."

"They might have been there for something else..."

"One of them was holding a picture of me and showing it to the receptionist."

"Wow, I never thought Jan would betray you," Nick said, shaking his head. "You two were always so close..."

"I don't know what I'm going to do," Bruce said, fumbling for his cigarettes. "Mind if I smoke?"

"Go ahead," Nick said. "You're safe here at least, while we decide what's the best thing for you to do."

"What happened in the office, after Plum called the police?"

"Can I get you a drink? Tea, coffee, something stronger?"

"Coffee would be fine," Bruce said, looking around the shabby lounge. Besides the stained fabric sofa he was sat on, a large leather chair was positioned at an angle in front of the television, which was perched on top of a black ash TV stand which also housed a Sony PS2 games console and two controllers. A matching black ash computer desk on the other side of the room contained several computer tower units, their lights constantly flickering, with dozens of coloured cables snaking between them. A single shelf was fixed to the wall, stacked with music CDs and DVD cases, which could have been films or PlayStation games.

"They spent a bit of time with each of us," Nick said, walking out into the small kitchen area and plugging his kettle in, which immediately made a boiling noise.

"Nice TV," Bruce said. "How wide is the screen?"

Nick replied but his words were muffled by the sound of the boiling kettle.

"What did you just say?" Bruce said, following him into the kitchen. "Bloody hell, that's a big chest freezer."

"It came with the flat," Nick said. "It's not mine, it's the landlord's."

Bruce lifted the freezer lid. The cabinet's sides were caked with thick ice and it contained a few boxed pizzas and a couple of ready meals for one. "Now that is a bachelor's freezer," Bruce said, closing the lid. "Maybe I should get one when..."

"They cost a lot to run," Nick said, handing Bruce a mug of black coffee. "I'd rather have one of those upright ones which also have a fridge built in."

"What were you saying, about what happened in the office?" Bruce said, noticing that the mug he had been given wasn't particularly clean.

"Yeah, like I said, the police just asked Plum, Alex and me some questions about you and Honey Peach," Nick said, walking back into the lounge.

"It's funny how the police are suddenly interested in her disappearance now she's been in the news," Bruce said as he followed him. "What did you tell them?"

"The truth – that you had been trying to find her, with her sister, though as we all now know, it wasn't actually her sister…"

"Did they ask about the phone?"

"Plum had already handed that over. They asked if it was hers and I said I couldn't be sure – I said it looked like it but there may be thousands out there like it."

"It must be hers," Bruce said, surreptitiously checking the pendant was still in his pocket. "Why else would it be in my desk?"

"I don't know," Nick said. "But it doesn't necessarily mean…"

"That I had something to do with her going missing?"

Nick stared at Bruce. "Tell me the truth, Bruce," he urged. "Did you?"

"I honestly don't know," Bruce said.

"Since you had that bang on the head…"

"Yes, exactly," Bruce said. "Since I had that bang, things have been a little crazy."

"Could you have tried it on with her, got rejected and then lashed out?"

"Do you honestly think I would do that?" Bruce said. "That would never have happened, no matter how drunk I was – and I wasn't actually drunk…"

"But we both saw that email to Jan, from Honey Peach…"

"Did you mention it to them?"

"I didn't," Nick said. "Maybe I should have but I didn't, out of loyalty to you…"

Bruce brightened. "Then maybe I'm not completely screwed."

"They said they would be coming back on Monday but that email doesn't prove anything on its own though, does it? It just said that she was afraid of being left alone with you because she thought you were obsessed with her."

Bruce stared at Nick. "When you put it like that, I feel practically exonerated."

"I know it sounds bad – given what's happened – but it doesn't necessarily implicate you in her disappearance, does it?" Nick said, taking his empty coffee mug into the kitchen. "I mean, I bet she felt like that about loads of blokes."

Bruce stood up and stared at Nick's CDs. They were all by artists he'd never heard of but the PlayStation games included Grand Theft Auto: Vice City, The Getaway, Tom Clancy's Ghost Recon, James Bond Nightfire, FIFA 2003 and Medal of Honor: Frontline.

"That's an impressive games collection," Bruce said. "It must have cost you a fortune."

"What else am I going to spend my money on?" Nick said as he came back into the lounge. "I'm a single bloke and I've got no one telling me what I can and can't do..."

"Is Jan's computer still in the office?" Bruce said.

Nick nodded. "They took your machine away for forensic examination but Jan's is still there. And the email is on her machine."

Bruce suddenly slammed his half-full cup down on Nick's computer desk, causing tiny droplets to splash the computer cases. "I need to speak to Plum," he said.

***

The man in the bobble hat and pungent coat was fully occupying the Marelli's restaurant host. His shouts of 'I've got just as much right to eat in here as they have, my money is just as good as theirs' were also attracting the attention of some of the Saturday diners, who tutted to each other over their scallops. In hushed tones the host explained that a reservation was required, and that the restaurant was fully booked for the foreseeable future, but that there were plenty of other eating establishments in the city centre where he would be welcomed...

The commotion allowed Bruce to walk in unchallenged and sidle into the chair opposite Plum, who was sat alone at his favourite table in the first floor window, watching the Saturday crowds swarming through the streets below from his elevated position. Plum raised his head, a gesture that usually resulted in an attentive waiter magically materialising, but with two of them now assisting the host it went unacknowledged. Well they can forget about a tip on this occasion...

"Plum, you've got to listen to me," Bruce said, his arm accidentally knocking over an empty water glass and an oversized salt cellar.

"Let me stop you right there," Plum said, raising his index finger in the air. "I haven't got to do anything."

"I need help," Bruce said.

"Now there I am in complete agreement with you," Plum said. "You certainly need help. With the benefit of hindsight, it's clear that your undiagnosed psychosis would manifest itself in some way but for it to culminate in such a tragic..."

"I don't believe that I had anything to do with her disappearance," Bruce said.

"You 'don't believe' it? If you were innocent you would know damn well that you had nothing to do with it. By saying that, you are demonstrating that you think you could have been involved. And by the way, your new haircut is dreadful. You have the sort of face that requires surrounding hair for it to be palatable."

Bruce poured a glass of water, his hands trembling slightly. "All I can remember is that I was standing outside the pub, with Jan, Nick and Honey Peach. Next thing I knew it was morning and I was lying in a shop doorway..."

"That's pretty incriminating in itself, don't you think?" Plum said. "Amnesia is invariably trotted out as an excuse by solicitors when their clients cannot explain something away. My client is suffering from memory loss, m'lud, but that doesn't mean he is guilty."

"Someone attacked me."

"Did they?" Plum said, casually buttering a small brown bread roll.

"What do you mean?"

"Did Jan see anyone attack you? Did Nick see anyone attack you? Did anyone see anyone attack you? Were there any witnesses at all to this alleged attack?"

"There were these two blokes who..."

"I must say, if I was attacked the first thing I would do is report it to the police, but you didn't do that, did you?"

"No but..."

Plum shrugged. "There you go then," he said, ripping off a portion of the bread.

"You can't think I'm involved in all this," Bruce said.

"Of course you are involved," Plum replied as his mouth enveloped the bread. "You were one of – if not the – last person to see Honey Peach alive..."

"We've known each other for a long time," Bruce said, his hand reaching out imploringly across the table to Plum's. "You can't believe I'm capable of..."

Plum pulled his hand away, avoiding contact. "I didn't think you were capable of passing yourself off as a representative of Her Majesty's Customs and Excise and fraudulently removing commercially sensitive documents," he said. "I didn't think you were capable of blackmailing a little old lady into giving up a confidential computer password by threatening her with prison..."

"I was trying to find out what had happened to..."

"And I certainly didn't think you were capable of falsely imprisoning someone in my boardroom and attacking them with one of my plants..."

"Milkman is the key in all this..."

"But Bruce, her phone was found in your desk. How do you explain that?"

"I can't, obviously..." Bruce wilted in the chair.

"Don't get comfortable," Plum said. "As soon as they've finished with that vagrant I am going to ask them to call the police."

"What would I have done with her body?" Bruce said.

"Far be it from me to speculate but it very much looks like you would have transported it to some destination, as yet unknown, in your car," Plum said, raising his finger in the air to summon the waiter.

"Why do you say that?" Bruce said.

Plum lowered his voice and leaned forward. "Because I understand – though this is unofficial and totally off the record at this moment in time, so I will deny ever saying it – that there were long blonde hairs discovered in the passenger seat of your Mazda."

Bruce felt his insides turn over. "In my car?"

"Indeed," Plum said. "It's not looking good for you, is it?"

Out of the corner of his eye Bruce could see a waiter approaching, belatedly responding to Plum's signal. Bruce stood up, moved around the table so he was next to Plum, and grabbed his arm: "Plum, please don't do this..."

Plum attempted to swat him away, leaning backwards on his chair to distance himself from Bruce, but Bruce yanked his arm even harder. "Let go of me, Bruce..."

"I need you to believe me..." Bruce pleaded.

"You're making a complete arse of yourself," Plum yelled, raising his foot in an attempt to kick Bruce away, conscious that he was now the centre of attention. "Have some dignity, man!"

Plum's portly body was now balanced precariously on just the two back legs of the chair. The waiter was standing patiently by the table, like a blinking cursor awaiting a command. He coughed: "Is everything alright, sir?"

Plum could feel himself starting to tip and his chubby arm tried to grab Bruce, to stop himself falling backwards. But Bruce still held Plum's other arm, so the two of them toppled over. Plum's dangling legs kicked the underside of the table, propelling cutlery, condiments and glasses several inches into the air. The waiter made an attempt at grabbing the bottle of wine but instead he knocked it sideways, scattering a shower of purple liquid in the direction of the next table – two elderly ladies who screamed in protest.

Bruce found himself lying on top of Plum, their faces – flecked with smoked haddock and leek risotto – just inches apart. Despite being winded, Plum pushed Bruce, who slowly rolled off him and landed on his back.

"Call the police!" Plum wheezed at the waiter. "This man is wanted for questioning."

"Don't do this, Plum," Bruce pleaded.

Raising himself up onto his elbow, Plum said to the still prostrate Bruce: "It goes without saying that you are sacked."

Bruce groaned.

"But at least you won't have to worry about keeping a roof over your head or fret about where your next meal is coming from," Plum said. "And I'm sure you will make plenty of new friends too…"

Bruce got to his feet. He looked across at the panting figure of Plum, who was being helped up by the struggling waiter, and sauntered out of the restaurant. An elderly gentleman with bushy white whiskers had just walked in through the entrance and he frowned disapprovingly at Bruce.

"I can recommend the haddock," Bruce said, licking flecks of yellow sauce from the back of his hand.

CHAPTER SEVENTEEN: SUNDAY 22ND JUNE 2003

For the second successive morning, Bruce woke up in a hotel room designed for tourists. This room was almost identical to the one from yesterday, apart from boasting two single beds instead of a double. This time it wasn't the sound of traffic acting as an alarm call though, it was the thunderous snoring of Nosh, curled into the foetal position on the other bed. Nosh had kicked off his quilt during the night, and his sinewy body, covered only by a grubby white pair of underpants, shook in time with his frenzied exhalations.

After acting as a distraction at Marelli's, Nosh's next task for Bruce had been to book a room at a city centre hotel. In retrospect, Bruce wished he had specified a single room and made it quite clear that Nosh's presence was not required, but he was in no position to complain after everything his new friend had done for him.

As Bruce sat up he noticed that the cabinet alongside Nosh's bed had six empty miniatures from the mini bar lined up on it. Bruce picked up the price list and totted up the additional charge that would be levied for the room. Nosh raised one of his skinny legs a few inches into the air and farted.

Bruce showered, dressed and turned on the television to drown out the snoring. He made a coffee, opened the window in order to diffuse the rather ripe aroma of Nosh, and lay back on the bed, deep in thought.

He walked across to the desk and wrote on the hotel's headed notepaper: 'Thanks for your help. I am leaving you £400, which will be enough to pay for the room and the drinks plus allow you to buy a new hat and coat'. Bruce counted out the cash and placed the note on top, using an unopened bottle of carbonated water from the mini bar as a paperweight.

Bruce crept out into the corridor and made his way down to the hotel's reception area. He pulled Nosh's bobble hat down and the collar of his thick coat up and, looking only at the floor, he walked out into the sunny streets of Bath.

The distant sound of bells, calling parishioners to church, battled with the hum of mechanical sweepers and vacuum litter collectors attacking the Saturday night detritus of burger wrappers, cigarette butts and empty beer bottles. Bath's streets are cleaned several times a day, seven days a week, and as Bruce returned a 'good morning' to a worker in a hi-visibility vest and watched another watering one of the city's many flower baskets, he suddenly felt a lump in his throat.

After handing over so much cash to Nosh, Bruce thought it prudent to obtain more. Even if it wasn't actually his. He inserted his debit card at his bank's ATM and tapped in his PIN. A few seconds passed and a message flashed on the screen. Instead of the usual polite question asking him about his intentions, the text bluntly informed him that his card was being retained and that he should contact his branch for further information.

He walked away, reasoning that he had no real grounds for complaint and that his wages, which were paid in electronically during the fourth week of the month, would cover what he had already withdrawn.

Deep in thought, he continued walking, up through Queen Square, along the bustling Royal Avenue where the lawns either side were filling up with dog walkers, joggers, old ladies feeding squirrels and divorced fathers playing football with their weekend sons. Two youths occupied the bandstand on the south side, strumming acoustic guitars, while the north side lawn which led to Royal Crescent was pock marked with picnickers and tourists taking photographs of each other.

He followed Royal Avenue, across Marlborough Lane, into Royal Victoria Park and stopped just inside the entrance, joining an elderly gentleman on a bench overlooking the obelisk dedicated to the monarch who gave the park its name.

"Lovely day," the man said, tipping his straw boater to Bruce.

"Bath is a lovely place," Bruce replied, and he felt like crying as he said it.

The man said something else but Bruce didn't hear it as his phone rang. Bruce removed the handset from his pocket and stared at the caller display. It continued to ring, much to the old man's annoyance. Bruce recognised the number and answered the call.

"Is that Britain's Most Wanted?" the caller said.

"Hello Rachel," Bruce said.

"Actually Rachel is my mother's name…"

"Is this the same terminally ill mother you were telling me about previously? I would have thought she would have popped her clogs by now."

The old man, his face aghast at what he was hearing, stood up and limped off in disgust in search of a bench with a better class of Sunday morning sitting companion.

"You do what you've got to do to get the story," Rachel said. "It's a dog eat dog world."

"So I understand," Bruce said. "Is there a point to this call? If so, can I suggest you get to it because my battery is about to die."

"I can imagine your phone has been red hot over the last couple of days."

"Not really," Bruce said. "You are one of a select few who has my number. How can I help you?"

"It's more about how I can help you," she said.

"And how do you propose to do that?"

"By getting you in next week's magazine," Rachel said. "I want to tell your story."

"You really are all heart, aren't you?" Bruce replied. "Not content with stringing me along with a cock and bull tale about a missing sister and a dying mother, leading me into a life of crime..."

"Life of crime?"

"Breaking and entering, impersonating an HMCE officer..."

"Bruce, that was investigative reporting..."

"Stealing the story from under me..."

"It was my story first..."

"Handing Gregan to the mob on a silver platter, trussed up with an apple in his mouth – while I end up as a suspect..."

"That's why you need to talk to me," Rachel said. "You're the prime suspect. I've been thinking about how I can help you – I do owe you, I'm obviously aware of that – and the best way is to get your side of the story across and set the record straight before they bang you up and restrict your access to the media."

"You know my side of the story," Bruce said. "You were there for most of it."

"I need to know all the details about everything else you got up to and how you ended up in this position."

"I was trying to help you," Bruce said, rather loudly. "That's how I ended up in this position."

"Oh bless you, Bruce. Look, I promise I will treat you sympathetically and I'll even let you see the piece before it goes to print..."

Bruce smiled at that one. "So you don't think I had anything to do with it?"

"Of course not!" Rachel snorted.

"But what about sub judice?"

"You really need to get up to date with the current law and journalism," Rachel said testily. "That went out of the window in 1981 following the introduction of the Contempt of Court Act. Do you know about this?"

"Remind me - which one is that?"

"The one that states that a media report can only prejudice an active case – as in when there has been an arrest or a warrant has been issued. Unless you are going to tell me differently, my understanding is that the police would just like to speak to you, and that no formal charges have been made yet."

"I wouldn't know, I've been staying in hotels for the last…"

"You've been staying with friends," Rachel corrected him. "Perfectly understandable due to the stress brought on by the situation you have been put in. And even if they do charge you, that will take a couple of days to process and we'll be on the newsstands a week tomorrow. You've seen how quickly we can move."

"But surely your legal department…"

"Everyone in the legal team of Celebs & Scandals has big balls," Rachel said. "That's why we're so successful – we get the stories no one else dares to."

"You sound like a renegade bunch of action heroes."

"Bruce, don't do this for me, do it for yourself."

Bruce looked at his phone's flashing battery indicator. "When were you thinking of?"

"How about right now?" Rachel said. "Unless you've got a more pressing engagement, I can be on the next train into Bath."

Bruce paused for a few seconds. "Okay," he said.

"Great! Where shall I meet you? In the cellar bar at Marelli's?"

"No," he said, looking around. "Meet me at the entrance to Vicky Park…"

"What's that?"

"Royal Victoria Park, you can't miss it – there are directions at the station. There is a large obelisk set just inside the main entrance to the park, with benches around it. I will be on one of them."

"Okay, I'll be there by three…" she said, before the battery in Bruce's phone finally expired.

***

As he watched her enter the park, Bruce's stomach did not do a little flip. He no longer had a crush on her. She was dressed in cropped blue jeans and a simple white blouse and she was sporting the same oversized sunglasses she wore in Da Vinci's. She was lugging what looked to be a heavy canvas bag over her shoulder. She walked up to the monument and read the inscription to check she was in the right place, glanced at her watch to confirm she was on time, and then stopped to take in her surroundings.

Wearing Nosh's overcoat and bobble hat, Bruce lay sprawled on the grass, just yards away from Rachel. He had collected several empty cider cans from one of the bins and arranged them in a little pile so that they hid his face from her but still allowed him to observe everything she did. Amongst the teeming Sunday crowds of families heading for the adventure playground, crazy golf and botanical gardens, he was just a shadow on the ground.

Rachel walked slowly around the monument several times and eventually sat on the ornate stone wall that surrounded it. An elderly lady was telling her granddaughter that the park was named after the eleven-year-old princess who opened it in 1830 but the girl, who was probably about the same age, just looked bored. She wanted an ice-cream, she said loudly.

Rachel delved into her bag and brought out a compact. After checking her eye makeup and applying lip gloss she retrieved her phone and stared at the screen for a few seconds. Like an experienced store detective, she carried out these routine tasks while simultaneously sizing up everyone who entered and left the park.

Stabbing her phone keypad in frustration, she made a call. After a few seconds she left a message: "Bruce, where the bloody hell are you? I'm at the entrance to the park, where you told me to be, and I've been here almost twenty minutes. Ring me when you get this."

Bruce, whose phone battery was now completely flat, grabbed a can and rolled over on the grass, manoeuvring himself closer to her. The movement attracted her attention and she stared at him. He settled himself into a prone position, head resting on the outstretched arm that held the can, and mumbled obscenities in a West Country accent. She wrinkled her nose in disgust and turned away.

After a further ten minutes she made another call, and she sounded even more frustrated this time: "Bob, it looks like he's a no show," she said. "I've been waiting almost thirty minutes and there is absolutely no sign of him. I've tried ringing him but his phone goes straight to voicemail. I know... I know... And the worst of it is I persuaded Gerry to give up his Sunday too. He's watching me from just outside the gates so he could pap the meeting..."

Bruce crawled a little closer to her. Should he reveal himself?

"Well I can only give him a few more minutes," Rachel said. "The police agreed to give me a half hour with him before they picked him up but if he doesn't show soon they'll be stood down – and there's no way that I'm going to meet him without backup."

That answers that question then, Bruce thought.

She waited a further ten minutes, during which she made notes in a small pad, left an additional message for Bruce and finally called Bob again. "No sign of him," she said. "It was worth a punt but still keep the cover free... I've already started jotting down my story about being on the run with him."

Rachel stood up, looked around one more time and then walked back to the park's entrance. She shrugged at a trendy looking guy, who Bruce assumed was Gerry – a photographer, judging by the SLR with telephoto zoom lens dangling around his neck – and the two of them marched off in the direction of the station.

***

One of the many benefits Legal House tenants enjoy is receptionist and secretarial support during office hours. Access to the building is also offered 24/7, with night porters manning the reception desk in shifts from 6.00pm until 1.00am and from 1.00am until 8.00am. According to the prospectus, the provision of a night porter enhances the building's security, permits cleaning and routine maintenance to be performed with the minimum disruption to tenants and also allows deliveries and collections to be made at any time.

On weekends there is also a team of Saturday and Sunday porters, and it was Pete the Sweet who Bruce wanted to catch before his shift ended. A retired policeman, Pete spent his shift reading large print detective novels and eating boiled sweets, and he had a particular fondness for Yorkshire Mixture.

Bruce bought a large bag from the newsagents on the corner and asked the assistant if he could have plenty of twenty pence pieces in his change. Armed with these, he went to the public telephone box at the end of the street and spent the next half hour making calls to Plum's home number. Every time Plum answered, Bruce would wait a few seconds and then hang up. After the eighth time this had happened, Plum stopped answering his phone.

Bruce sprinted the short distance to Legal House and rapped on the door. He could hear Pete grumbling as he put down his book, trudged across the reception area and put his eye up to the peephole.

"What do you want, Bruce?" Pete asked.

"Can you open up One East for me please?" Bruce said. "We're on deadline and I've got a piece to write before tomorrow."

Pete opened the door. "I can't let you up there without the permission of the keyholder, you know that," he said.

"I know," Bruce said. "Ring Plum for confirmation. I'm pretty sure he's out and about today so you may have to try his mobile."

"Okay," Pete said, returning to the desk and opening the large diary that contained all the keyholders' contact details.

"I'll wait outside and have a smoke while you're doing that," Bruce said. He handed over the bag of sweets and added: "Oh and I thought you might like these."

Pete thanked him and Bruce let himself out.

Bruce put his ear to the door and heard Pete tap in Plum's landline number. Straining, Bruce could just about hear the sound of Plum's phone ringing, unanswered. After letting it ring for almost a minute, Pete hung up and called the secondary number listed for Plum.

The phone in Bruce's jacket burst into life, emitting a tinny version of the theme from Indiana Jones.

"Yes," Bruce said, in his fruitiest voice.

"Mr Harvey, I've got one of your lads here," Pete said. "Young Bruce said he wants access to your office because you're on deadline."

"That's quite correct Pete," Bruce drawled. "And when you go off shift make sure that he's not disturbed by your replacement, will you? The lazy bugger doesn't need much of an excuse to down tools…"

"Right you are, Mr Harvey," Pete said. "So it's okay for him to stay here indefinitely then?"

"Absolutely," Bruce said.

"I'll make a note of that. Are you enjoying the sunshine today, Mr Harvey?"

"Yes thank you, Pete," Bruce said.

"I don't get to see much of it, stuck inside…"

"Is there anything else?" Bruce said, as impatiently as Plum would have.

There wasn't and Pete shuffled out from behind the reception desk and opened Legal House's front door. "Mr Harvey says that's fine," he said to Bruce. "If you'd like to follow me, I will open up for you."

It took several minutes for Pete to ascend the stairs and out of courtesy Bruce walked up at the same laborious pace. Normally he would either vault up the stairs two at a time or crawl up, head heavy with hangover, but now, for the first time, he actually looked at the artwork that adorned the walls; vintage prints of long forgotten cricket and rugby teams, lined up on benches like soldiers. The men, sporting tasselled caps and matching moustaches, glared at the photographer, as if daring him to try taking their silver cups.

Bruce saw One East in a new light too. It was no longer the place where he would be spending eight hours of each day. Even though he had turned up for work as normal on Friday, which was just the day before yesterday, he now felt disconnected from it, like that time he'd revisited his primary school as an adult. As the fluorescent tubes flashed on, he noticed that someone had moved the water cooler a few feet to the left – why would they do that? The cable was now a health and safety hazard, coiled like a snake on the carpet.

He walked across to his desk. It looked empty without his computer and everything in his drawer had been removed. Bruce Baker has left the building, it said. On Nick's desk were grey scale printouts of his Blowup Babes Beauty Parade feature, with red felt pen suggestions from Plum on how the layout could be improved. In a nutshell, by removing elements. One of Nick's downfalls as a graphic designer was his insistence on using every tool in his toolbox.

The printout of the layout looked good, to be fair. It featured pictures of the dolls sunbathing on Weston-super-Mare beach and floating on their backs in the sea. Bruce smiled as he saw that Nick had given top marks to the inflatable Honey Peach doll – which looked absolutely nothing like her.

The office had never been so quiet but Bruce could still hear something humming. Had someone left their computer on? Alex hadn't. Nick hadn't – oh actually he had, his laptop's lid was closed but its fan was whirring. Bruce lifted the lid and the screen burst into life. It demanded a password so he closed it again. It was Jan's machine he was here for, and he was grateful she had never used password protection. He fired it up and availed himself of the newly positioned water cooler while it went through its start-up sequence.

He wandered across to Plum's office and gently pushed the glass door. It was locked. That was a shame. He would have taken great delight in polishing off a bottle or two of Plum's stash of Merlot.

He opened the door to the archive. Walking in, he gazed at the rows and rows of films, all featuring variations on the same thing, and laughed at the absurdity of someone being employed to 'review' complete strangers performing the sex act. What would his mother have said if she'd lived long enough to see the career path he took?

On the third shelf down his eyes were drawn to a gap. Volumes one to six of California Cum Whores were missing. Looking a little closer at the rows, he also noticed that there were some cases without artwork. He pulled one out. It was just an empty DVD case. The second one he pulled was the same, and the third. Oh well, it wasn't his problem anymore if the cleaner was stealing the samples and replacing them with blank cases to hide the gaps.

Emerging from the archive, he slumped into Jan's chair. He couldn't recall ever seeing the office from this vantage point before, which made him smile, and he noticed that her chair seemed more comfortable than his. No doubt several years' exposure to his overweight arse had compressed the padding in his seat.

Bruce opened Jan's mail program. With messages after her accident being routed to Alex, the one he was interested in was still close to the top. He stared at the sender's name and clicked on it to read it again. Why would Honey Peach say those things, if they weren't true?

His recent adventures danced through his mind. It felt like he had packed more living into the last three weeks than the last three years – ten years, even. He smiled at the exhilarating memory of running across the Brighton gardens with Rachel, bluffing his way into Milkman's office, hiding in Honey Peach's wardrobe... But there had also been the disturbing incidents, such as finding the pendant and Honey Peach's phone in his drawer, the bank transfer from her account to his and, of course, the contents of this email to Jan. Add in his bunch of keys suddenly sprouting one for his desk drawer, and news stories he had written disappearing, and the result was... what exactly? Someone who should be locked up? After the plant incident in the boardroom with Milkman, quite possibly.

He read Honey Peach's email again, aloud this time, and attempted an impression of her voice: "Please don't leave me alone with Bruce... I think he's obsessed with me... Last time I was over he asked me out and gave me a pendant and he asked me to wear it every day..."

Neither his impression nor those words sounded like her.

"When were you last over?" Bruce said to Jan's monitor. "It must have been back in May when you signed some of your posters for competition prizes. You were only in the office a few minutes and you didn't even speak to me, so when would I have asked you out? And the first time I saw that pendant was in Marelli's – I wouldn't even know where to buy such a thing."

It was still in his trouser pocket. He tossed it onto the desk and stared at it. He was here to delete the incriminating mail but reading it again made him angry. He clicked on Reply and typed 'None of this is true' and then hit Send.

Across the office, an incoming mail alert bonged on Nick's laptop a few seconds later. Intrigued, Bruce clicked on the message again and replied once more. This time he typed 'You are a liar', and for the second time, Nick's laptop let him know it had received a new message.

He wandered across and lifted the laptop's lid. He stared at the invitation to input a password. Then he opened Nick's desk drawer and removed the CD labelled Emergency Boot Disc.

CHAPTER EIGHTEEN: MONDAY 23RD JUNE 2003

The expression on Nick's face suggested he was surprised to find the office door unlocked and the lights already on.

"Hello?" Nick called out. "Plum?"

"I didn't know you were a keyholder," Bruce said, swivelling dramatically in Jan's chair, like a villain in a James Bond film.

"Bloody hell mate, what are you doing here?" Nick said. "My flat's only a few minutes away so I can be here pretty fast if there's a burglary or something."

"I wish I'd known that Saturday," Bruce said. "It would have saved me quite a bit of time – but you probably wouldn't have opened up the office for me, would you?"

"What's going on?" Nick said, looking around and ignoring the question. "How come you are here?"

"Can I get you a drink?" Bruce said, walking to the water cooler. "I promise I won't drop any roofies into it."

Nick stared at Bruce. "Mate, what are you talking about?"

"That's what you used, wasn't it? One or two crushed tablets of Rohypnol? I understand it dissolves very quickly, certainly in the time it takes to walk from the bar to the corner table in Marelli's. It's quite bitter though, so for it to be undetectable to the victim you'd really have to add it to something that already has a vile taste."

Nick ignored Bruce. He slowly walked to the far side of the office and gazed through the glass doors of Plum's office and then the boardroom. After establishing that they were both locked and empty, he walked back and closed the door that leads out from One East to the third floor landing of Legal House.

Bruce continued: "You almost had me believing that I might have been involved in her disappearance but, yet again, you overegged the pudding. You gilded the lily. You... actually I can't think of a third example but you get the picture. If you'd stopped at just planting her phone in my desk, that would have probably been enough – not just for the police but for me too – but you added too many other elements."

Nick tensed the muscles in his burly arms. He glared at Bruce but said nothing.

"I'm thinking of the bank transfer in particular," Bruce said. "I wouldn't have had a clue how to do that."

Nick sat down at his desk and picked up his phone. "Dee, can you call the police, please? We've got an intruder in the building and it happens to be someone they want to talk to in connection with a missing person."

"They'll probably take about twenty minutes to get here," Bruce said. "So do you mind if we continue chatting?"

Nick patrolled the perimeter of the office, staring at the skirting boards where all the electrical sockets were located. He yanked one thick black plug out and traced the cable back to its point of origin – a mini disc recorder hidden under Jan's desk. Smiling, Nick popped the lid and removed the recordable disc.

Bruce tried to grab it but Nick effortlessly swatted him away. Bruce went sprawling across the office, his momentum causing him to tumble into the desk and chair that he formerly occupied, before collapsing in a heap on the floor.

Nick held the disc in the palm of his hand for a couple of seconds, ensuring Bruce could see what he was doing, and then closed his fist around it, crushing the plastic case into splinters. Grabbing a pair of heavy duty scissors from his desk drawer he then removed the thin metal disc from the centre and cut it into fragments. He scooped the fragments into his hand, walked across to the front window and yanked it open. Smiling, he threw the tiny shards of plastic and aluminium up into the air and they shimmered like hi-tech confetti in the early morning sun, before dispersing with the breeze into the streets below.

"That's going to confuse the pigeons," Bruce said from his position on the floor. "Why are you so quiet today, Nick?"

Nick pulled the front window closed and then opened the rear one that overlooked the courtyard, before returning to examining the electrical sockets. "Because I don't know what you're talking about, Bruce," he said.

Bruce rose unsteadily to his feet. "I think you do, Nick. I must say that planting the pendant was a good ploy, because no one else knew about it apart from me. That was pretty effective at getting me doubting myself. The email to Jan from Honey Peach was clever as well. How did you get it to arrive in the past?"

Nick paused from his task to stare at Bruce.

Bruce continued: "I couldn't figure that out so I spent hours online last night and in the end I joined a couple of forums. Eventually an IT engineer told me about a firm he once worked at which used a separate server for routing its chargeable invoices through. Its internal clock was set for fourteen days previously, so it made the finance manager's job a lot easier when he chased for payment – the client had already had the invoice two weeks. Highly illegal, apparently. Hey, now I think about it, wasn't that a server I saw in your flat?"

"Bruce mate, you should listen to yourself, you sound like a madman," Nick said. "It looks to me like you have invented all these conspiracy theories to deflect attention away from your own guilt. It wasn't that long ago you told me you thought Spaghetti had killed her. Then you very publicly accused Milkman of doing it. Do you remember that? When you attacked him in the boardroom with a plant?"

"I remember it very well," Bruce said. "Not my finest hour, if I'm honest."

"Remind me – was that before or after you gained entry to his office, removed confidential documents and threatened his personal assistant?"

"That was after," Bruce said. "And I'm sure she wouldn't mind me pointing out that she's more of a part time receptionist than a PA. She's not even on the books."

"And didn't you break into Honey Peach's house in Brighton and steal her laptop?"

"You know very well that I did," Bruce replied. "But it was no help to me because there was nothing on it…"

"Life's a bitch, ain't it?"

"Or so I thought," Bruce continued. "But that was because the machine you gave me, after you'd kindly examined it in my absence, wasn't the machine I brought back from Brighton. It was very similar to your laptop so you peeled off the pink unicorn stickers and applied them to your old machine and banked on me not being able to tell the difference. And you were right – I didn't."

"Once again, I don't know what you are talking about."

"Oh you do," Bruce said. "You wiped your hard drive before handing it over to me, though you archived everything that was useful to a USB drive first and then transferred it to Honey Peach's laptop, which now has both your stuff and hers on it."

Nick glared at Bruce.

Bruce walked across to Nick's desk and pointed at the laptop, which he powered up. "I only realised what you'd done after I replied to that email you fabricated from Honey Peach to Jan, and your machine bonged. When I looked at it, I saw all my messages to Honey Peach were there, apart from those ones with big attachments, which you deleted."

A vein on Nick's forehead began to pulsate.

"Oh and before I forget, thanks for leaving the Emergency Boot CD in your desk – I would never have been able to confirm any of this without it. And isn't online banking great? I didn't realise how easy it is to transfer thousands of pounds from one account to another. All you need are the log-in details, password and memorable word – and I noticed there was a text file on your laptop which contained all of them. I assume you used the Boot CD to get into Plum's machine and look up my bank account details, so you had somewhere to transfer her funds."

Grim faced, Nick grabbed Bruce by the arm and hurled him away from his desk. He then started tapping frantically at his laptop's keypad.

"Will you have time to format the hard drive before the police arrive?" Bruce said. "I don't think you will, unless you've got some trick program that only IT professionals know about. But I understand nothing ever gets truly deleted anyway. If you've got the right tools you can recover anything from a hard drive."

Droplets of sweat started appearing on Nick's face.

Bruce sat in his old chair and put his feet up on his now empty desk. "Going back to the start of it all," he said. "I assume your plan was to have your wicked way with Honey Peach so you drugged her drink when you bought that round of cocktails. But she only drunk a little of it, and Jan and I helped her out."

He continued: "You had about twenty minutes until the roofies kicked in, which would have given you plenty of time to follow her to the station and 'rescue' her when she started wilting. That was why you were so keen to expedite our exit, but I messed your timings up by ordering another round. Sorry about that."

Satisfied with what he'd done on his laptop, Nick took a step towards Bruce. "What a vivid imagination you've got," he said. "Have you considered writing a murder mystery?"

"By the time we got up to street level the three of us were starting to get woozy, with Honey Peach the first to go. You had to get me out of the way though, so I wouldn't see what you were doing, so you attacked me with something like a brick."

Nick shook his head and pointed to his fist. He took another step towards Bruce.

"That was a punch?" Bruce said, sliding his legs off his desk and standing up. "That's impressive, though in my defence I was drugged a bit. I seem to remember those two sales guys being there, so you presumably chased them away and then dragged me into a doorway, out of sight. Then you caught up with Honey Peach, who must have been a bit out of it at this point, and guided her to your flat."

Nick made a grab for Bruce, who dodged and brandished his chair in front of him.

"But Jan was the problem, wasn't she?" Bruce said, pushing the chair at Nick. "She was also out of it, staggering back to her car. You couldn't risk her being found and tested for drugs, because then we might all be rounded up and awkward questions would be asked. So you restrained Honey Peach somehow and then went back for Jan. You knew where she was going and when you found her she was probably only half conscious. So it would have been easy for you to force her to drink that bottle of gin. Then you put her in her car and sent her down the hill. She looked like just another drink-driver when she was picked up."

Nick continued walking towards Bruce, his face now rigid with determination.

"By the time you got back to your flat, I'm guessing something had happened to Honey Peach. Perhaps you gagged her and she choked? What you probably didn't know was that she had a heart condition, so that may have contributed towards whatever happened to her."

Nick attempted to grab Bruce again. This time Bruce hurled a telephone at him as he backed away.

"Why didn't you call an ambulance?" Bruce yelled. "They might have been able to save her."

Nick's hands had both formed fists and his breathing grew deeper as he got closer to Bruce.

"Was it because if Honey Peach had gone to hospital she would have been tested for drugs? And someone might then have looked into what happened to Jan a little closer? And if the same drug had been found in her – or even me – then that would have put you in a bit of a pickle. Not least because the penalty could be up to ten years in prison."

Nick swung a fist at Bruce, who managed to duck in time but found himself cornered by the open window overlooking the courtyard.

"So you panicked," Bruce said, a slight tremble creeping into his voice. "You probably stored her body in your freezer while you considered what to do, which was why you took the next day off. And what you came up with was to set me up for it, and make me think I'm going nuts so I'd even suspect myself. First it was the little things, like the news stories going missing. Obviously you remotely deleted them from my machine over the network."

Nick slowed. His prey was trapped – though it wouldn't shut up.

"Oh and while I was poking around the office last night I discovered that every desk drawer can be locked by the same key and there's a handful of them in Jan's drawer. So you used one of them to lock my drawer – after you put Honey Peach's pendant in it – and then attached it to my keyring…"

Nick leapt on Bruce, the weight of his body forcing him to the floor and pinning him down.

"It would have been good if someone else had discovered the pendant but I found it and kept quiet about it, so then you planted her phone too, and made sure everyone knew it was there by ringing it when we were all in the office," Bruce continued, gasping under Nick's sixteen stone. "Then you sent the email from Honey Peach to Jan, dated it several weeks before and routed it through your server, transferred her bank balance into my account, and I also understand you planted some of her hair in my car?"

Nick's bulk pushed down on Bruce's chest, causing him to gasp as he continued: "I'm guessing you intended placing some incriminating strands of her hair in the boot, until you broke it open and saw it was far too small to hold a body – Jesus, you are heavy, Nick, you're crushing me – so you slashed my roof, in about ten different places so it wasn't obvious, and dropped the hair in the passenger seat."

Nick whispered into Bruce's ear: "Where's the other mini disc?"

"I made your job a heck of a lot easier by getting involved in all sorts of scrapes myself too," Bruce wheezed. "As you mentioned, there were the adventures in Brighton and Chepstow…"

Nick pulled Bruce up by his shirt collar and dragged him across to the rear window. "Where is it, Bruce?" he whispered again, far more threateningly.

"Of course, while all this was going on, you still had her body in your freezer," Bruce said. "So it was in your interest for me to be banged up as soon as possible…"

"Where is it?" Nick repeated, twisting Bruce's arm behind his back. "You obviously wouldn't be making this elaborate speech unless it was being recorded…"

Bruce bellowed with pain but continued: "To get rid of her body you hired a van and filled it with dolls. You inflated them in your flat and carried them out to the van early in the morning – it would have been quite easy to smuggle a real porn star's body out among a dozen inflatable ones. If anyone saw you they would have just assumed it was one of the expensive models."

Nick twisted Bruce's arm further behind his back, pushing him part way out of the window. "I mean it Bruce," he said. "Tell me where it is or you're going down, quite literally…"

"If there was another one," Bruce said, struggling to hold on to the frame of the window with his free arm. "You wouldn't know where it was if you dropped me. And someone else could find it…"

Nick pushed him further out through the window, so the whole top half of his body was outside. "That's a chance I'm just going to have to take, mate," he said.

With only his legs keeping him from falling, Bruce relented: "Alright," he gasped. "I'll show you where it is."

"I know you will," Nick said, pulling him back in with one hand while still keeping Bruce's arm twisted behind his back with the other.

With a defeated look on his face, Bruce pointed to the drawer of his desk.

Nick could just see the tip of a microphone wedged into the drawer. He released his grip on Bruce and yanked it out, along with the second mini disc recorder it was attached to. "Belt and braces," Nick said approvingly. "Plum would be pleased. And full marks for running it off batteries – no power cord, so I wouldn't be able to find it as easily as I did the first."

Bruce collapsed into his chair, his arm burning with pain.

"Don't be too downhearted, mate," Nick said, as he popped the lid of the second mini disc player. "You were pretty much bang on. It was roofies…"

"Which you got from someone at the gym in exchange for some porn DVDs you stole from the archive," Bruce said.

"Full marks again!" Nick said, slapping him hard on the back. "I started using them as currency earlier in the year, just the odd one or two a week."

"And you plugged the gaps with empty cases so I wouldn't notice them going missing," Bruce said, rubbing his arm as he watched Nick destroy the second mini disc in the same manner as the first. "That's how you could afford black market steroids."

"That's right," Nick said, tensing his biceps until they shook. "You don't get guns like these without a little help. And that's where my PS2 games came from as well."

"But with me out of the way you don't need to cover your tracks, so you took all six of the California Cum Whores series."

"They're worth more if the wrapping is still on them," Nick said.

"I thought you were going to break my arm just then," Bruce said, flexing his fingers in an attempt to restore feeling to his aching limb.

"I was, it's a dog eat dog world out there."

"I have heard that," Bruce said.

"But mate, I didn't plan this," Nick said. "If Honey Peach had just drunk the cocktail none of it would have happened. You and Jan would have gone home, I would have had a bit of fun with Honey Peach and she'd still be here today – and probably none the wiser. But she turned her snooty little nose up at the Red Hot Dutch and you and Jan got involved. I had to knock you out, get Honey Peach off the street and then sort Jan out. And by the time I got back…"

"Nick, if we explain it was an accident…"

"What?"

"And that your judgement was impaired at the time because of the steroids you've been taking…"

"Mate, I'm afraid that's not going to happen," he said, grabbing Bruce by his arms and pulling him out of his chair.

"What are you doing?" Bruce said.

"Just tidying up the last loose end," Nick said, dragging Bruce back towards the open window.

"Nick," Bruce pleaded. "You don't need to do this."

Nick once again forced Bruce's upper body out through the window. "The thing is, the police are going to be here soon, or Alex and Plum will be coming in, and it's going to look awkward you and me being here together."

"We can explain…"

"No, I'll explain," Nick said. "I'll explain that I went to grab you but that you tried to escape through the window. Everyone thinks you're mental anyway, so it won't surprise anyone. And it's not like anyone will even care."

"Please, don't do this Nick," Bruce yelled, desperately trying to hold on to the frame of the window.

"I'm sorry mate, I really am, but I've got to be sure – belt and braces sure – that you are, quite literally, the fall guy."

"Help me!" Bruce cried, his voice echoing around the walls of the empty courtyard, his arms scrabbling wildly to find something to hold onto.

Nick punched Bruce in the mouth, causing a splattering of blood to burst out of his bottom lip. "Shut up, Bruce," he snarled, punching him again. "You're causing a scene."

Bruce howled with pain as his head smashed back against the window frame. His feet were off the ground, his legs kicking wildly at Nick.

"Hey, you prick, that bloody hurt," Nick said, as one of Bruce's kicks caught him in the ribs.

The door to the archive creaked opened and Alex slowly emerged. She had the office video camera in her hand, its red light indicating that it was recording. "In all fairness, you did provoke him," she said to Nick.

Wild eyed, Nick tried to grab the camera from Alex but she deftly backed away. He swung a fist in her direction but missed, throwing himself off balance and allowing Bruce to scramble back in from the window ledge.

"Don't bother," Alex said to Nick. "I've already sent a text to Plum in reception, and given him the signal to come up."

Winded and bleeding from the lip, Bruce collapsed to the floor. "Could you have left it any longer?" he said to Alex.

"What's your problem?" she retorted. "I had to get the money shot, didn't I?"

Nick stared incredulously at Alex. "Why would you help him?" he said. "You hate him."

Bruce looked up and saw Plum arrive, along with several burly police officers. "She does," he said. "But it's a dog eat dog world out there…"

CHAPTER NINETEEN: FRIDAY 27TH JUNE 2003

"You seriously expect me to believe it was the old biddy in the next bed who ratted me out?" Bruce said, removing a handful of grapes from the bunch by Jan's bed and popping them into his mouth one at a time.

"She might have looked comatose but it was all an act," Jan said. "Apparently she does it in the care home too. When they were taking her out, one of the porters trod on her toe – she miraculously regained the power of speech then."

Bruce sighed. "I really thought it was you."

"Why would I have told the police you were at the Hicks?" Jan said. "You were the only one bringing me nice things. True, you tended to eat them yourself but..."

Bruce shrugged. "In my defence, I had been abandoned by everyone else and Nick made me think I was losing my marbles."

"This is going to make quite a story for AMG."

Bruce laughed. "It will, but it won't be me writing it. I think I've done my last piece for Plum."

After a break in the conversation, during which a nurse made some notes on the pad at the end of the bed, Jan said: "Have you heard what's going to happen to Nick?"

Bruce shook his head. "We're not going to know for months. There's going to be psychiatric reports, negotiations between teams of lawyers... then there's the question over the footage Alex recorded of him, which he was obviously unaware of..."

"It might not be admissible as evidence but..."

"Worse than that, filming him without his consent or knowledge may have been a breach of his Human Rights," Bruce said, plucking more grapes from the bunch.

"What about Honey Peach's Human Rights?" Jan frowned. "What about your Human Rights not to be thrown out of a third floor window?"

"His solicitor will claim that the balance of his mind was disturbed due to the illegal anabolic steroids he was taking."

"This country really does make me cross sometimes..." Jan shook her head.

"Against that though, everything he did was so calculated," Bruce said. "He very methodically downloaded incriminating stuff to my computer – such as articles about how to dispose of a dead body."

Jan sighed. "That poor girl. Why did he drug her, Bruce?"

"So he could boast he had sex with her?" Bruce shrugged. "I honestly don't know."

"Has he said what happened to her?"

"Not that I know of," Bruce said. "But my money would be on him taking her out to sea."

"How did you reach that conclusion?" Jan said, moving the last few grapes closer to her.

"It was when I saw the printout of his feature," Bruce said. "And all the dolls were on the beach, looking like cadavers. It suddenly struck me that it would be a perfect cover story if someone wanted to transport a dead body. He also saved on my machine the times of the tides at Weston-super-Mare, so if her body was found it would look like I'd been planning to take her there. He probably drove the van onto the beach and took Honey Peach out to sea in his dinghy. Or perhaps he went a few miles north to Sand Point, the peninsular that marks the start of the Bristol Channel, and just let the tide take her."

"Surely someone would have seen him, though? People walk their dogs…"

"Even if they did, he had a load of inflatable dolls with him – and if she was frozen she would have looked like a doll herself from a distance. Don't forget, he was out at sunrise, so the light wouldn't have been ideal for identifying dead bodies. And while you or I would have struggled to carry her, Nick would have found it a doddle."

After a pause of a few seconds, Jan said: "On a more cheerful note, Plum came to see me yesterday."

"How lovely for you," Bruce said, plucking the last of the grapes from the bunch.

Pointing at the giant cuddly toy at the end of her bed, Jan said: "He wants to know when I'll be coming back. Of course, he was full of apologies about not visiting before, due to the increased workload everyone was under…"

Bruce smiled. "You were persona non grata when he thought you were going to be charged. If that homeless guy hadn't come forward after seeing you in the local paper…"

"The power of the media…"

"Why didn't he report it at the time, if he saw what Nick did to you?"

"He was sleeping in the back of someone's car, and he didn't want to give up such a comfy bed. A relatively benign form of breaking and entering – no one was hit on the head with a kettle – and he didn't actually do any breaking as the car was left unlocked."

"So you're in the clear now?"

Jan smiled and nodded. "What about you?"

"My legal team are confident something can be worked out about the impersonating a HMCE official charge."

"Your legal team? Get you! Is Plum paying for that?"

"The publishers of Celebs & Scandals are…"

"You're going to work for them?" Jan said, aghast. "Alex will be so jealous!"

"No, I'm co-operating with them on a piece about the whole Honey Peach affair, and in return their solicitors are going to defend me, should there be any problems. They'll argue that everything I did – even all the shenanigans with Milkman – should be excused because I was a journalist pursuing an investigation which was in the public interest."

"Poor Milkman, he was innocent all along."

"Not quite innocent," Bruce corrected her. "He did break into Honey Peach's house and attack Julian Gregan with a kettle. The irony is he probably will be investigated by HMCE now."

"I'd have loved to have seen you and him fighting in the board room," Jan said, suppressing laughter. "Though you shouldn't have destroyed Plum's plant. He's had that for years."

"Collateral damage," Bruce shrugged. "The solicitors are confident that I'll get off. I've been told that they've got away with far worse in the past. They're also applying pressure on Plum on my behalf for a severance payment in lieu of a claim for wrongful dismissal."

"Oh that's wonderful, Bruce," Jan said, offering him a hug. "I'm so pleased. How's your lip, by the way?"

"It's fine," he said, awkwardly embracing her. "It just needed a couple of stitches."

"What are you going to do now?"

"They have offered me a job," Bruce said, uncoupling from Jan. "Not on Celebs & Scandals but on a new lad's magazine they are launching, called Men Come First – it's going to be all about football, gambling, video games and porn…"

"Sounds right up your street."

"It does, but it means I will have to move to London."

"Well," Jan said, avoiding looking at him. "You should do what's best for you."

"I will," Bruce said. "Opportunities like this don't come along very often, and I'm told that while my name has got a certain cache, I should exploit it."

"A happy ending then, thanks to Alex," Jan said. "And after all those nasty things you said about her."

"She didn't do it for me," Bruce said, laughing. "I had to ask Spaghetti to ring her – luckily I had his mobile number so I could reach him on a Sunday night – and she only went along with it because he promised to take ads in every issue for the next three months."

"There's not much that girl won't do for a good ad booking," said Jan. "She'll go far."

***

The string quartet busking outside the Roman Baths had attracted quite a crowd, so much so that a pair of jugglers moved down from their own pitch further up Stall Street in an attempt to poach those on the edge of the gathering. It wasn't just the centre that was packed with people. In every direction Bruce looked there was a swarm of shoppers darting in and out of doorways, clutching brightly coloured carrier bags.

Bruce had forgotten how hectic Friday afternoon was in Bath. For the last few years he had been confined to the AMG office, due to Friday being deadline day. Alex would be chasing advertisers if their artwork hadn't arrived; Jan would be dropping non-time sensitive features, if space was tight, or commissioning last minute ones if the page count had risen; Nick would be rushing through layouts for Plum to approve; and Bruce would be watching porn films with his feet on his desk, making critical notes every now and then. It all seemed a very long time ago.

The aroma of freshly ground coffee seduced Bruce into making a purchase at a branch of a High Street chain and he wandered further down Stall Street, window shopping as he supped. He considered treating himself to a music CD from the huge branch of HMV but he couldn't face fighting his way through the mob milling around the entrance.

He continued south in the direction of the railway station. He took several diversions down side streets, where the chic shops gave way to takeaways, and was shocked to see a life-size image of Honey Peach ahead of him.

With only two Amazonian plant leaves protecting her modesty, her platinum blonde hair and tanned body was set off beautifully by the blacked out windows each side of her. The promotional cut-out had been stuck to the inside of the shop's glass door with sticky tape and while Bruce was staring at the image, two long haired youths in school uniform took great pleasure in opening the door inwards by pushing her breasts. Bruce doubted the terms of Love Shack's licence would allow such imagery to be showcased in what was, in effect, its shop window – but by the time this was pointed out to the store manager the display would have served its purpose.

An A4 sign, also stuck to the shop's front door with sticky tape, next to the one warning the public that no one under eighteen was allowed to enter the premises, announced 'Exclusive Honey Peach promotion – while stocks last'.

Bruce followed the two giggling youths into the shop. The left side and rear walls of the narrow store were devoted to videos and DVDs, while a counter, with shelves of sex toys behind it, ran the length of the right hand wall. In the centre was a free standing display unit, containing hundreds of small bottles of lubricant and massage oil, plus a hastily assembled shrine to Honey Peach: a green felt-covered trestle table loaded down with a stack of Legend of the Amazon Women DVDs, plus out-of-the-box samples of her Signature Series of toys: Head Master, Spasm Chasm and Hand Job.

Taped to one of the DVD cases was a hand-written sign which stated, 'Free bottle of lube with every purchase of Honey Peach's Spasm Chasm. Also get a second DVD half price when you buy Legend of the Amazon Women (selected titles only)'.

One of the youths picked up the sample of the Honey Peach Spasm Chasm. He forced his fingers into the rubber vagina and waggled them about aggressively, shrieking with laughter.

His mate picked up the Head Master sample and held it to his groin. "Suck it, you bitch!" he roared.

The single member of staff behind the counter had a queue of four blocking his view of the youths so Bruce said: "Guys, come on…"

"Fuck off," the first youth replied.

Bruce suddenly stumbled forward, pushing both youths into the trestle table, which collapsed like a deck chair, scattering the DVDs and knocking over the plastic tower of lotions and potions. Dozens and dozens of bottles rolled across the shop floor, with several of the tester units spilling their sticky contents as they did so. As Bruce tried to stand up, he accidently stepped on the first youth's hand and his elbow caught the second one a nasty blow to the side of the head. They both squealed with pain.

The commotion brought the member of staff from behind the counter. Seeing the vandals who had destroyed his display were clearly under eighteen, he grabbed them by their ears and dragged them out of the shop, threatening to kick their heads in if they ever came back. Terrified, they ran off.

Bruce stared at the offending area of carpet he had tripped over. "Somebody should take a look at that," he said as he left the shop.

CHAPTER TWENTY: MONDAY 7TH JULY 2003

"Thanks so much for coming to get me," Jan said, as she hobbled out through the hospital entrance.

Bruce, trekking ahead and grappling with Jan's suitcase and several canvas bags, could already feel beads of perspiration forming on his forehead. "I'm pretty sure Pink Floyd went on tour with less than this," he grumbled, gesturing at his load.

They walked the short distance to the hospital car park and Bruce paused, as if trying to remember where he parked.

"Will we fit all this in your Mazda?" Jan said. "I can't say I'm looking forward to being crammed into that pokey little thing."

"You'll be fine," Bruce assured her.

"But it's so low down to the road," Jan said. "It's like being on a skateboard and I don't know if my back will be able to stand it."

"You'll be fine," Bruce repeated.

"And will you have to take the roof off to fit my suitcase in? Because that will mean my hair gets blown all over the place, especially the way you drive..."

"Would you prefer to drive?" Bruce put the bags down and ferreted in his jacket pocket.

"I'm not sure," she said. "My doctor told me I should get back behind the wheel as soon as possible but I don't know if I'm up to it."

"Catch," he said, retrieving from his pocket a key fob with a single key attached. He gently tossed it towards her.

She caught it. "I've never driven a two-seater before. People will think I'm on the pull."

"It always worked for me," Bruce said, picking up her bags and marching along the rows of cars, one of which was a bright orange Volkswagen T2 Camper.

"Oh stop a minute Bruce," Jan said, peering through one of its long side windows. "I love the material they have covered the seats with. Look, the pattern is like one of those pop art paintings."

She walked around the rear of the vehicle and stared at the number plate. "It's immaculate for a 1973 model, there's no sign of rust at all."

"And it's done less than sixty thousand miles from new," Bruce said.

"How can you tell?" she asked, peering in through the driver's side window.

"Are you going to unlock it, so I can load your bags into it?"

Jan held up the key Bruce had thrown to her a couple of minutes earlier, and noticed its distinctive VW roundel glinting in the sun. "What's going on?" she said.

"Believe it or not, I rather fancy just buggering off around Europe in a camper van and seeing what happens," Bruce said. "All I need is the right person to go with."

If you enjoyed this book, and even if you didn't, it would be hugely appreciated if you could spare a few moments to post a review of it online, either on Amazon or wherever else you usually post book reviews. Thank you.

Also available from Dale Bradford

From Sex Shops To Supermarkets: How Adult Toys Became A Multi-Billion-Pound Industry

With almost every major UK supermarket now devoting shelf space to adult toys, From Sex Shops To Supermarkets chronicles the phenomenal growth of the sector, and how mainstream television, cinema, and celebrities have rushed to embrace it.

The book features many of the industry's milestone moments, including the consumer electronics giant that launched its own sex toy, the private prosecution that could have threatened the Ann Summers business model, and the great jiggle ball shortage of 2012.

It also explains how Lovehoney used clever PR to build its business and reveals the strategies behind some of its most successful campaigns. The book concludes with venture capitalists investing in leading players and merging them into 'supergroups'.

The Time-Travelling Estate Agent

It's December 2019 in a small Welsh town, and 60-year-old estate agent Eric Meek discovers a property which boasts a truly unique garage conversion. Instead of the more customary home office or gym, it contains a hole in space-time that has been developed into a traversable portal.

The portal allows movement between 2019 and the day it was first powered up, 3rd July 1976, which just happened to be the best – and worst – day of 16-year-old Eric's life.

Presented with a chance to right the wrongs of the past, Eric revisits the moment he believes defined his future. His adventures in time also find him caught up in a decades-old missing persons case while he attempts to improve the lives of those close to him, including his long-dead father.

Will Eric change history? Or will history change Eric?

The Time-Travelling Estate Agent is the story of a first love, a second chance, and a third age redemption.

Printed in Great Britain
by Amazon